About the Author

John Gillick is a retired social worker and former stand-up comedian, being a former member of Glasgow-based comedy collective, The Funny Farm. A comedy writer, actor and voice over artist, he is widowed, has two children and two grandchildren. And a dog. He lives in Glasgow.

The Scars of Fate

John Gillick

The Scars of Fate

A Sam Meredith Novel

Olympia Publishers
London

www.olympiapublishers.com
OLYMPIA PAPERBACK EDITION

A CIP catalogue record for this title is
available from the British Library.

ISBN: 978-1-83543-149-8

This is a work of fiction.
Names, characters, places and incidents originate from the writer's
imagination. Any resemblance to actual persons, living or dead, is
purely coincidental.

First Published in 2024

Olympia Publishers
Tallis House
2 Tallis Street
London
EC4Y 0AB

Printed in Great Britain

Other Books by this Author

One for Sorrow

For my mother

Acknowledgements

Thanks to Billy, Mel and Vanessa for their support, dedication and constructive criticism, without which I wouldn't have got there, wherever that is. I will also be forever grateful to Anna Smith for her sage guidance and invaluable advice. Lang may her lum reek.

Prologue

As a boy of thirteen, he had watched his father die after he had been stabbed trying to apprehend a burglar who had broken into the family home. He and his mother were forced to look on helplessly as his father lay, bleeding to death in front of them. The robber then ransacked the house before leaving with cash and jewellery amounting to over £20,000.00. The masked murderer was never caught, and his mother never really recovered from the ordeal and the loss, subsequently suffering from chronic depression for over twenty years before taking her own life aged fifty-five. He was only twenty-seven at the time.

There can be no doubting the significant traumatic effect that such horrific events and experiences would have had on him at such a young age and on his subsequent development, with it almost certainly having influenced and perhaps even determined many of his future life choices, possibly even including that of his occupation.

Certainly, as his life developed, he found that he had become more determined to 'make a difference,' and address or prevent what he perceived as injustices and transgressions against innocent victims, whenever possible.

Chapter 1

Sam Meredith was driving home from Prestwick airport, with the thoughts of recent events still preying heavily on his mind, to the extent that he realised that he could not remember driving for the last few miles and/or how he got to where he was. However, instead of calming his mind and slowing down he decided that he just wanted to get home as quickly as possible and pulled out to overtake a slow-moving articulated vehicle in front of him. Unfortunately, he did so just before another large truck appeared over the hill on the other side of the road, and when he attempted to pull back in, he realised that he couldn't do so because the large, slow-moving truck he had just attempted to overtake was blocking his way. He couldn't slow down and move in behind it because there wasn't enough time as the oncoming truck was moving too fast and would hit him before he could get out of the way. Which it did, and Sam Meredith's world descended into oblivion.

Chapter 2

Farouk hated Glasgow. It was cold and dark, and the sky was low and grey, and when the sun did shine, it wasn't for long, unless it was a freak heatwave, which also tended not to last for any length of time. This was maybe just as well, given his current job, and ironically, the other thing about the weather was that when it rained, which it did a lot, he didn't tend to have much work at his job, at least not his day job. Farouk hated his day job, it was hard, and he worked long hours for very little pay, six days a week. And when he finished his work at the car wash, he had to go home and get washed and changed for his job at the nightclub, or more precisely 'Gentlemen's Club', where he worked as a Barman/Steward. He also did some odd jobs and handed out leaflets around the streets of the town centre and outside big hotels, particularly when there were events being held there.

He liked his job at the night club, when he wasn't exhausted from his day job, and sometimes he wasn't finishing until three or even four a.m., and then he was expected to start working again no later than nine a.m. the next day at the car wash, weather permitting. In saying that, he was fed and watered at the club and there was also the occasional perk of a girl or two, as long as the bosses didn't find out. There actually was one of the girls that he liked, and he was sure that she liked him. However, he had been down that road before, and he couldn't afford to make that same mistake again.

The flat that Farouk shared with several others was pretty much a hovel, whereas the ones the girls lived in were much more comfortable, but that was because they had to 'entertain' there. However, his current situation wasn't anywhere near as 'cushy' as the job he had had in Spain, where the money, conditions and weather had been much preferable. He was still annoyed at himself for getting involved in something that had led to his being moved to Glasgow.

He had protested vociferously but been unceremoniously dismissed out of hand and made aware, in no uncertain terms, that he was lucky to be offered anything other than being summarily dismissed to fend for himself or make his way back to Algeria, which he did not consider to be an option. And because you did not argue with his benefactors and paymasters, he would just have to lump it for the time being.

Chapter 3

Sam woke up with a start, hyperventilating and covered in sweat, as he always did when he had the dream, or more to the point, nightmare. Except that it wasn't a nightmare or a dream, it was real, apart from the end thankfully. He will never know how or why he did what he did that day, other than that it was the only thing he could do, and it was out of pure survival instinct. But it was undoubtedly the craziest, most dangerous, and singularly terrifying experience he had ever had, bar none. And what he did was to drive across the path of the oncoming truck, and disbelieving driver into a passing space on the other side of the carriageway, missing the truck by seconds and probably traumatizing the driver forever. Against all odds, he also managed to swerve and stop before hitting the wall and then ploughing into a field. It was probably the nearest thing to committing suicide he could have done without accomplishing it.

He could still hear the truck's horn blaring and see the disbelieving panic and terror in the driver's face, and he still shivered and felt lightheaded whenever he recalled the incident. He also remembered that at the time, after his miraculous escape, he had just sat staring, unbelieving, into space, trembling with shock for what seemed like an age, before eventually dissolving into tears when he realised how close to death that he and probably the truck driver had come. As he gradually regained his equilibrium, he half expected the police or the truck driver to turn up and either arrest and/or beat the shit out of him, respectively, for being such a crazy, dangerous maniac and with good cause. At one point he had thought about turning back and trying to catch up with the truck driver to try and explain his actions but realised that there probably wasn't an acceptable or reasonable explanation. He also had realised that in his existing state of mind he was more likely to end up accomplishing what he had just somehow managed to avoid. He remembered a quote from a film, whose title he couldn't bring to mind which went something like 'Sometimes a man can meet his destiny by taking the very road he took to avoid it', which he thought sounded apt and profound.

He had eventually managed to compose himself sufficiently to drive home, although he was still an emotional wreck for some weeks after the event and was very reluctant to get behind the wheel unless he really had to. It was only a few months ago, and he was still experiencing recurring nightmares and unexpected panic attacks. And of course, there was the nightmare, which, if anything had become more frequent in recent weeks. In the days, weeks and months after the incident he had many thoughts about why it had happened; he wondered whether this was meant to be some kind of reminder of his mortality and/or a consequence of his actions, during that fateful and traumatic 'holiday' in Benidorm, which he had been returning from.

Sam suddenly realised that he had still never told anyone about the incident, even close friends and family, probably because of the feelings of guilt and shame that would be forever associated with it and also because he couldn't have done so without becoming emotional and probably tearful.

He had actually considered telling Kim, his estranged wife, when they met up after he returned from Benidorm, but felt that it would have been insensitive as she was having enough difficulty dealing with her own, not inconsiderable, highly personal and emotional issues, which she only revealed to Sam following on from the dramatic events in Benidorm. In particular the murder of a man with whom she had had an affair while she and Sam were together. And a man whom Sam had never met but who he had come to know quite well before his death, a death he had been accused of causing. Interestingly, it was a question that Kim had never asked him for whatever reason; Sam reckoned that it was either because she believed that he had nothing to do with it or that she didn't want to know if he did. Sam also found himself rationalizing the situation to the extent that he had speculated whether justice might have been served if he had been killed by the truck. However, the one thing that he was unquestionably sure of was that he had cheated death that day. He just wasn't sure that he deserved it. But he realised that he would have to learn to live with it thankfully.

Chapter 4

8 January 2018
Monday

Sam had had a good day at work, gradually winding down in preparation for his forthcoming holiday, having spent it planning and preparing all the necessary briefings and handovers prior to his departure to his colleagues in the advertising department at the Cambusglen Chronicle the paper that he had worked at for over thirty years. He had worked all over Christmas and New Year, so he was ready for his well-earned break, Sam told himself, musing over the use of language routinely employed to describe the concept of holidays: 'break; getaway; escape,' the implication being that we are all being held prisoner or permanently existing in some sort of captivity.

After work, Sam headed to the Tesco supermarket in Cambusglen to pick up the basic supplies required to last him until he left on his much-needed holiday. However, as he headed towards his car in the supermarket car park, his face fell and his heart sank, in that order.

Everybody knows that horrible sinking feeling when you arrive back at the car to find that piece of paper under the windscreen wiper—the dreaded parking ticket. But there's something worse, and that something worse had just happened to Sam, and that is to find a piece of paper with nothing on it. It took Sam just a few seconds to realise what it meant; and what it meant was that some devious, despicable, scheming, immoral dirt - bag had banged into him but didn't have the decency to wait, so instead pretended to write their name on the bit of paper to both deceive and hopefully reassure any concerned onlooker or fair-minded citizen.

But the thing that got Sam was that they hadn't written anything—nothing at all. Evidently, they couldn't even think of one thing to say, so not only was he, or she a terrible driver, but they were also obviously totally devoid of any creativity. *They could've put anything,* thought Sam, even just stated the glaringly obvious; 'Sorry, I'm such a shit driver but I'm not insured either, signed, a well-wisher!' But to write nothing – nada, zero, zilch, zippity fucking doo dah! They could even have been a bit of a smart arse and put something like; 'Dear Crash Test Dummy, had a little bash while you were away, sorry you missed it, maybe run into you again. But no—nothing! Not a bloody sausage. They could've had a laugh, mused Sam, introduced a bit of humour, something like; 'Sorry about the mess, can't stop,' – obviously! 'Anyway, must dash as I'm late for an optician's appointment. Oh, and sorry about the writing, I'm a bit pissed!' But no – nothing, diddly squat, absolutely hee -fucking haw! Sweet F all-not even the name of a half decent panel beater!'

Sam surveyed the damage, it didn't look too bad, mainly superficial, but he needed to get it repaired before it started to rust. He decided that he would get a couple of quotes from local garages before he made the decision whether to claim his insurance, given the substantial excess on his policy. So, he asked a few people at work and one of his neighbours, who was always messing about with his car. He also looked in the local paper for adverts and after due consideration he decided to take it into a place that he had noticed whilst out shopping and which was quite near to him.

So, he drove in on his way to work and asked for an estimate for a repair, whilst making it clear that it was for him and not his insurance company, as he was aware that the prices were invariably hiked up in the latter scenario. The guy he spoke to asked him to take a seat whilst he arranged for someone to have a look at the damage and showed him into a small seating area and told him to help himself to coffee from the machine there, which Sam did.

As he sipped the grey liquid, whatever it was, because it certainly wasn't like any coffee he had ever tasted, he noticed that there was a car wash a couple of units up from the garage and realised that his car was well overdue a clean. As he was considering whether to take advantage of this, he saw something which made him start and stare in disbelief. He was looking at one of the men working in the car wash, who was foreign, possibly of North African descent, and who Sam was convinced was Akmal Samir, the man whom he had encountered and had 'dealings' with during his holiday in Benidorm the previous year.

You the Merc'? Sam's thoughts were interrupted by one of the garage mechanics speaking to him, which he didn't register immediately so had to apologise and ask the guy to repeat what he said.

'Sorry what? I was dreaming,' he said.

'You the Merc?' he asked again, adding, 'damage repair estimate?'

'Oh… yes,' said Sam, and the guy handed him a printed invoice, detailing the work required and the breakdown of the cost involved, which Sam thought was reasonable.

'OK, thanks,' said Sam adding, 'how soon can you do it?'

'Bring it in first thing Wednesday. It should take about 2/3 days. Cash only, is that OK?'

'Yes, that's fine,' said Sam, then 'see you Wednesday,' on his way out. Sam had also decided that he would also pay the car wash a visit on Wednesday, thinking that there wasn't much point whilst the car was damaged. However, he did drive towards and past it slowly to take another look at the subject of his curiosity. The more he looked, the more he was convinced that it was the same guy.

Chapter 5

9 January 2018
Tuesday

Sam's mouth was killing him, and it was all Jamie Oliver's fault. He had watched the young celebrity chef's show the previous week and had decided to have a go at making one of his creations, which was a pasta dish that involved crushing peppercorns in a mortar and pestle to make a 'husk'. Jamie had also recommended that you sprinkle some of the remaining crushed peppercorns over the completed dish, in one final flourish of flavour and presentation—which Sam had done. Unfortunately, however, some of the remaining peppercorns were not crushed into husk, and when he bit into them, they had removed a filling, and not just a filling but half of the tooth as well. And the pain was getting worse, so he had gone to the chemist and bought some oil of cloves, which had helped.

However, he needed to get an appointment to get it seen to before he headed off on holiday, because it wasn't going to go away anytime soon, much like his nightmares, which were also becoming more frequent and upsetting.

The encounter with 'Akmal' at the car wash had unexpectedly brought back a lot of thoughts and feelings about what had happened in Benidorm for Sam, and he found himself experiencing a range of differing emotions, and most of it not pleasant. He realised that in the past year he had managed to put most of it to the back of his mind and that he hadn't really thought about any of it since his return, other than the dream and the other nightmares he was having. He knew that there was a clear reason for that, and that reason was self-preservation, as he had found the thoughts and memories of that time to be very unsettling and still did. Some things were best forgotten about, he reasoned, for some reason, recalling another phrase, 'Rivers are for crossing and bridges are for burning', which also seemed apt.

However, since his sighting of 'Akmal' it had been different; it had been conscious reflection, contemplation and even evaluation of what had taken place and why, with no clear conclusions reached. It had also made him quite apprehensive and quite anxious about his forthcoming holiday to Tenerife scheduled for the following Monday.

And, as it turned out, he would have good reason to be.

Chapter 6

10 January 2018
Wednesday

Sam was supposed to pick up his car later in the day but instead he got a call from the garage informing him that it wouldn't be ready until the Friday, whilst offering the standard and predictable; 'We're waiting on parts', as the reason for the delay. Sam couldn't say that he was surprised, as he had never really trusted what he was told by garages, recalling the occasion when on contacting a garage to enquire if his car was ready to be collected after repair, was told, 'You're not going to believe it, your car was ready, job done, but when we road tested it, we heard something that we didn't like.'

What the hell does that mean? thought Sam at the time, 'Was James Blunt on the radio at the time?' Thankfully, however, there was no more delays, and the car was ready to be collected on the Friday, as promised, even if it was after work rather than before, as hoped. However, the main thing was that he would have it back, as he needed it to drive to the airport on the Monday.

Chapter 7

11 January 2018
Thursday

'Samuel Meredith' said the dental assistant, indicating that the dentist was ready for him. Sam had always hated the dentists, ever since he had a tooth removed, unnecessarily, as it turned out, as a child. This was in the days before the introduction of Novocaine, when the dental surgery was performed with the use of Nitrous Oxide, which was simply referred to as 'gas.' He was anxious before it, so when he came out from under the anaesthetic, covered in blood and in some pain, he was, unsurprisingly, traumatized and distraught. Unfortunately, the switch to Novocaine didn't significantly improve his mindset, because he was also not that keen on needles. His dentist still hid the needle behind his back, and he just shut his eyes and gritted his teeth and thought of better days.

However, despite his phobia, he was also able to see the funny and ludicrous side of the situation as he had come to regard the dentists as a quite ridiculous place, where you're allowed to spit, somebody's actually asking you to spit, but it's practically impossible to do so. Mainly because your mouth feels like it's made of Play Doh. And then you're told to spit into a basin the size of squirrel's anus whilst, invariably, a quite attractive young dental nurse watches you slathering all over yourself like a stroke victim. And you can't eat anything without chewing half your face off. He also recalled that, incredibly, he was once breathalysed after a jag at the dentists, which was even more awkward than trying to spit. He was sure that the officers thought that he was on drugs. And strictly speaking, they were right. As the dentist was seeing him on an emergency basis, he was only able to make a temporary repair to the filling and broken tooth, and he was given a further appointment for a full and permanent repair to be undertaken after his holiday, which he told Sam to enjoy.

Chapter 8

12 January 2018
Friday

Sam picked his car up from the garage and was pleasantly surprised to discover that they had made a really good job of it. And, thankfully, they hadn't washed it, otherwise it would have looked a bit strange him driving into a car wash. Sam paid and thanked them before driving off towards the car wash, where he joined a short queue of cars, at the head of which 'Akmal' was cleaning cars with a brush, prior to them going through the automated wash. Sam couldn't stop looking at him and then suddenly realised that he was next in line and was coming face to face with his quarry.

'What you like?' asked the guy of Sam, leaning in the car and looking straight at him with no hint of recognition. He had half expected him to say, 'You like a massage from sexy girl?'

'Just the basic wash please, I'm in a hurry,' thanks, said Sam, handing over the required amount plus a tip, whilst maintaining eye contact. But still, there was no hint of him recognizing Sam. Also, up close, Sam began to doubt whether it was in fact Akmal, as there was just something different about him. The guy handed Sam his change, but Sam motioned for him to keep it, adding; 'I hope you get to keep it,' and then decided to chance his arm by adding, as casually as he could, 'Sorry, I don't know your name?'

'My name is Farouk,' he answered, then seeming to look

29

unsettled, added hesitantly; 'And I don't tell about tips because they take all the money.'

'Good for you,' said Sam closing his window and driving into the wash.

Sam knew from previous research, relating to the situation he had experienced in Benidorm, that workers were trafficked from Asia and Africa with the promise of highly paid jobs and then made to work long hours in menial, hard jobs like car washes for a pittance, with there being illegal workers in Glasgow, Clydebank and many areas of Lanarkshire. Some workers, Sam knew, arrive and claim asylum, and anyone claiming asylum is legally entitled to stay in the UK while awaiting a decision, which can take months, even years.

When they arrive in the UK they are put to work and often paid in only food and accommodation in unhygienic and overcrowded, cramped conditions. Sam also thought that 'Farouk's' voice sounded similar but not quite as he remembered, but the resemblance was still striking. However, he was realised how ridiculous an idea it was and reluctantly accepted that it wasn't Akmal. *I mean, think about it*, thought Sam, *what would he be doing in Glasgow?*

Chapter 9

13 January 2018
Saturday

Sam was looking forward to his holiday, even if it was on his own again. Holidays were something he really valued, as it was something that his family had not been able to afford when he was growing up.

It was also not something he had enjoyed as a young adult, for different and complex reasons relating to his childhood and upbringing. Whilst he wouldn't have said that his family were living in poverty when he was a child, Sam remembered that they went through some tough times, when they had no money for food or gas and electricity; when they couldn't pay bills and his mother telling him to be quiet when debt collectors came to the door so they wouldn't know they were at home. He recalled frequently being sent a 'message' to an aunt's house, which was code for borrowing money. He could also remember watching his father rubbing old pennies on the roughcast wall at the back of the house until they fitted into the electricity and gas meters.

He could also recall quite vividly having to cuddle the dog for a heat and remembered thinking that it was an amazing coincidence that they got central heating installed by the council not long after the dog died. Obviously, they had not satisfied the criteria prior to this; 'Do you have any other form of heating at home, Mrs. Meredith?

'Yes, we have an electric fire in the living room?'

'Just in the living room?'

'Yes'

'Is it portable?'

'What?'

'Can it be moved from room to room?'

'Yes.'

'Ok, just one final question. Do you have any pets?

'Yes, we have a dog,'

What kind?

'A Labrador.'

'Oh, I'm sorry, that qualifies a source of heat I'm afraid. You'll just have to freeze for a while longer but be sure to let us know if anything changes.'

Chapter 10

14 January 2018
Sunday

Sam was all packed and organised for his holiday to Tenerife the next day. He had set his alarm on his mobile 'phone for four a.m. as his flight was at nine thirty a.m. from Glasgow Airport. He fell asleep as soon as his head hit the pillow, so, when the alarm went off, he felt rested and rose instantly. After showering and eating some cereal he decided to head off and either have a more substantial breakfast at the airport or just buy some sandwiches to take on the plane, or both, depending on how hungry he felt.

It was a typically 'dreich' Glasgow day, the kind that you are glad to be leaving behind. Unfortunately, it was usually the same kind of day that you inevitably found yourself returning to. *Enough of the negativity,* thought Sam, *just enjoy the fact that its two weeks away from it* all, determined to be positive. Well, it was fifteen days for some strange reason, but that was the deal he had been given by the travel agent.

As he sat in the airport, enjoying his first beer of the day at seven a.m., as was his tradition when he set off on holiday, taking advantage of the airport's magical licensing laws. After his beer Sam felt hungry, so he ordered a Scottish breakfast, which cost him nearly as much as the deposit he had paid for the holiday. After his breakfast, which hit the spot, he checked and saw that his flight was on time. He had time for another beer, after which he headed to the departure lounge, as per the instructions on the screen. Sam had never liked flying, regarding it as a necessary evil and the least enjoyable part of his holiday, which he just wanted to be over as soon as possible. He did not see the attraction of blasting through the sky in a pressurized metal tube, and consequently, he had avoided travelling to certain faraway destinations, which he would otherwise have liked to visit, because of the distance and flying time involved. He recalled with some bemusement that, ironically, one of the most pleasurable flying experiences that he ever had was when he and Kim had gone to Tenerife in 2010, during the drama of the 'dust cloud', formed from volcanic ash, following the eruption of a volcano in Iceland.

Incredibly, amidst some considerable concern and uncertainty surrounding their flight, they received a 'phone call from the airline to say that they should make their way to the airport as planned, which they had done, whilst still feeling a bit apprehensive. If they had not been able to travel, they would have accepted it, as, clearly, safety had to be the ultimate priority. In saying that, they were equally as happy to accept that the airline had taken all necessary precautions and checks and that there was nothing to worry about.

On arriving at the airport, they found it to be almost deserted, and consequently, there was no queue or waiting time, and the flight was also on time. Also, when they boarded the plane, they found it to be half empty, and accordingly, they were allowed to stretch out in extra legroom seats and enjoy the flight. Sam even ordered champagne to celebrate, and perhaps, unsurprisingly, the time flew in – no pun intended.

The fact that this almost idyllic set of circumstances came into play during such a freak and concerning meteorological phenomenon was, Sam thought, particularly ironic and unexpected, but welcome, nevertheless. It was the most relaxed he could ever remember having felt on a flight, particularly considering the reservations he had had about the situation. Unfortunately, the rest of the holiday had not gone quite as smoothly.

On today's flight, he had booked an aisle seat as usual because he didn't like a window seat and particularly hated being in the middle between two complete strangers, whose personal hygiene often left a lot to be desired. He was also a bit claustrophobic. Kim, on the other hand always had to have a window seat as she didn't like being disturbed by other passengers getting up to go to the toilet, etc. This meant that he was left with the middle seat, because he usually had had a couple of beers in the bar, had to get up at least once to go to the toilet, thereby inconveniencing the other passenger, whereas Kim never went to the toilet ever, on a point of principle, regardless of the length of the flight.

She clearly had a very determined and resilient bladder, whereas he had a problematic prostate. After he and Kim had split up, he had met and gone on holiday with someone else, who was happy to sit in the middle so that he could have the aisle seat. He had suggested that they could book two aisle seats, but she rejected this out of hand because that meant that they wouldn't be able to 'have a blether and a cuddle'. Whilst Sam had found this to be both romantic and flattering at the time, unfortunately, the reality was that she spent most of the flight asleep. Sam had never managed to sleep on a flight, probably because he hated flying and couldn't relax enough to do so. Also, he very rarely drank much on the actual flight—maybe one or two beers maximum—and never wine, as drinking it from a plastic cup was anathema to him, regarding it as sacrilege.

He needed to drink his wine from a nice big glass, viewing it as all part of the enjoyment of the experience; it was like eating pasta without wine–totally unacceptable.

Sam hadn't felt particularly hungry because of the substantial breakfast that he had enjoyed at the airport, so hadn't bought any sandwiches to take on the plane. Nor had he ordered any food on the flight; instead, just purchasing a couple of bags of peanuts to eat with his beer. He bought two because, *the bags are so small that they wouldn't fill a squirrel,* thought Sam. He also noted with some amusement that there was a warning on the bag that read, 'may contain nuts! No shit Sherlock.

Sam quite liked it when bars gave you little ramekins filled with peanuts, but only when they were exclusively yours; he didn't like it when they or some hotel foyers put out bowls of peanuts for everyone to dip their fingers into, regarding it as particularly unhygienic.

He also hated those nuts that the bars in Spain give you for free, or 'miseria', as they are called, and for good reason, having caused him considerable orthodontic misery and pain in the past. Accordingly, he had since made it his business to find out the Spanish word for peanuts, which is 'Cacahuetes', to separate the 'wheat from the chaff' in future. He had also felt the need to do so following a particularly hilarious misunderstanding some years before when he and Kim were on holiday in Nerja, in Costa del Sol. After a walk, they had sat down at a pavement cafe on the Balcon de Europa, which is a delightful promenade above Calahonda and Caletilla beaches, which along with the Burriana are amongst the best in the Axarquía area. In the evening, the locals get dressed up and enjoy a *paseo* along the Balcon, when it is brightly illuminated and alive with vendors, artists and performers of all kinds. It also has a hotel built into the side of a cliff from where you can look over the Mediterranean. You can also have your photo taken with the statue of the late King Alfonso XII who named the balcony after the earthquake that hit Nerja in 1884.

They had ordered some drinks and tapas and on finishing their food, ordered some more drinks. Sam had the notion for something savoury to go with his beer and asked the waiter, in his Glasgow accent, if they had any nuts. The camarero looked at him quizzically, before saying, 'Wait please' and headed off to fetch their drinks. On returning, he delivered the drinks and then said to Sam, apologetically, 'Sorry, we don't have Javenni nuts. What are Javenni nuts?' They couldn't explain to the guy for laughing.

Chapter 11

15 January 2018.
Monday

Sam stepped off the plane to that very familiar and welcoming blast of hot air and sun on his face, which, for him, was the moment when his holiday really began. He was travelling light, with only cabin luggage, so he had no need to wait at the baggage carousel. After he was through passport control all that remained was for him to find his taxi, and then he was only around thirty minutes away from his hotel pool and bar. Like the rest of the day up until then, everything went according to plan, and in just over an hour, he had indeed checked in to his hotel, the Mediterranean Palace in Los Americas, having booked a room with a pool view. He dumped his luggage, changed into swim shorts and a tee shirt, applied the necessary sun spray and was sitting at the pool bar with a cold beer within fifteen minutes of arrival.

He still had time for at least a couple of hours at the pool before he needed to get ready for dinner and the only other thing, he needed to do was buy some wine and beer to put in the fridge.

The sun was still high in the sky, and he had a book, a lounger, a beer and at this moment in time, not a care in the world. *Still, it was early days*, thought Sam, light-heartedly chiding himself, it can't possibly last. Little did he know how prophetic his thoughts would prove to become.

Chapter 12

15 January 2018
Monday

When the sun disappeared behind the clouds after a couple of hours, removing that almost amber glow and hue from the early evening landscape, Sam took the opportunity to go to the supermarket to fetch the required supplies for his fridge, after which he showered and changed before heading out to enjoy the first night of his holiday. He had a beer in Harry's bar in the Safari Centre before heading off for food, making his way along the Paseo los Andes, where there were many and varied bars and restaurants. However, he kept walking, and as he came to the end of the road, he found himself directly facing an Irish bar on Avenida Santiago Puig. He also noticed, from the signs outside, that the bar was showing the Liverpool v man City game whilst also displaying an impressive food menu, which led to him deciding it ticked all the boxes.

Whilst the food was expensive but of very poor quality, the football, by contrast was a seven-goal thriller, with Liverpool coming out of it the victors. After the football finished, Sam left and on walking up Avenida Santiago Puig on the way back to his hotel, he noticed someone standing on the corner opposite the Hotel Columbus, stopping people and handing out leaflets. The guy looked strangely familiar, so much so that he thought that he must be hallucinating. Because yet again he thought that he was looking at the man he knew as Akmal from Benidorm. What the fuck is going on? thought Sam. What is happening to me? Am I going insane? Am I hallucinating or obsessed with this guy? Why do I keep thinking I am seeing him everywhere I go?

Whilst Sam realised that this was something of an exaggeration, nevertheless, that's how it was beginning to feel. And yet, as he watched the guy animatedly stopping people (all male it must be said) and thrusting leaflets in their hands, there was indeed something compellingly and convincingly familiar about him.

Sam decided that he had to get closer and see for himself to put his mind at rest, despite his reservations about his steadily deteriorating and seemingly delusional state of mind.

So, he started to walk towards him, and as he got ever closer, he was even more convinced that it definitely was Akmal. When he was almost beside him the guy noticed him and handed him a leaflet for some 'nightclub' saying; 'You like beautiful girls, you like to have sex with beautiful girls?' Unlike in Glasgow and his encounter with Farouk, this time the voice was right, everything was right. As Sam stared at him searchingly, the guy also seemed to sense something about him was familiar. And Sam, emboldened by this realization decided to trust his instincts and confront him.

'Hello, Akmal, long time no see, still working hard, I see.'

As he spoke, he could see the dawning realization gradually transform the look on the guy's face from confusion to disbelief, as he recognised him, or his voice, or both.

Akmal stared at Sam disbelievingly and seemingly stunned into silence. 'What's the matter Sparky, cat got your tongue all of a sudden?' said Sam. 'A couple of minutes ago you were giving it plenty, like a Town Crier. Back in the old routine I see, eh'?' he added sardonically.

'Why are you here, what do you want from me?' said Akmal, finally finding his voice.

'I am here on holiday if that's okay with you, what's your excuse?'

'You're not stalking me, are you?' Sam asked a still perplexed Akmal.

'No, I think it is you are stalking me, how you know I am here?'

'Calm down Sparky I didn't know you were here until I heard you touting your wares from across the road,' said Sam, pointing across the road. I am just on my way back to my hotel.'

'You are staying there, at the Columbus?' asked Akmal, nodding in the direction of the KN hotel directly opposite.

'No, I am staying at the Med Palace,' said Sam and instantly regretted it. He wasn't sure why, but it just occurred to him that it was probably a mistake to tell Akmal anything about his situation.

'So, you are truly on holiday?' How long you here for?' asked Akmal.

'A fortnight... two weeks, well, fifteen days actually,' said Sam, and then thought, 'Nice one Sam so much for not telling him anything, why don't you tell him your bank account details, while you're at it.'

'So, you don't want nothing from me?' asked Akmal, sounding relieved. Sam ignored the forgivable grammatical double negative from the Algerian particularly as his English was much better than Sam's Spanish or French and simply said, 'No it would appear that it's just a coincidence after all,' said Sam, looking pensive, as he wasn't a great believer in coincidences, before adding, 'So how did you end up here. What happened to Benidorm?'

41

'I get moved because of my problems with… with you… our fight… and then the other thing, so I don't have to answer questions. Too much attention from the police… it is not good for business.'

'Well, you could have done a lot worse than here,' said Sam, 'you could have ended up in Glasgow.'

'Like my brother,' said Akmal, 'he is there now. He used to be here in Tenerife, but I get his job after he make a big mistake, much worse than me.'

'Your brother is in Glasgow?' said Sam, as the wheels in his head started to turn and a gradual realisation began to take shape in his mind. *Surely, not*, he thought, now that would be a fucking amazing coincidence. 'Where does he work?' asked Sam, followed by; 'Do you look like each other?' as he became quite excited by the prospect of another very unlikely co-incidence.'

'He work in a nightclub,' said Akmal, looking puzzled and asking; 'why you want to know this?' Why you need to know about where my brother is?'

'What, no nothing, no reason, just curious?' said Sam not seeing any reason to explain the highly unlikely scenario that he had been contemplating, instead asking, 'so what did he do wrong to get moved?'

Akmal, who had almost missed a group of guys passing and had rushed to hand them some fliers, smiled and said, 'He fuck the wrong girl.'

'No luck, women eh,' said Sam, for no reason other than for something to say. 'I'll bet he's happy about that,' he added casually.

'He like the nightclub OK, with the girls but he also works in a car wash in the daytime, and he does not like it as it is hard work for not much pay.'

'Wait, what? You… your brother works in a car wash? Are

42

you kidding me? Is his name Farouk?'

'What? Yes... no, how you know this?' said Akmal surprised.

'Because I, I... saw him, working at the car wash, I mean. I thought he was you, but when I spoke to him, I realised that it wasn't you,' said Sam, realising that he was rambling.

'You spoke to my brother?' asked Akmal incredulous.

'Yes, but only when I was paying him for my car being washed. So, when I saw you tonight, I thought that I was losing it.' He saw Akmal struggling to understand his idiomatic phrase and corrected himself.

'I thought that I was going mad, imagining things,' becoming obsessed but it's okay, because you're you and obviously I'm happy to say that I'm not-going mad I mean.' *But it is still a helluva coincidence,* he thought. Or maybe even a sign.

'You say you are not mad, but you talk crazy,' said Akmal, obviously confused.

'It's okay Sparky, everything is fine, nothing to worry about. Have a good night and don't work too hard,' said Sam, smiling.

'I work hard, every day and night,' said Akmal.

'I am sure that you do Sparky,' said Sam, smiling and then holding out his hand saying, 'well goodbye, I know where to find you if I need to,' laughing and then adding, 'appearing nightly at a street corner near you.'

Akmal initially made as if to shake Sam's hand but then hesitated, saying, 'Why you need to find me?'

'Only kidding Sparky, just a joke, I hope that we never see one another again,' said Sam, over his shoulder, as he walked away without looking back and headed back to his hotel. He had a drink in the hotel bar, which was quiet, before deciding to call it a night- without any further incident for a change.

43

Chapter 13

16 January 2018
Tuesday

Farouk thought back to the girl that he had become close to and latterly intimate with in Tenerife; Carmen, who worked at the Mantasy club, amongst others. Normally, the bosses weren't too bothered if the girls and the male workers had some fun together, as long as it didn't interfere with business, i.e.: the formers' output and productivity. However, Farouk had made the mistake of becoming involved with one of his bosses' 'favourite' girls, whom he was very possessive and protective of. And, whilst she was initially very receptive to his advances, basically it was doomed to end in disappointment, as he had nothing to offer her as an acceptable alternative to her existing position, such as it was. Furthermore, his subsequent ill-advised defiant and volatile reaction to being put in his place also incurred the wrath of the 'Zaeim' to the extent that he was lucky to still have any kind of job at the end of it.

Then his phone rang and on looking, he saw that it was his brother, Akmal calling. Akmal and his brother Farouk spoke regularly on the phone catching up with each other about their respective situations. Ironically, Akmal had been given his brother's position in Tenerife, following the latter being moved to Glasgow as punishment for his indiscretions with Carmen, which had met with the disapproval of his superiors in the organisation. Equally, Akmal's move to Tenerife was designed to take him out of the firing line in Benidorm, following his encounters with Sam and the subsequent arrangement that had taken place prior to a murder being committed. As far as the authorities in Benidorm were concerned, he had had to return to Algeria for personal reasons, and in the absence of anything connecting him to the murder had no reason to pursue it any further. Akmal, for his part was quite happy with his lot, in contrast to Farouk, who clearly wasn't happy with his move to Glasgow, or the reasons behind it.

However, there was no bad feeling between them, as the latter realised that his brother, like himself, had no say in the situation and was merely following orders. However, when Farouk had taken the 'phone call from Akmal on Monday, he had sensed a degree of animated excitement in his brother's voice; he then listened as he informed him that the man with whom he had found himself in conflict prior to then subsequently brokering a 'contract' with, in Benidorm in November of the previous year, was currently in the same resort as he was, in Tenerife. Akmal breathlessly described his meeting with Sam, whilst the incredulity in his voice at the odds of their paths crossing again in such circumstances was clear. He also told Farouk that the person in question lived in Glasgow and had been to his car wash and spoken to him. Farouk stated that he could not recall having a conversation with anyone but did ask his brother why the guy was in Tenerife. Akmal then went on to reassure his brother that he was simply there on holiday, whilst also admitting that initially he was shocked and worried as to why he was there.

When Farouk didn't seem convinced by his brother's reassurances about Sam only being a tourist, Akmal attempted to reassure his brother further by providing him with the details of the hotel where he was staying and for how long, as Sam had advised. However, Akmal remained insistent that it was only a coincidence and that he did not anticipate having any further contact with him.

If only he had known how wrong he was.

Chapter 14

16 January 2018.
Tuesday

Sam didn't go to breakfast the next morning instead opting to have a lie in and not rising to face the day until around ten a.m. After having some cereal and a cup of tea on the balcony, he lay on a lounger at the pool for a couple of hours with a his Kindle before deciding to go for lunch at the Palapa Beach Club, which, depending upon your point of view sits at the start, or the end, of El Camison Beach, across from and actually forming part of the Mare Nostrum complex: which is comprised of three hotels, the Mark Anthony, the Cleopatra Princess and the Mediterranean Palace, where Sam was staying. He had previously stayed at both the Med Palace and the Cleopatra Princess, both with Kim and on his own, respectively, and as he sat there looking on to the glorious, crowded beach from his wonderful vantage point, he smiled and shook his head as he recalled something which had happened on the latter occasion.

He had arrived at the Cleopatra Princess on his own on a day when the rain was bouncing off the ground and whilst being checked in, he watched from the foyer as a group of young, seemingly inebriated English holidaymakers frolicked on the beach and in the sea across from the hotel, seemingly oblivious to the abysmal weather conditions.

'Feeling no pain,' Sam had said to the very pleasant and

attractive female member of staff who welcomed him with smile and a glass of fizz on his arrival. 'Welcome to the Cleopatra Princess Mr Meredith,' let's get you checked in then,' she said, adding, 'now let's see if we can get you a nice room. What kind of room would you like?' she asked, smiling that friendly smile of hers, which was working for him big time. The thing was, Sam had booked his room online and thought that he had booked a standard room. However, for whatever reason, he got the impression that she seemed to be giving him, if not necessarily preferential treatment, certainly a choice over and above that.

And he wasn't wrong, because after she handed him his key and his paperwork and said, 'Enjoy your stay and have a lovely holiday,' again with that same lovely smile, he followed the directions provided only to discover that she had given him a double room with a balcony looking directly on to El Camison beach. He remembered hoping that his luck, rather than the rain, would last for the rest of the holiday.

And indeed, the next day was a beautiful sunny day, and the beach was very busy, and so, after breakfast Sam had taken himself out to the balcony with a coffee, to read his book and watch the world go by, when to his disbelief, the patio doors locked behind him. Following several failed attempts at trying to prise them open, he was forced to accept that he was stranded, and he was reduced to shouting at passers – by walking along the promenade for help. *Not surprisingly,* thought Sam, they probably thought that he was either drunk or demented, or both, as he hilariously alternated between English and broken Spanish in his desperate attempts to communicate his predicament to all and sundry.

Thankfully, someone eventually realised the reason for his seemingly bizarre behaviour and went into the hotel to alert them accordingly, at which point a member of staff came to the room to release him from his solitary distress and put him out of his misery. Incredibly, the same thing had happened to Kim on an earlier holiday together in Tenerife, at another hotel in the Fanabe area of Costa Adeje.

On that occasion he had gone to watch the 2012 English Premiership title being decided, as Manchester United played Sunderland and Manchester City played Queens Park Rangers, in one of, if not the most exciting conclusions to a football season ever. Such was the level of anticipation and excitement that both games were broadcast simultaneously by Sky Sports. Both teams needed to win their games have any chance of lifting the Premier League trophy and Sam had gone to Los Christianos to watch the tense showdown, choosing a location where there were two pubs adjacent to each other, showing the respective games.

Fortunately for Sam, he had ended up in the one showing the Manchester City game, so he was able to experience the full euphoria of the extra time winner for Manchester City live and the now legendary 'Agueroooooo! commentary moment by Martin Tyler, when the little Argentine legend scored to win the title for City in the dying moments. It had echoes of the moment, five years previously, when his team, Glasgow Celtic, were playing their long term rivals Rangers, which had produced a similar magical outcome and response, only instead of 'Aguerooooo 'the commentator had screamed; Nakamuraaaaa'!, when the little Japanese genius scored a wonderful free kick against Kilmarnock in a 1-0 victory to win the Scottish Premier League title. A year later he had also blown the title race wide open and the roof off the stadium when he scored his first Old Firm goal, an absolute screamer which, co-incidentally Sam had also watched in Tenerife, whilst there with Kim. However,

49

unsurprisingly, and predictably, on the day of the Manchester City victory he got caught up in the resultant euphoria and celebrations of the Manchester City fans and then lost track of time – again!

Unfortunately, Kim, unlike Sam, had not been rescued from her confinement on the balcony, but instead had been both stared at and flashed at by an elderly male pervert on the rooftop nudist pool. So, whilst Sam's return to the room was welcomed it wasn't with open arms and a warm smile. He had suggested that Kim report it to the hotel management, but she was clearly more annoyed at Sam, believing that he was more to blame for her predicament because of his drunken, selfish behaviour, than anyone else. And to be honest she probably had a point.

Chapter 15

16 January 2018
Tuesday

Sam had showered and changed into smart but casual attire, before heading to the Palapa for lunch, where he enjoyed some stew and Canarian potatoes with a couple of glasses of red wine. After his lunch he returned to his lounger and kindle at the poolside for a few more hours, as it was still sunny and hot, not leaving until early evening to shower and change again before heading out for dinner and drinks. He headed to the Hole in the Wall Bar across from the hotel where he had another beer and watched the second half of the Chelsea v Barcelona game, but after only one beer he suddenly felt ravenous and decided to treat himself to a steak at the Prime Steak House in the Safari Centre, which did not disappoint.

After his meal he went to the Hard Rock Café, where he enjoyed live music in both the main bar downstairs and in the more bijou and intimate space of the upstairs bar, where he ended his night, due to feeling the effect of his travels and his consumption of food and alcohol. Fortunately, the same factors also combined to ensure that he enjoyed a sound night's sleep in his second night in Tenerife. Sadly, it was not to last.

Chapter 16

17 January 2018
Wednesday

Despite the alcohol he had consumed the night before, Sam awoke late feeling quite refreshed after his surprisingly peaceful and settled sleep. As he had missed breakfast, he decided to have lunch at the pool bar at the Cleopatra Princess, where he ordered a Chicken Caesar Salad and a couple of glasses of wine, which went down very well. After finishing his lunch, he decided to walk along El Camison beach, which faces the Mare Nostrum resort and runs parallel to the Avenida de Americas, before turning off and heading down Paseo Orinoco to Las Americas beach, buying a newspaper on the way. He found a seat at a café looking out to sea, where the waves crashed up on to the rocks on the shore bordered by the boardwalk, which he found very calming and relaxing. He ordered a beer and read his newspaper before turning his attention to the crossword, which he was making light work of before finding himself stumped at a couple of questions. His puzzled expression obviously revealed his predicament because he heard a voice say, 'You look stuck, can I help?'

He looked up to see an attractive, middle aged, redhead smiling at him sympathetically from the table diagonally across from him.

'I'm a bit of a crossword and puzzle geek, and my nose was

bothering me to be honest, sorry!' she said smiling, half apologetically.

'I've got two to get,' said Sam, standing up and offering her the paper for her attention, which she took from him, smiling. She smiled a lot. And it was a nice smile too; one that made him think that there might be room for further endeavour and conversation.

'No pressure,' she said, 'it would serve me right if I ended up with egg on my face here, wouldn't it?' she replied, making a mock grimace.

'Would a drink help?' asked Sam, pointing towards her wine glass, which was empty and adding, 'I was just about to have another one anyway,' which wasn't strictly true, as he had been just about to leave. She seemed to hesitate slightly before replying; 'Yes, that would be nice, a white wine thanks,' tapping the pen on her teeth and picking up the paper to look at the crossword.

'Coming right up,' said Sam heading towards the bar, where the waitress took his order before informing him that she would bring the drinks out to the table. Sam asked to use the toilet and she directed him accordingly. When he returned to the table the drinks had been delivered and the crossword had been completed.

'All done,' said his new drinking companion, with a look of smug satisfaction on her face.

'Well done, you,' said Sam then adding, 'I'm sorry I don't know your name.'

'It's Emily,' she said, holding up her glass and Sam responded accordingly saying, 'Sam.'

'Cheers, Sam, pleased to meet you,' said Emily, clinking her glass with his. Sam responded accordingly, whilst picking up the newspaper to inspect the completed crossword. He smiled ruefully and nodded his head, acknowledging the accuracy of her input. She responded with another smile, before saying;

'Just a fresh pair of eyes, that's all it was.'

'Such modesty… and a fair bit of knowledge obviously,' said Sam and decided to take the opportunity to gain some knowledge of his own, by asking, 'So Emily, what does an attractive and intelligent woman like you do to keep mind and soul together?'

Emily told him that she was a carer and he told her what he did and after a couple more drinks they found out a bit more about each other.

They also exchanged phone numbers and agreed to be in touch with a view to meeting up again. Sam had actually asked her out to dinner that night, but she said that she needed to go and sleep as she was not used to drinking as much during the daytime and she felt very sleepy. Her hotel, the Siesta ironically was closer than his, so he walked her there and said his goodbyes, with a very polite and respectful kiss on the cheek, which was reciprocated.

As Sam made his way back to his own hotel, he realised that he also felt quite tired and decided to have a nap. However, the 'nap' lasted nearly three hours and when he woke up it was dark, and his stomach was rumbling with hunger.

He got up, showered and dressed quickly, with the intention being to find somewhere to eat, and, after due consideration he decided upon the little Chinese Restaurant situated in the strip of bars just behind the Safari centre across from the Mare Nostrum complex.

He regarded the food there to be every bit as good as the much more up-market and expensive Teppanyaki Restaurant, above the dancing fountains at the Safari Centre, where you paid through the nose to be entertained by staff performing dramatic fire theatrics and circus tricks.

The place was still busy, the staff pleasant and the food very good, so after his meal of a Salt and Chilli Chicken starter, followed by Singapore Chow Mein and a free bottle of red wine - which he only had a glass from as unfortunately it wasn't of the same standard as the food - he decided that he needed a refreshing drink to cool his palate and ordered a beer. He was happy to sit there with a drink after finishing his meal and watch the world go by, apart from being constantly pestered by what he thought were African guys wearing Asda hi - viz tabards trying to sell him everything from flowers to wristwatches, bags and kids' toys.

On leaving the restaurant, Sam, after scouting the various establishments in the immediate vicinity, found himself at the Bull's Head, a bar just a few doors along which had a band on playing covers of rock classics from his era and making a very good job of it too. In fact, they were absolutely brilliant. The bar staff, who were Spanish, English and even Scottish, were all very pleasant and he had a few beers there before calling it a night. All in all, he reckoned it had been a very enjoyable day and a nice start to his holiday. But then he had been in that situation before, and it hadn't exactly turned out that way. However, he had decided that on this holiday, given the events in Benidorm the previous year and the resultant trauma experienced, that he would be more than happy with some female company and conversation without any complications. He had had enough drama and stress to last him a lifeline and he wasn't going through all that shit again.

At least that was the plan.

Chapter 17

18 January 2018
Thursday

Sam was awakened the next morning by a knock on the door and then what sounded like something being pushed under his door. He got up and saw a long white envelope on the floor with his name written on it, not his full name, just 'Sam'. He opened it and found that it was an invitation to a 'Singles Evening' for all the 'unattached guests of the hotel, travelling on their own,' to be held in two days' time on Friday 19th January. It also informed that this entitled him to purchase a ticket for the event, available at reception, for the 'very reasonable' amount of 25 Euros, which included all drinks and a meal.

Whilst he had initially not given it much thought, but the idea had gradually grown on him during the day, *why not?* he thought, *what have I got to lose?' if it turns out to be shit, I can always leave.*

Sam showered and then went for breakfast at the hotel before heading to the Med Palace pool, as it was a sunny day. However, he was able to find a bed quickly and after applying liberal amounts of sun spray, settled down with his book. However, he found himself thinking about the planned 'Singles Night' at the Cleopatra, which brought to mind the occasion when he and the band were booked to play at a singles night in a hotel in Perth, in what unexpectedly proved to be a wonderful 'fly on the wall' experience. There were about forty participants, some of whom had booked into the hotel and others who weren't and who were either travelling or lived local. The potential 'dates' had been divided up into four separate tables by the organisers and Sam and the other members of the band had each been allocated to a table allowing them to meet and chat with the guests for the meal, prior to them taking up their performance duties.

There were several bottles of wine placed on all tables and initially it was all quite civilised and respectable, until the drink was consumed; by some more than others, and in the case of Sam's table, mainly by one particular man and a woman, who embraced it with considerable gusto to the extent that most of it was finished before the first course had been served, leading to loud demands for further refreshment. The woman had arrived at the table already the worse for wear and announcing her presence/arrival by throwing her room 'key', which was attached to a lump of metal the size of Thor's hammer, on the table, to the alarm and amusement of all and sundry. (This was before the introduction of the slick keycards in use today. In saying that at least the actual keys always opened the door first time, and you didn't find yourself heading back down to reception for a replacement due to the new technology not being able to perform the basic intended function or 'do what it said on the tin').

Her melodramatic and loud actions with the key were amplified by her declaring, equally as subtly, 'Right that's me checked in, now I need a drink.' This, it seemed to Sam, was also designed to make it clear that she was staying the night, had an 'empty' and was 'available' to anyone who was brave or desperate enough to go there.

Sam also became aware of rather hostile glances and attitudes being directed towards him whenever he engaged in any friendly dialogue with any of the female guests, with the resentment and annoyance being palpable. Clearly, the males in attendance didn't appreciate the invited entertainment cramping their style or chances of 'pulling.'

And on the subject of 'style' some of the men's dress sense had to be seen to be believed, everything from 'Teddy Boy garb, brothel sneakers, drainpipe trousers and lace ties and 'winkle pickers' to western style shirts and cowboy boots. But they all obviously thought that they were the 'bee's knees

Contrastingly, there were several very attractive and stylish women in attendance, who in truth looked really out of place and incongruous with the situation; in particular a young, attractive and clearly very intelligent American woman, who Sam got chatting to- to the obvious annoyance of Mr loud and inebriated. Sam found her to be very interesting, charming and likeable and had he not been in a relationship, troubled as it was, he may even have made a move himself. However, if truth be told, he thought that she was probably out of his league too and accordingly, he complimented her on her style, thanked her for her company and wished her all the best for her future endeavours, both romantic and personal. Meanwhile, Mr Loud and Inebriated staggered drunkenly around the hall and could be heard above the music shouting loudly and angrily; 'How do you get a fucking drink in this shithole', whilst his female drinking partner echoed his sentiments by banging her substantial and weighty 'key' on the table, to the clear annoyance of the other members and staff alike.

The bar, for some unknown reason, had been closed. *Probably to stop him and his female counterpart from drinking it dry* thought Sam. He also remembered thinking that alcohol really made some people look very unattractive, which, ironically, had been an observation made by his ex, Kim, shortly before the subsequent demise of their relationship.

As Sam and the rest of the band were leaving the venue, Sam saw the very drunk woman from his table, standing outside the entrance to the hotel smoking a cigarette and talking to the singer, who had mischievously engaged her in conversation. He had apparently asked her if she had enjoyed the night and if she attended regular events like this and she had answered yes on both counts. *The bass player had then, quite cheekily,* thought Sam, asked her how much it cost her in membership fees.

However, the considerable lubrication from the alcohol had clearly loosened her tongue and she was only too happy to inform him that she was required to pay the handsome sum of £60.00 a year, plus the costs relating to individual events, before taking a long drag of her cigarette and then exclaiming, 'And quite frankly I don't really think I'm getting my money's worth!' Sam remembered thinking that she wasn't referring to the entertainment.

Sam's thoughts then drifted into his own plans for the evening's entertainment and, after checking his phone, he discovered that Barcelona were playing Espanyol in the Copa del Rey and thought that would do for starters. He also thought that he would play it by ear as far as food was concerned but then, unexpectedly, the thought of food made him feel peckish, leading to him heading to the pool bar for a burger and chips, which was sufficient to tide him over until a more substantial meal later in the evening.

After his lunch Sam returned to his lounger and book at the poolside for a few more hours, as it was still sunny and hot, not leaving until early evening to get showered and ready to head out for the evening. On leaving the hotel, Sam went for a walk around the immediate area and decided upon a seafood restaurant looking out towards Las Vistas beach which stretches all the way to Los Christianos. It was a very mild and pleasant evening, and the place was quiet with a nice ambience, making Sam feel quite calm and relaxed. The food was also fantastic, and he enjoyed some oysters with a Bloody Mary dressing, followed by Sea Bass with Salsa Verde and Canarian Potatoes and a Greek salad, all washed down with a couple of glasses of Rioja Blanco. This had only served to put him in the mood for a few cold beers and so, after thanking the staff for the lovely meal and service and tipping them accordingly, he decided to stay local and headed for the nearby strip of bars again, this time deciding upon the nearby Soul Bar, which was very lively.

He had a few beers there, listening to a black singer performing very impressive covers of Motown hits, prior to calling it a night, despite receiving several requests for a dance from various attractive but seemingly intoxicated females standing at the bar. He most definitely wasn't intoxicated enough to think about dancing, whilst also realising that he was looking forward to meeting up with Emily again and resolving to contact her the next day to arrange it.

Chapter 18

18 January 2018
Thursday

Following Farouk's conversation with Akmal on the Monday, he had thought long and hard about the information his brother had given him, which he had never previously discussed with him in such revealing detail. Then, after some more reflection, he also realised that a certain Glasgow 'businessman' would be very interested in that information; however, he also knew that it would hold a serious threat for his brother should it fall into the wrong hands. When Akmal had called his brother Farouk was on a very rare night off and had gone out for a few drinks with a few friends, who worked in one of the other nightclubs and car washes, like himself.

Unfortunately, following a few beers he had relaxed and become quite loose lipped and voluble, carelessly blabbing about the conversation he had with Akmal about the 'arrangement' that had been made in Benidorm involving his brother and some guy named Sam Meredith. As is the way of these things, one of the guys had then blabbed to someone, who also blabbed to someone else, until eventually all of the information had finally reached the ears of said 'businessman'- one Terry Lindsay - the brother of Rab Lindsay, who had been murdered in Benidorm - allegedly as a result of the aforesaid 'arrangement.'

Only this time, the fact that the information emanated from one of the people reportedly involved more or less confirmed the veracity of the allegations, as far as Lindsay was concerned, which unfortunately did not augur well for Sam, or Akmal. Terry Lindsay also just happened to be part of a group of Glasgow 'businessmen' involved in an ongoing feud with a Syrian named Naseem Akim, who was one of the owners of the Car Wash and 'Gentleman's Club' where Farouk worked; each being just one of several such businesses in the city. One of the consequences of the feud was that several car washes had been bombed and burned down over recent years, the most recent having been six months earlier. On that occasion the emergency services fire crews had to battle the fire for eight hours, requiring five fire engines to extinguish the blaze. Six men were subsequently jailed for a total of one hundred years after being found guilty at the High Court in Glasgow of trying to murder Akim, who also 'just happened' to have well established links to the criminal 'cartels' in Benidorm and Tenerife, and other places- involved in drug and people trafficking - amongst other things.

Whilst Akim had survived all the attempts on his life to date, the feud and the unrelenting struggle for power continued unabated between the two factions, with no quarter given or asked, but with no great benefit to either side.

Terry Lindsay, however had not been slow to see how the recent revelations could be used to his advantage, by making some inroads into resolving the feud, whilst also taking revenge for his brother's death; he had already set the wheels in motion in that regard by making contact with certain individuals. However, there were other loose ends that needed to be attended to, whilst a contingency plan was also needed, just in case things didn't work out as planned. A telephone call to Akim was all it took to set things in motion.

Chapter 19

19 January 2018
Friday

Sam had forgotten to close the blackout curtains before he had gone to bed the previous evening, and he awoke to find the room flooded in sunlight, which had the effect of making him feel that he should be up and about. Accordingly, he decided to head down to breakfast early, leaving his towel and a book on a sun bed on the way. *Well, everybody else does it,* he thought. However, after a hearty breakfast, he found that the pool at the Med Palace was too busy and loud for his liking and headed through the connecting corridor to the pool at the Cleopatra Princess, which was much quieter and peaceful. He found a vacant bed in no time and settled down, applied liberal amounts of lotion to everywhere but his back and lay in the sun until it got so hot that he needed to cool down with a swim in the impressively ornate pool, surrounded by Greek statues and Doric columns and capitals and statues. And it was wonderfully refreshing.

This is the life, he thought, as he dried himself off after his swim, before settling down to read his book, which for some reason wasn't really grabbing him, and he hadn't bought a newspaper, as normal. Accordingly, his thoughts began drifting back to Emily, at which point he decided to call her, reaching for his mobile phone, when it suddenly and on looking at the screen he saw that it was Emily's number. 'Good afternoon, how are you this bright sunny day,' she asked, then adding, 'Are you busy?'

'Why, do you have something in mind?' Sam asked, and then adding, 'I was just about to call you,' and on being met with a loud silence, added 'Honestly.'

'I believe you,' she said, laughing that delicious laugh and then informing him, I thought that we could meet for lunch at the Papagayo Beach Club. My treat,' she offered, which he was more than happy to accept.

After a quick shower, shave and a change into stone linen shorts and a blue linen shirt, he made his way along Avenida Dominguez Puig before cutting down Paseo El Dorada until he reached Avenida Rafael Puig. He then headed down Paseo Mexico towards the shore, turning right and walking along the boardwalk of Playa de Las Americas at a leisurely pace until he arrived at the Papagayo. On realising that he was early Sam ordered a beer for himself that he paid for, advising the waitress that he was there for lunch and was waiting on someone else arriving. She nodded her understanding and smiled a friendly smile as she left him to await his guest's arrival. Sam sat outside and sipped his beer looking out to sea from the comfortable surroundings of the Beach Club. '*It really is a lovely setting,*' thought Sam, never having been there before now, but happy to be there on this day, he thought, as he waited for Emily to arrive, which she did within minutes.

Sam was taken aback by how lovely she looked, despite having very little make-up on and being dressed very casually in sandals and a short sky-blue sundress, which showed off her lovely, toned legs. She looked so fresh and bright, and she had done something with her hair. It was all he could do not to stare. 'You look nice,' he said, stating the obvious.

'Thanks, Sam, have you been here long?' she asked.

'Just this long,' said Sam measuring the gap between the top of his glass and the level of his drink with his thumb and forefinger.

'What would you like to drink?' he asked, to which she replied, 'No, it's on me, I'll get it, and waved to attract the attention of a passing waitress, who arrived and asked Emily; 'Would you like a drink?'

'Another beer for'... but Sam interrupted her, saying, 'At least let me buy you a drink.'

'Ok, I'll have a Gin and Tonic thanks, and can I have diet tonic please,' Emily said to the waitress.

'And another beer,' said Sam.

'Is that everything?' asked the waitress.

'Yes thanks, but don't put it on a tab.'

'Sorry, what you want?' asked the waitress, clearly not understanding his idiomatic phrase.

'I'll pay for it now with cash,' said Sam and then just to make sure she understood, added; 'Yo quiero a pagar ahora con dinero, por favor Senorita.'

'Si, yo entiendo Senor, Gracias,' said the waitress, who was quite clearly a senora rather than a senorita, by virtue of the ring on the third finger on her left hand, which Sam may or may not have noticed.

However, she seemed quite pleased at this oversight, simply smiling and asking, 'Esta todo Senor?' whilst placing particular emphasis on the last word.

'Oh, and can you bring some peanuts please,' asked Sam.

'Senor?' she asked, seemingly confused again.

'Tienes Cacahutes ?' asked Sam, thereby ensuring that they avoided any repetition of the Javenni nuts episode.

'Ah, si Senor, Muchas Gracias,' said the waitress, smiling as she went. *Probably at my woeful Spanish* thought Sam. Emily, however, was impressed and complimented him on his linguistic prowess, but then followed it up with 'You'll put yourself off your lunch eating peanuts,' said Emily.

'I don't think so,' said Sam, 'I'm feeling very hungry. I just won't have a starter.'

'You can have whatever you want,' said Emily, as the waitress arrived with the drinks and menus-and the peanuts, which Emily began to pick at saying, 'Sorry, I've got a cheek, particularly after giving you grief for asking for them. I love peanuts but they normally give you the other ones which are hard and tasteless.'

How did you know what to ask for? Sam told her the Javenni nuts story, which she laughed out loud at but then said that she didn't believe it was true, accusing him of making it up.

'I wish, I'm not that clever-or funny,' he said, protesting, whilst continuing to maintain the honesty and accuracy of the story, which she grudgingly accepted, but in a very good humoured way. If nothing else, the anecdote served to put them both at ease and they chatted happily, to the extent that they forgot about the food, until the waitress reminded them.

They ordered tapas type food which they were happy to share and which they both enjoyed, along with each other's company, so much so that they lost track of time, with several hours having passed, without them having realised it. When the waitress appeared and asked if they wanted any more food or drink, Emily demurred, whilst asking for the bill.

Sam offered to pay or at least go Dutch, but Emily was adamant that it was on her. 'Well, the next one's on me,' said Sam, before adding, 'sorry... if you want to that is?' looking expectantly at Emily. However, in truth, he would have been surprised if she hadn't agreed, as he thought that they were clearly were enjoying each other's company.

'Of course, I do,' I enjoy your company Sam,' she said conforming hat his instincts were sound. Sam assured her that the feeling was mutual, and she reached over and held his hand. Sam was just about to kiss her when the waitress arrived with the bill, which Emily snatched away before he could see it or do anything with it.

'Where to now?' asked Sam, whilst being almost certain that he knew the answer.

'I'm afraid I'm a bit of a lightweight when it comes to drinking, particularly during the day, so I need to head back for a siesta again,' said Emily.

'No problem,' said Sam, as that was exactly was what he was expecting her to say. 'We could walk along the shore towards your hotel, and I'll head back to mine from there,' he offered.

'I was thinking that maybe you could join me, and we could have a siesta together,' said Emily, taking his hand again and pulling him towards her.

'*Now that was definitely not what I expected to hear,*' thought Sam, and all his previous cautious resolve evaporated as he took Emily in his arms and kissed her.

'You smell and feel lovely,' he whispered softly in her ear, as he gently caressed her lustrous red hair.

They went to Emily's hotel and on entering her room, which was very spacious, bright and airy with a very large bed, which made Sam think back to the hotel where he and Kim had stayed at in Croatia, as the bed had been so big that he remembered thinking at the time that there would be very little likelihood of

67

them coming into contact with each other by chance. At one stage Sam, who couldn't sleep, had thought about moving over and attempting to negotiate some 'contact', but had looked over and thought better of it as it was too far to travel.

On entering the room, Emily put the kettle on and made them coffee, as she said that she needed to 'sober up a bit', adding that she was 'a bit of a lightweight'. She took the coffee to the separate lounge area which had two sofas at ninety-degree angles and a coffee table between them.

She sat down on one and placed the coffees side by side, inviting Sam to join her on the same sofa which he did. However, as he sat down, he sensed an uneasiness in her demeanour and some tension between them.

" Are you okay Emily?" he asked, feeling both concerned and uncertain, given her presentation, which had altered dramatically in a very short space of time. She smiled at him briefly before dissolving into tears and then apologizing profusely, initially reaching out to touch him and then getting up and walking away from him in no particular direction. 'What is it Emily? What's wrong?' asked Sam, getting up and gently leading her back to the sofa and then sitting her back down and wiping the tears away.

'I'm sorry Sam, I thought that we could just come back here and spend some nice time together,' she said.

'Look Emily, it's all right, don't worry, there's no need to be upset. I don't mind, we can just sit and talk, or I'll leave you to sleep if you like. Or if you don't think you can't sleep, we can talk about each other, and I can put you to sleep no problem at all.'

Emily forced a weak smile and said, 'You're so nice Sam,' I don't know what you see in me or why you would want to be intimate with me?'

'What? Why are you saying this, Emily? You're lovely. I'm the one who's privileged to be with you. Anyone would be. And I'm not talking about sex either. I mean just having your company. I have enjoyed being with you so much these past couple of days and I was looking forward to spending more time with you.' Whilst Sam was trying to reassure and comfort Emily, he also realised that he meant every word that he was saying.

However, he also realised that maybe it wasn't the right thing to say as Emily burst into tears again, this time wrapping her arms around him and holding him tight until her sobbing ended. "I'm sorry, Sam," she said, easing softly away from him. 'You must think that I'm a basket case and maybe I am. You don't have to stay, you know, you can leave if you want.'

'I don't want, but I do want to know what's going on in that head of yours that makes you think the way you're thinking. It's so wrong. I'll make us another coffee and you can tell me,' said Sam, wondering what could make someone so nice feel that way. Initially Emily was quite guarded and reticent in opening up, appearing embarrassed and ashamed because of her behaviour. She told him that she had lied about being a carer but didn't know what else to say as she was currently unemployed and had been for a number of years. However, she considered that her last job had been nursing her father prior to his death, so she believed that strictly speaking she was actually telling the truth.

'Is that all you're worried about?' asked Sam, in disbelief, concerned that she could be so upset by something as trivial and attempting to reassure and comfort her again. However, she gestured with her hands and her head to indicate that that certainly wasn't all. Then she stood up, saying; 'I need a drink,' and poured a glass of red for both of them.

'I need this if I am to get through this. I don't quite know why Sam, because I hardly know you, but I need you to know about my past.'

At this point Sam, despite his affection for Emily, wondered what was coming next and, whether for right or wrong reasons, began to think back to his not so distant experience in Benidorm with a woman called Trish who had also furnished him with unsolicited dramatic and troubling background information, which turned out to be a well-planned web of deceit and which had ultimately led him into a deeply disturbing odyssey of revenge and murder. However, for whatever reason, and even though – as Emily had observed – they hardly knew each other, he felt that he could trust her, and hoped that he wouldn't live to regret it. Possibly sensing this, Emily seemed to relax and revealed a lot more about her past.

And what a past it was; she told Sam that she had been married for over twenty years and had a son and a daughter with her husband, who she was still very much in love with, and he with her–or so she thought. She knew that he had been married before and had children with his first wife; he had been very open about that.

However, he hadn't had any contact with his children in all the time that she had known him, and he was also estranged from his parents and siblings. She had asked him about it, but he had more or less said that he didn't want to talk about it, and she had left it at that, albeit reluctantly, as she was curious to know what had happened to bring the situation to such an unsatisfactory outcome. 'Well what woman wouldn't be?' she reasoned. However, his view was that he was divorced, and it was all in the past. Unfortunately, it hadn't stayed there. Emily told Sam that her husband, as far as she believed, worked as a sales representative for a software firm which took him all around the country and sometimes Europe, which meant that for the duration of their marriage, he had been away from home for half the week and every other weekend. She advised Sam that she had never really thought to question his absences, even when he missed her and his children's birthdays and on occasions, Christmas. He even missed his son's graduation and his father in law's funeral, protesting that he needed to work to provide for his family.

However, she had always had nagging doubts, particularly as she had never been invited to any work-related social events or been introduced to any of his colleagues. She also began to wonder about his absences, even worrying that he might be seeing other women—indeed one woman in particular, but she told herself she was just being silly and insecure. And, so, she was definitely not prepared for what was about to come, following her being contacted by her best friend out of the blue whilst her husband was away working, who gave her news that took her breath away. She had previously confided in the same best friend, against her better judgement at the time, about her suspicions, who said that she knew someone that worked as a private detective whom she could ask to keep an eye on him as a favour and let her know where he went and if he met anyone. Whilst she thanked her friend for her offer of help and support, unfortunately and ironically, it was her best friend that she had suspected of having the affair with her husband.

However, she decided to go along with the charade as she was curious to see how they handled it, but mainly because she wanted to create the impression that she had no idea about the deception. As it turned out, her husband really wasn't having an affair with her best friend, which she was relieved about. However, she knew it wasn't good news when her friend, who

71

telephoned her to give her an update about the investigation, asked her if she was 'sitting down'. She then went on to tell her that her husband was still living with his ex-wife in Paisley, along with their three children, and that they were still married. When Emily asked her how she knew this, she informed her that she had a friend who lived in Renfrew, who, on being shown some photographs of her and Emily's families together- which unusually featured the latter's husband- she recognised him, saying that she knew 'his family' who lived nearby. This was then confirmed by the private detective who had both tracked and observed him at the address in question over a period of several days.

After several exchanges of 'Are you sure' and; 'She must be mistaken', Emily then found herself reflecting on how wrong she had been in her own flawed assessment before finally accepting that what her friend was telling her was true; that her 'husband' had another wife and family and that he had been living a double life for their entire married life. Despite being totally distraught, she had called him on his mobile and confronted him, and whilst being obviously taken aback and shocked, he admitted it whilst offering no reason for his behaviour. She informed Sam that she had not seen or spoken to him since that day, as his son had picked up all his belongings and everything else was dealt with in the courts, including his prosecution for bigamy, for which he was sentenced to two years imprisonment, of which he served a year, before being released.

Emily hated her 'husband' because of how much his actions had affected her family, particularly her dad, as she had watched his health steadily deteriorate in the year following the revelation.

She also stated, with some emotion, that her children were also distraught and had questions to which she had no answers, which almost destroyed her. From talking to her Sam was struck by how much the situation had affected and almost defined her as a person. She had, of course, blamed herself and still did, feeling that she should have acted on her suspicions. She felt that she should have known, and, cruelly, that's what most people said to her when it became public, 'How did you not know?' She also felt that she had let down her kids, which Sam felt had contributed massively to her developing an apparent sense of guilt and worthlessness.

Emily advised Sam that after seeking medical help, she was finally diagnosed with depression and prescribed anti-depressants, which she had then eventually managed to wean herself off, realising that she was becoming more and more dependent upon them to cope, whilst all they were really doing was impairing her level of functioning.

Sam felt that Emily seemed to have benefited from having told him, appearing much calmer and to have been reassured by his reasoned and, he hoped, sensitive response. However, Sam also believed that she clearly seemed to need his approval of her as a person, 'warts and all' if they were to move on from this point, whatever that would involve. Sam, for his part, wondered what she would think of him if she knew about his own not so distant redoubtable, and morally questionable behaviour and whether she would be as accepting of him as a person if she did. Somehow, he doubted it, but he certainly wasn't about to test this theory. In saying that, he also wasn't about to be a hypocrite and judge her in any way, viewing her as much more of a victim than he had ever been. He also realised that, in all probability, he had had significantly more personal, practical, and fiscal resources available to him in dealing with the challenges that he had been confronted with, whereas she had apparently been so personally and emotionally disabled by the traumatic events that she had clearly felt totally unable to deal with the situation.

Sam convinced Emily to lie down on the bed and rest, and then he lay on the bed beside her. He told her that he would stay with her until she fell asleep, which she accepted on the condition that they meet up again soon − as long as he wanted to − there was that self-doubt again.

He reassured her that he very much wanted to and would be in touch the next day. Before she drifted off, she looked into Sam's eyes and said, 'I hardly know you Sam but you're the first man I have felt able to trust since… 'I know, it's okay Emily,' interrupted Sam, stroking her head until she closed her eyes. Sam almost drifted off himself but stopped himself from doing so as he needed time on his own to reflect on things and also didn't think waking up beside Emily would be a good idea until he had the opportunity to do just that. He then found himself questioning the wisdom of his actions in promising to meet up with her the next day, thinking back to his previous experience of meeting strange women with complex histories, issues, and, unfortunately for him, hidden lethal agendas.

Chapter 20

He is known as a professional 'hit man', a contract killer who only deals with serious people—people who are serious about wanting someone dead, for which he is paid a serious amount of money. The only thing he doesn't take seriously is relationships, not having had any for several years, which is entirely deliberate because the nature of the job presents a serious risk to anyone's private life. His parents are both dead, and he has no family or friends or family to speak of, other than very close but secret colleagues, which means that he doesn't need to worry about anyone else being threatened, hurt, or used as a way of getting to him. That is also one of the main reasons that he has never had a family because his 'occupation' would unavoidably leave them vulnerable to harm from those looking to exact revenge or perhaps even to exert influence over him.

But now all that has changed, as, against all the odds and his better judgement, he has met someone who knows everything about his secretive and perilous profession. And, with whom he wants to spend the rest of his life. Unfortunately, there is a problem; he is also a wanted man, there currently being several 'contracts' out on him, sanctioned by serious crime bosses whom he has crossed or offended.

He also has another secret.

Chapter 21

18 January 2018
Thursday

After leaving Emily, Sam turned left from the Hotel Siesta towards Avenida de Las Americas and headed back to the Mediterranean Palace. On entering his room, he felt like lying down and closing his eyes, but instead showered and changed, realising that if he did close his eyes, he wouldn't open them again until the following day, and he was determined to enjoy as much of his holiday as he could. He headed out of the hotel, turning left on Avenida de Las Americas and then walked diagonally across the road, arriving at a large open-air bar/restaurant with cabaret entertainment on offer. He sat down at a table and ordered a beer. Whilst the place was busy and lively, the music wasn't to Sam's taste, leading to him deciding on a change of scenery.

So, he drank up and headed in the direction of Las Vistas beach and then up along Paseo las Vistas, deciding to have another drink inside one of the bars overlooking the beach and enjoying the wonderful views from above the shore. After finishing his drink, he went for a wander along the streets full of a wonderful variety of shops including, curiously, a proliferation of opticians, on Avenida de Suecia.

On heading down towards the shore, Sam found himself amidst

the familiar warren of bustling bars and restaurants of Los Christianos, surveying his surroundings and the throng of likely candidates for his custom before deciding on a small tapas bar. Sam liked the look of the place because it was both bright and busy with what seemed to be Spanish people – always a good sign – whilst looking spotlessly clean. Also, the music being played was neither loud nor annoying.

As he sat with a drink, awaiting his food, Sam found himself thinking about Emily and her obvious emotional fragility; he also still had a deep feeling of unease about the recent sequence of events and unlikely coincidences which had occurred since his arrival. The main reason for this, Sam acknowledged, was that, strictly speaking, he didn't really believe in coincidences whilst, contradictorily, being a great believer in gut feelings and instinct. And his was telling him that something just wasn't quite right, whilst not having any clear reason or evidence to justify him feeling that way. However, he knew that he had an almost sixth sense about these things and was very rarely wrong when it came to instinct and intuition, which was why he was good at his job. It was also inescapably true that the last time that he had had similar thoughts and feelings, he had been absolutely on the money, which was in Benidorm, only a matter of months ago, in November of the previous year.

Unfortunately, he hadn't heeded the signs on that occasion, resulting in both dramatic and traumatic consequences for both himself and certain others. He told himself that he needed to ensure that he didn't make the same mistakes as he had in Benidorm ever again. However, he also had to acknowledge that *when you're as impulsive as I am, that is easier said than done.* But he told himself, 'Forewarned is forearmed,' saying it out loud and realising that he was trying to convince himself of his ability to learn from experience and be rational and sensible. He also had to acknowledge, however, that these qualities were only ever in evidence whilst he was sober.

After enjoying a very tasty tapas selection, Sam sat sipping a beer and decided that he would head off in search of some entertainment, particularly as the restaurant and the others nearby had started to empty. He asked for the bill, which the waiter brought directly with a bowl of nuts. Sam knew that the reason bars provided nuts, crisps, and even popcorn, was that they were salty and made people thirsty and therefore likely to order more drink.

However, because Sam had not asked for 'cacahuetes' the nuts that the waiter had brought weren't peanuts but 'miseria'; the ones that Emily had described as 'having no flavour and as hard as nails.' However, unbelievably, he ate them, the ones that he had sworn he would never eat again. And he instantly regretted his actions, wishing that he had stuck to his guns, as no sooner had he bitten into one when the last of his filling came out, prompting him to curse loudly, drawing both concerned and disapproving looks from the remaining diners, at which point he paid and left.

As he made his way through the brightly lit, vibrant streets of Los Christianos, Sam decided that he would just keep walking and follow his nose and ears, which he did. This eventually brought him to a bright, lively street which was home to a clutch of bars and restaurants, from which emanated a syncopated cacophony of noises and sounds, ranging from football commentary and restaurant muzak to actual live music and comedy.

He decided to have a beer in a bar showing the dying embers of a Copa del Rey game involving Real Madrid and Leganes, which Madrid won 1-0, to his dismay, as he was an out and out Barcelona fan. When the game ended, almost at the same time as his beer, he decided to move on and ended up in a bar a short walk away called Beau Jangles, which was offering a Michael Bublé tribute act and an 'outrageous' camp Scottish musical comedy act.

Sam ordered himself a beer and sat on stool at the bar, which was situated at the other side of the room from the stage, which, as it turned out, proved to be a good choice as the 'outrageous' comedy act had a tendency to pick on people in the audience, and in particular guys called 'Gary', for some unknown reason-to hilarious effect.. Sam, thankfully, from his point of view, had successfully managed to avoid attracting his attention, as he was mainly concerned with slanging and riffing off two separate groups of men and women in the audience, who, it has to be said, were absolutely loving all the attention, mainly because he was very funny and not at all nasty with it.

These factors all combined to produce a very pleasant, friendly, and relaxed atmosphere in the room, whilst the Michael Bublé tribute act was also of a particularly high standard. There was an announcement that after the live entertainment finished there would be a DJ and dancing, however, Sam began to feel quite weary and decided to call it a night. Accordingly, he drained the remains of his beer and headed outside to the balmy Canarian night to find a taxi to take him back to Las Americas. As he sat in the taxi heading to his hotel, Sam considered that he had had a most enjoyable evening indeed, apart from losing the remainder of his filling – which was causing him some pain and discomfort due to the tooth being rough and sharp and having caught his gum and tongue on a few occasions. However, in the coming days, these mundane issues would be dwarfed into inconsequence by concerns and pain of much more serious dimensions.

79

Chapter 22

19 January 2018
Friday

The next morning Sam awoke early, to a bright, warm, sunny day, feeling relatively refreshed, despite his indulgences of the previous evening. He got up, showered, dressed and had breakfast at the hotel, before spending most of the day by the pool, taking the sun. Whilst he would normally have had a beer at the pool bar he had decided not to have any alcohol during the day, preferring to save himself for the immediately imminent singles night at the Cleopatra Princess later that evening, which he found himself feeling particularly nervous about, never having been personally involved in anything of that nature, other than his hilarious and eye opening 'fly on the wall' episode at the singles night in Perth. He sincerely hoped that it would be a more positive and refined experience.

Sam left his room fifteen minutes before the evening was scheduled to start, dressed casually in navy blue denims and a light blue cotton shirt, stopping at the bar in the Med Palace for a beer to settle his nerves. On arriving at the event, which was being held in the 'pyramid,' he was made to feel at ease by a very friendly and beautiful young woman, who, Sam thought, was Asian, and who introduced herself as Aja, pronounced Asia – which she both spelled and pronounced for him- which also just happened to be the title of an album, by one of his all-time favourite bands; Steely Dan, and provided him with a drink of 'champagne', which he thought tasted more like Cava, but it was pleasant enough. She then chatted effortlessly with him, advising him that she was Indonesian, before introducing him to some other people at the bar, who, she informed, were at the same table where he had been placed.

'I think you will like where you are seated,' she said, smiling, and as they approached the table he noticed several very attractive women seated there, one of whom he had been seated next to and who was being chatted up by another man, sitting in his seat and who was not for moving until Aja indicated that it was Sam's seat. However, even then he seemed reluctant and Sam, rather than make an issue of it, said 'It's okay, take your time, no rush,' and indicated to his hostess that he was happy to stand at the bar and wait to be seated, which was what he did. Aja, however, was less happy about the situation and made a point of speaking to the guy to make him aware that he would have to move soon. She then approached Sam at the bar to apologise and to tell him that she would make sure that the other man would be moved soon. He then watched as she consulted with a large, burly male standing at the entrance to the room, who then made his way to Sam's table to carry out her instructions, to the other man's obvious annoyance.

Maybe it was just Sam's imagination, but he got the impression that the woman wasn't that upset at his departure, and, almost as if to confirm this, she looked round and smiled at Sam as he stood at the bar. Sam politely acknowledged this with a smile but didn't immediately return to the table, thinking; *There's no rush the night is young, even if the women are considerably outnumbered by the men. It will also give the other guy some time to cool down after his abrupt removal.*

81

He had also worked out that standing at the bar he had a better viewpoint from which to check out the demographics of the room, which was slowly filling up. It seemed to Sam that it was mostly single men on their own but that there were also clearly small groups of men, maybe on a stag holiday, whilst the females were either on their own, in pairs or also in small groups. Consequently, Sam reasoned, it was perfectly probable that strictly speaking, they were not all 'singles.

His forensic diagnosis of the assembled participants was then interrupted by someone lightly touching his arm, and on turning round he saw that it was the woman whom he had been seated next to at the table. 'Sorry about that, she said, gesturing towards the table and in particular the guy who had been sitting in Sam's seat, who was now attempting to ingratiate himself with one of the other women at the table. 'He was being a bit of a nuisance, and I think he's maybe had a bit too much to drink already,' she said, looking at Sam. But I think it's safe for you to sit down now.'

'It wasn't a problem,' said Sam, surprised to hear that her accent was American and even more surprised to see that she was wearing a ring, and she, noticing this, responded by stating, 'I wear it to put off people like him, but he was oblivious, or maybe chose to be,' she said.

'Or maybe he didn't care or want to notice,' said Sam,

'Well, you were very patient and diplomatic,' she said.

'I didn't see the point in making an issue of it, particularly as the seats are allocated so I was happy for somebody else to sort it out.'

'Very sensible, and I think they are watching him closely now, she said, adding, I see he's moved on to someone else.'

'Well, just be grateful for small mercies, at least he's leaving you alone.'

'Long may it continue,' she said, taking her drink from the barman, before adding, 'well, I'll see you back at the table, nice to meet you Sam.'

Sam looked at her, surprised, saying, 'How do you know my name?'

'It's on your place setting,' she said smiling. 'And 'I'm Jill,' she said.

'Very observant, Miss Marple, pleased to meet you too Jill,' he said, smiling back. 'And I will see you as soon as I fetch myself another drink.'

'I'll wait,' she said. And she did.

Chapter 23

19 January 2018
Friday

Sam had always found Americans, up close, to be on a different planet, in terms of their general behaviour and attitudes, with the notable exception of a guy he had worked with some years previously, who was from Missouri, or 'Mizzura' as he had pronounced it. Whilst he had loved his colleague's accent, he realised that whilst he was used to American accents in films and on television, he found that he just couldn't get used to hearing certain ones in everyday, real life. Also, most other Americans that he had met always seemed to him, annoyingly, to have bucket loads of confidence, which he both admired and resented in equal measure. He also hated the way that they changed the English language by making up their own words, like; 'interpretate', or saying 'addicting' instead of addictive and 'normalcy' instead of normality.

They seemed, in his view, to have this natural in-built reluctance to accept perfectly adequate words, instead, displaying a need to change or add bits on to them for no good reason. It was as if the words weren't descriptive enough in their existing form and required some much-needed amendment or supplementation, which they were more than happy to provide. However, Jill wasn't like that at all, he found, after spending most of the night in her company. He also found out that she wasn't American, she was, in fact, Canadian, from a place called Niagara on the Lake, in Ontario, which, she informed him was nothing like Niagara, which she described as bigger and more vulgar version of Blackpool. Niagara on the Lake, 'on the other hand', she was quick to point out, had, in her opinion, more in common with Bedford Falls, the lovely little town in It's a Wonderful Life' the Frank Capra film starring James Stewart as George Bailey, who is saved from himself by Clarence, a trainee angel who is trying to earn his wings. Coincidentally, it was also Sam's favourite film and he recalled being taken to see it at the Glasgow Film Theatre at Christmas, as a surprise by an ex-girlfriend, which he still considered to be one of the nicest gestures and presents, Christmas or otherwise, that he had ever been given. And yes, he did cry at the end, to his extreme embarrassment.

Jill advised, when asked by Sam, who was just being playful, that it didn't have a Building and Loan, but noted that it did have a theatre, cinema and beautiful colonial architecture and was situated in a beautiful area famous for vineyards.

'Sounds lovely,' said Sam.

'Yes, it is,' she agreed, then adding, 'but so too is Scotland, I believe,' whilst advising that she had never visited.

'Large parts of it are,' he agreed, advising her that he was from Glasgow, where he still lived and which, he said, 'Isn't exactly scenic but has some impressive architecture and beautiful scenery within less than an hour's drive.' Jill told him that she 'Absolutely loved his Scottish accent,' saying, 'I could listen to it forever,' which is the kind of things that American's – and now apparently also Canadians-say, he thought. And she was also quite forward and said things like, 'So are we going to your room or mine'. Sam, whilst quite surprised, also had to stop himself from responding with the line from the old joke, which is 'Both, you go to yours and I'll go to mine,' thinking better of it, believing that it would be neither appropriate nor well received.

Whilst he was considering a more acceptable response and also trying to balance his libido and reservations - based upon his previous experience of being seduced by an attractive woman on holiday- the now very drunk and even more obnoxious guy from earlier suddenly appeared from nowhere and demanded that Sam give him his seat back, telling him that he 'was sitting there first' and had been speaking to the woman (Jill) before he 'butted in'.

'Who the hell do you think you are anyway?' he asked Sam, whilst staggering unsteadily and holding on to a chair. Sam tried to placate him and reason with him by saying, 'I'm nobody and I don't make the rules, I just sat where I was told, so you'll need to speak to the organisers about that.' However, this only served to make him even more aggressive, replying, 'I'm speaking to you,' and when Sam ignored him, he made a lunge and swung a punch at him. The punch never landed however as he was lifted into the air by the massive hands of the large, burly guy who had spoken to him earlier.

The guy's feet never touched the ground as he was unceremoniously ejected from the premises. Whilst the incident was all over in an instant it had the effect of sobering Sam up somewhat, both physically and mentally and he found that he was reconsidering his position regarding Jill's offer. He then told her that he was feeling quite drunk and didn't think that he would be any use to her anyway and if it was okay with, he was going to take a rain check.

Jill, whilst clearly being surprised at this, nevertheless accepted it with seeming good grace. As Sam headed to his room, he was already questioning and maybe even regretting his decision.

Chapter 24

20 January 2018
Saturday

Sam awoke the next day to cloudy, overcast conditions and, surprisingly, due to his relatively early night and sensible behaviour the previous evening, made it to breakfast. There was no sign of Jill, but the obnoxious drunk guy was there looking suitably sheepish and hung over. Sam wondered if he remembered the events of the previous night or if he had recognised him. If he had, he wasn't letting on and was keeping his head down.

After breakfast Sam went back to his room and made himself a cup of tea and took it out to the balcony. As he sat there looking at the grey skies, he thought back to something that had happened to him the last time he had stayed at the Mediterranean Palace when he was there on his own.

It was also in January and on that occasion, he had again awakened to a dull, grey, cloudy day and was so disappointed that he went back to bed and fell over again, before rising again around ten thirty, feeling very hungry. So, having missed breakfast, he decided to head to the pool area for something to eat, buying a newspaper en-route. Whilst the weather had brightened up a little, the beach was almost deserted; much like the hotel pool area was when he arrived there soon after. He ordered a coke and a burger from the pool bar and the waitress told him that she would bring it over to him at his table. He sat down and looked at the sports section of his newspaper which informed him that Andy Murray was playing in the Australian Open later in the day and the match was being shown on both Eurosport and BBC, both of which were available on the television in his room. As he was pondering the likelihood of this being his entertainment for the day, given the weather conditions, the waitress arrived with his food and drink.

As he looked up from his newspaper, he noticed a very attractive brunette sitting at a nearby table, seemingly struggling to organise paperwork without it blowing away in the wind that had suddenly appeared from nowhere. She also had what looked like samples of sun creams and other products and he naturally assumed that she was a sun product representative or advisor who either worked at or was visiting the hotel to sell and /or demonstrate her wares. However, he reckoned that she would not be doing either today, given the unfortunate lack of sun and people, then noticing that they were quite literally the only two people left at the pool. He also noticed that the waitress hadn't brought him any condiments or sauces and headed to the bar to fetch them. Unfortunately, on his way back to his table he saw that both his drink and his burger had left the premises, having been blown away by a sudden gust of wind and were now lying on the ground at the foot of the sun cream woman, who was covering her face with her hands trying to hide the fact that she was trying very hard not to laugh at his predicament.

'I'm so sorry,' she said, in an English accent, again from behind her hands as she tried, unsuccessfully to stifle another laugh. 'It was the look on your face,' she said and then burst out laughing again this time not even trying to stop. 'Oh god, I'm so sorry, it's not funny,' she said again the tears of mirth in her eyes belying her words.

'It is a bit funny I suppose,' said Sam, 'Other people's misfortunes and all that,' as he stooped to try and retrieve his lunch from the ground. The 'rep' seemed reassured at Sam's words, which had assuaged any guilt that she was feeling, and she then got up from her seat to attempt to help him pick up the debris.

'It's okay, I'll get that,' said Sam, shoo-ing her away.

'At least let me buy you another burger and drink,' she said, 'as penance for my sins,' but Sam wouldn't hear of it, 'Not at all, don't be silly, it wasn't your fault, "You were only watching," he said, before adding, 'as Billy Connolly once reassured his audience.'

'And laughing,' she said, smiling apologetically, before saying;' I'm Beverly, Beverly Jordan, but you can call me Bev.'

'I'm sure Billy would approve,' said Sam, offering her his hand adding, 'I'm Sam and you can call me Sam,' and smiling mischievously. 'Bev' responded by shaking his hand and then giving him a gentle peck on the cheek, which Sam returned, then adding, 'Anyway, looks like I've had my lunch Bev,' and smiling wryly.

'Well, if it's any consolation I'm not exactly having a great day either,' she said making a sad face and again looking to the sky.

'Yeah, I noticed that business wasn't exactly booming,' said Sam,

'Actually, it's like being back home in Glasgow,' said Sam laughing.

'I know what you mean, Hull isn't much better,' said Bev, and as they relaxed, they chatted easily, mainly about her and her job, which she loved and had been doing for almost three years, previously having been a holiday rep, which she hadn't enjoyed as much and was looking to give up anyway.

This led to Sam asking her about the different products she had and recommended and what factor and level of protection he should be using. Which, in turn, led to her talking about the different kind of skin tones and sensitivities, touching his skin and hands, for what seemed, to Sam, much longer than necessary. Not that he was complaining.

Sam didn't ask Bev if she was single, but he noticed that she wasn't wearing a ring so assumed that she was. She, however, maybe noticing his appraisal of the situation, did ask him if he was on his own and seemed pleased to find out that he was.

'The worst thing about going on holiday on your own is that you can't put sun cream on your back,' and then realising what he had said, instantly felt the need to apologise, saying, 'I'm sorry I wasn't hinting, honest,' which she laughed at and found quite endearing.

'It's okay I didn't think you were and I would have been more than happy to help you out had the weather been better, but somehow, I don't think you'll need it today,' she said gesturing towards the grey skies overhead and handing him a complimentary bottle of spray lotion adding, 'for when you do need it, the spray makes it easier to do your back.'
'Thanks so much, that's very kind of you,' said Sam, pleasantly surprised. 'And hopefully I will need it at some point. But you know what I mean don't you? You can't really ask a total stranger to put sunscreen on your back,' said Sam. 'I only ever did it once and to be honest the guy was really good about it' said Sam, before bursting out laughing, quickly followed by Bev, who wasn't expecting such a sharply humorous response. 'I'm sorry I

tried but I couldn't keep my face straight,' said Sam. At least I didn't tell you the boring story about the time I got burnt walking to the supermarket to buy sun cream. I think you're right, about today though' he said looking to the same sky. Hopefully it'll clear up by tomorrow,' said Sam.

'Unfortunately, I won't be here tomorrow,' said Bev looking at Sam, holding his gaze and adding, 'You can only have me for today. It's a one day only deal.'

Sam's estranged wife Kim, used to tell Sam that he had no idea when women were flirting with him and, intentionally or otherwise, she had raised his awareness in that regard. Accordingly, he could feel his pulse quicken at his realisation of the implication of the unfolding scenario. Unfortunately, he then discovered that being aware of it and knowing what to do about it were two different things. Consequently, whilst he didn't know quite how to respond initially, he was determined not to let the moment pass without saying or doing something about it, because he knew that he would never forgive himself if he didn't. Eventually he managed to respond with 'So what will you do for the rest of the day?'

'Probably just head back to my hotel and read my book in my room, I suppose. There's not really anything else to do in this weather is there,' she said, smiling seductively, before asking;

'What about you Sam?'

'Do you like tennis?' asked Sam tentatively and then smiled as he saw the confusion and surprise in her face.

'What? Yes… yes, I do but… do you mean do I play? Because I think it might rain.'

'I think there's no doubt it will, but no I meant watching,' he said informing her of Andy Murray's imminent match, before telling her that she was free to watch it with him in his room. 'We could order some food but take it to my room rather than risk another runaway burger disaster. I also have plenty of wine and beer' It seemed like an absolute age before she responded to his invitation, and initially she didn't respond at all, whilst just holding his gaze for what seemed like an age, leading to Sam breaking the silence with 'It's a one day only offer.'

'In that case how could I refuse,' she replied. 'But... only on one condition.'

'What's that?' asked Sam curious.

'You let me buy the food.'

'Deal,' said Sam.

They ate burgers and French fries and drank beer and wine in his room and chatted effortlessly about everything and nothing, until there was nothing else to talk about and the talking gave way to the inevitable. They made love whilst Andy Murray played his match in the background, their bodies illuminated by the fluorescent glow of the television. And then they made love again before taking a break to refresh their drinks and to order some more food from room service, which they devoured with the same appetite that they had demonstrated towards their lovemaking.

Jill was an enthusiastic and imaginative lover, receptive to his own inventive and passionate endeavours and they made love again before drifting off to sleep, their needs and desires met and satisfied respectively. When Sam woke the next morning Beverley was already awake and dressed and obviously preparing to leave.

'You're up, bright and early,' said Sam noticing that, so was the sun – at last.

'I was just about to wake you, and it's not that early, sleepyhead,' she said, 'But it's a beautiful day and I must quite literally 'make hay while the sun shines' as the saying goes so, I will have to love you and leave you.'

'Quite literally,' said Sam rising from the bed.

'And regrettably,' said Beverley, moving towards him and kissing him on his forehead. 'Thank you for a lovely day... and night, she added, softly.

'My pleasure,' said Sam.

'It wasn't all yours, I can assure you,' said Beverley, 'but I really have to go, sorry.'

'Can I ask you to do one more thing before you go?' said Sam.

'What? Yes of course,' she answered, curious as to what was coming next. Sam went into the bathroom and emerged holding the bottle of spray that she had given him the previous day. He handed it to her and smiled, as he said; 'Could you put some of this on my back please'?

Chapter 25

20 January 2018
Saturday

As Sam sat on the balcony, reflecting on the memory of his experience with Beverley, he thought, ruefully, That was in the days when you could get it on with somebody without having to worry if they were going to be murdered or try and blackmail you, reflecting upon and his traumatic and not too distant experience in Benidorm the previous year. And here he was again, enjoying the company and seemingly affectionate interest of two very attractive women. *It was almost Déjà vu,* thought Sam, the difference being that both were still alive- so far. And then there was the meeting with Akmal too- an unbelievable coincidence - if that was indeed what it was- bearing in mind that he didn't really believe in coincidences. And if he was honest, he was still having some difficulty in accepting it as that.

And then he began to wonder, '*if the situations could be connected in any way. No, surely not,*' he thought. '*He was just being paranoid. Wasn't he?*'

***

Following the weather brightening up, Sam decided to head to the beach for a change, which turned out to be a particularly good decision, as, by midday, the sun had rediscovered its mojo and had asserted its presence with a vengeance. Sam then set about correcting the belief that only 'Mad Dogs and Englishmen' sit out in the midday sun, by positioning himself on a spot opposite La Palapa Beach Club, appropriately protected with liberal amounts of the appropriate skin protection, of course (as previously recommended by Beverley) and taking regular respite from the heat in the gloriously refreshing sea. Eventually, when it got too hot for him, he headed to the beach club for some lunch and much needed shade.

Normally he would've headed back to the hotel and changed but he was feeling lazy and, from his position on the beach, he had noticed that there was a vacant table in the restaurant looking on to the beach and decided to go for it before someone else did, beach towel and all.

However, as he entered the premises and approached the table, he saw that Jill was sitting at the table adjacent, reading the menu and apparently oblivious to his presence. Initially he thought about turning around and walking out; just leaving, without even acknowledging her presence, partly because of his extremely casual garb and somewhat scruffy appearance and partly because he felt awkward, because of how they had left things on their previous acquaintance. And then his curiosity piqued and rendered all his previously held insecurities and reservations inconsequential, as he decided that he was very interested to see how she would react to seeing him again, particularly given that he had effectively rejected her advances. It was while he was pondering these thoughts that Jill noticed him and beckoned for him to join her at the table, which he did.

And he was pleasantly surprised to discover that she appeared really pleased to see him and made no comment about his appearance or the circumstances of their previous parting, instead offering to buy him lunch, which he declined. He did however agree to join her but only on the condition that they split the bill, which she reluctantly agreed to. However, she then suggested that they have lunch somewhere else and asked him if he had ever been to La Caleta, which he hadn't, saying that he didn't know where or what it was, whilst asking if they could walk there, which brought a smile to her lips as she informed him; 'Well we could I suppose but it would probably take about an hour and a half, maybe more, and I wouldn't recommend it in this heat. We can probably get a bus or else we can get a taxi for about 10 euros. I don't mind paying. It's a lovely place and they have great restaurants there, particularly if you like seafood'.

'I love seafood,' said Sam.

In the end they took a taxi - after Sam had dropped his towel off in the room and freshened up with a quick change of clothes – as there wasn't a bus to Caleta due for nearly an hour.

On the way there Jill told Sam all about their destination, 'It's a fishing village situated on the southwest coast of Tenerife, near Adeje Costa. However, in recent years it has been transformed by significant building developments in the form of hotels and holiday housing, which have been purchased by mainly British and German people. Also, during the last few decades, La Caleta has become well known for exceptional culinary provision and some of the best seafood on the island. It also has quite a chilled vibe.'

Sam was intrigued by Jill's extensive local and historical knowledge but reasoned that it was just borne of a keenness to learn more about the island after many years of holidaying there.

The taxi dropped them off at a man-made sandy beach near the main drag of La Caleta, where they decided to have a drink at a nearby beach bar. As they sat there Sam noticed two very attractive women on the beach flouncing around playfully, removing and trying on items of clothing. He pointed this out to Jill, saying, 'Look at these two, they're having a great old time to themselves.' Jill burst out laughing, explaining that they were models, who were displaying beachwear for sale to the other holidaymakers on the beach. 'I need to get out more,' said Sam, 'preferably to places like this,' and laughing at his naiveté.

After finishing their drinks, they went for a walk, before stopping at another bar which offered a spectacular view overlooking the bay at Playa Diego Hernandez, which is regularly voted one of the most beautiful beaches in Tenerife.

As they sat looking over the bay and all the fishing boats moored there, the barman, who was very friendly and spoke very good English, explained to them that many of the fishermen swam to shore with their catches, rather than sail in dinghies or small boats.

Jill asked the barman if he could recommend somewhere to eat which was not overly expensive, informing Sam that the average cost of eating out in La Caleta is slightly higher than other parts of the island. However, the barman informed them that it was possible to find some reasonably priced restaurants there and recommended a place called El Varadero, in Calle las Artes, which was nearby.

Unfortunately, they never made it for lunch as they were enjoying just sitting and chatting idly about everything and nothing and simply watching the world go by; so much so that they lost track of time, to the extent that they sat until sunset, witnessing the spectacular sight of the last of the sun disappearing behind the neighbouring island of La Gomera. It was truly idyllic but unfortunately Sam couldn't help thinking that he wished he was there with Emily instead.

They eventually made it to El Varadero, where they were fortunate enough to get booked and to enjoy delicious seafood and wine and more convivial conversation - without giving away too much about each other. Which was fine with Sam as he still wasn't sure how he felt about the situation and again mentally cautioning himself along the lines of; 'Once bitten twice shy.' However, despite his reservations, he had to admit that he was very relaxed and enjoying being in Jill's company, and that he also still found her very attractive; *and who wouldn't*, he thought. He was toying with the idea of having another drink, however as the sun disappeared into the horizon Jill suggested that they head back to Las Americas. Sam agreed with his usual 'Sounds like a plan,' but was surprised at having to admit to feeling a pang of disappointment, if it meant the end of their time together for the day.

However, this was only momentary, as Jill then asked him if he had any other plans for the rest of the evening and if not whether he wouldn't mind heading out for more drinks in Las Americas, which despite his determination to be cautious, he agreed to with little sign of restraint; and again replying 'Sounds like a plan.' However, inside he was thinking '*So much for all that "Once bitten..." stuff then.*'

Chapter 26

20 January 2018
Saturday

Akmal's phone rang, and he answered it. He said hello and then nothing else. He just listened. This wasn't a social call or a normal conversation; this was someone receiving information or instructions, from a totally anonymous, faceless entity, as it had been in Benidorm- and that's the way he liked it, because what he didn't know he couldn't tell. And that meant that no one else had to worry about it or his part in it. No, this was a one-way street, strictly business transaction and the business being another 'arrangement.' Only this time, the unfortunate beneficiary was someone who had previously been on the other end of such an 'arrangement.' Akmal knew that he really didn't have a choice, as it was made abundantly clear that his co-operation was expected as payback for his previous reckless and maverick behaviour in Benidorm, which, again, had run the risk of attracting unwanted attention to the organisation.

And there was no room for discussion, debate or denial, just do it or else; and what he had to do was to use his influence to identify a suitable and willing candidate to carry out what had been agreed. And, when it came down to it, he really had no problem with it, as he was of the view that this was payback for all the inconvenience and hassle caused to him because of their previous encounter. There was absolutely no acknowledgement that the situation was of his own making, because of his immoral and illicit behaviour which had set the subsequent, equally as reproachable, sequence of events in motion. What goes around comes around.

Chapter 27

20 January 2018
Saturday

They went to Harry's bar and had a couple of drinks watching the 'dancing fountains', outside the Safari Centre; brightly lit, coloured flumes, synchronised with everything from rap to classical music. Sam's memory took him back to a time when he and Kim were on holiday in Montenegro and the restaurant, they were eating at played a particular piece of classical music and she had inexplicably burst into tears. She never did explain why, and Sam was left to wonder if it was related to a significantly happy or unhappy memory from her life before she had met him, before reflecting ruefully that they had probably accrued enough of both during the duration of their ill - fated marriage.

Sam and Jill then had more drinks at the Hard Rock Café where they watched a band with a very glamorous and charismatic female singer, who performed a selection of cover versions of pop classics in a very professional but sanitized performance. At least that was Sam's view, whereas Jill appeared to absolutely love them, even asking him up to dance, which he did, albeit very reluctantly. He also realised that he was feeling a bit on edge but wasn't entirely sure why. Jill, perhaps sensing this, asked; 'What's wrong Sam, are you not enjoying yourself?'

'What?' Yes of course,' he replied, whilst being a little taken aback by the question, as he hadn't thought that his discomfort was that obvious and then asking, 'Why do you say that?'

'It's just that you seem a little on edge.'

'Do I?' No, I feel fine, probably just a bit tired' he lied, annoyed at himself and then realising that the reason for his 'edginess' was because of the uncertainty he was feeling about what the rest of the evening held for them; ironically, because of what happened between them, previously, or, more to the point, what *hadn't* happened.

Did that then mean there was an expectation that something would happen between them tonight? he wondered. He wasn't sure whether he was he more worried about that or how he could possibly reject her advances again? Presuming, she made any of course.

God, what do I sound like? Anybody would think I was an impotent, neurotic sad bastard worried about the prospect of having sex', he thought, which made him smile, albeit briefly. But that wasn't what was concerning him. It was more about what happened if they did. Because yes, it was all about trust, and he couldn't help feeling that he had 'been here before.' And he wasn't ready to go there again.

He knew that he enjoyed being with Jill, but he just wasn't sure that he trusted her, or her interest in him as genuine, without knowing why, other than his acquired suspicion of people's true motives. And yes, he thought that she probably wasn't expecting anything other than what the duration of the holiday offered, but he was still having difficulty in taking her interest at face value. And then there was issue of the persistent, nagging unease he was having trouble shaking, about the various 'coincidences' he had experienced since his arrival in Tenerife. So, at the end of the evening when Jill, quite hesitantly, he thought, invited him up to her room in the Cleopatra for a nightcap, he again begged off, repeating his lie that he was tired. He wasn't sure if her expression was one of disappointment or despair, but she managed to squeeze out an excuse of a smile and bade him goodnight with a swift peck on the cheek. Sam couldn't help thinking that he had seen the last of her.

Chapter 28

21 January 2018
Sunday

Sam woke early the next day but wasn't in the mood for breakfast, so decided instead to have a long lie. However, after dropping off quickly he was roused from his slumbers by the sound of the chambermaid firstly ringing the bell and then entering the room and loudly announcing 'Chambermaid, room cleaning.'

He responded in the negative, asking her to come back 'mas tarde' until he realised that she was at the foot of his bed. However, she complied with his request, leaving without comment. Sam thought it strange as maids do not routinely enter a room while the guest is in it, but then, he thought, she may have thought that he wouldn't still in be in bed, given the late hour. Sam suddenly felt really awake and felt quite guilty about still being in bed. So, realising that he wouldn't be able to sleep, he decided to go for a shower instead.

Whilst in the shower, he thought that he heard the door again but then thought that he was just imagining it. After his shower, Sam dried himself and instead of wrapping the towel about himself, as he usually would, realising that he had closed the curtains to assist in helping him to drop off, simply threw it to the floor, thereby indicating to the chambermaid that it needed washed and walked out to the room naked to get dressed.

Unfortunately, he hadn't heard the knock on the door and walked straight into the chambermaid, as she entered the room. Sam spluttered an apology before jumping back in the bathroom, where he continued to apologise profusely, telling her that he hadn't heard her knock on the door. He then began to think that maybe she hadn't bothered to knock, but decided against having that conversation with her, if she was even still there. He listened carefully, before shouting 'Hello' a few times and, on getting no response, opened the door and entered the room, this time with a towel wrapped around him.

However, she had indeed left and as he absorbed the uncomfortable feelings of embarrassment, he found himself thinking, 'I don't know who got the biggest fright there.' This caused him to smile as he recalled it being said to him some years previously on a particularly hot summer day in a park, by the owner of a Pit Bull terrier. He had been lying on the grass sunbathing and had momentarily dozed off, only to be awakened to find said Pit Bull's head on his groin. His subsequent screams of alarm had only served to agitate the animal, leading to it growling loudly and displaying an impressive shark like jaw full of terrifying teeth. As Sam was envisaging a DIY castration by the chastened canine, thankfully, it responded to its master's voice and instructions to desist, with the owner also adding 'I've told you to stop doing that,' leading Sam to conclude that this was something of a favourite pastime for the beast. The guy had then apologised to Sam before uttering the immortal words. Sam remembered thinking that he could probably help clear up his dilemma, given that he had never, at any point been contemplating biting *it's* bollocks off.

Sam made it to breakfast and thankfully there was no sign of the chambermaid on his way either to or from the dining room, or, when he left the hotel later in the day to head to the Gaelic Corner bar to watch Celtic play Brechin in the Scottish Cup. He would normally have chosen to frequent Leonardo's' *al fresco* courtyard environment to watch the game, but as the weather was again dull and overcast and quite chilly and breezy, he chose to watch it inside.

As it turned out he was warmed both by the indoor temperature and the result, as Celtic trounced the opposition by five goals to nil.

If he had been a betting man, he would have made quite a bit of money, as his 'other' team, Barcelona, were also victorious in their game recording an identical score against Real Betis- which he was also able to keep a weather eye on, due to the number of screens on show. After the football finished Sam felt hungry and walked along Avenida Raphael Puig, crossing the road and stopping at Sugar and Spice, a small Italian Bistro diagonally opposite. After viewing the menu on display, he decided to have lunch there, which proved to be a good choice, as the food was lovely and the staff pleasant and accommodating. After his lunch Sam headed back to his hotel passing Emily's hotel en-route, causing him to wonder what she was doing and, despite the emotionally charged nature of their previous meeting, looking forward to seeing her again.

There was no sign of the maid on his return to the hotel and he made his way back to the room, deciding to have a nap before heading out somewhere for dinner. He didn't get undressed but on lying down on top of the bed he found that he dropped off almost immediately. However, he was awakened by the sound of the door opening and of someone entering the room and asking; 'Hello, is anyone there'?

He opened his eyes to find the maid standing over him

smiling.

He sat bolt upright and immediately apologised to her for any embarrassment or shock caused to her and assuming that she was looking to clean the room, said that he would leave to allow her to do so.

However, to his surprise, she sat down on the bed beside him and, still smiling, said; 'It's ok, you don't need to apologise, I wasn't shocked, I liked what I saw. I was hoping to see more and thought that maybe you would like to see me too?' she added, starting to unbutton her blouse. Sam was only half awake, but he was surprised to hear her speak such good English, having assumed, wrongly, that she would be Spanish Mediterranean or European. However, her accent sounded Australian, whilst her manner and body language were very casual and provocative. Then he completely surprised himself by what he did next, because he stopped her saying, 'Woah, woah, no, no, no, wait just a minute, let's just hold on now'. Maybe it was his previous salutary experience with Audrey, the woman whom he had met and been intimate with in Benidorm the previous November, which stopped him. In truth, he wasn't really sure if that was the reason, but whatever it was, alarm bells were ringing and something just didn't feel right.

However, whilst he was saying this, the chambermaid was running her hand up his leg and over his crotch area, which unfortunately was producing a predictable physical reaction, which was clearly obvious to both.

'Why do you want me to stop? I can see that you like it,' she asked, whilst starting to unbutton his shorts. How Sam managed it he will never know but he pushed her hand away and got up from the bed, saying; 'I don't think you should be doing this. I think you should go before I have to call the manager. If you go

107

now, I won't mention this to anyone.'

The maid's expression changed to a scowl, and she simply stood up and stormed out of the room, to his relief. Sam found that he was shaking and had to sit back down again to steady himself and catch his breath, as he was hyper-ventilating. After he had calmed down and stopped shaking, Sam got up and took a bottle of water from the fridge, which he nearly drained in one gulp, before deciding that he needed something stronger and opened a beer. *'What the fuck was that all about?'* he thought trying to make sense of what had just taken place. He had heard stories of people getting it on with chambermaids, even songs about it (Last Summer by Rod Stewart sprang to mind) but thought that was all they were – stories, anecdotes, urban myths, flights of fancy and products of people's fantasies and overactive imagination. He had certainly never imagined that anything like it would ever happen to him, reluctantly acknowledging that it had thrown him and that he had panicked. But he also realised that that was not why he had rejected her advances. No, it was more than that; it was because something hadn't seemed quite right; in much the same way as he had felt about Jill's attraction to him.

Or was it simply the case that he was imagining things and had started to believe that every attractive woman who displayed any affection towards him had an ulterior motive because of what had happened in Benidorm? He realised that he had not been intimate with anyone since then and started to wonder if he had deliberately avoided it. Could it really be the case that his experience there had left him damaged and unable to trust women ever again, in much the same way as Emily's experience had affected her willingness to trust men?

He didn't really want to believe that was the case but decided that whatever the truth was he was determined that, unlike the last time he found himself in such a predicament, he wasn't going to let it ruin his holiday. Experience should also have told him that that was the least of his worries.

Chapter 29

20 January 2018 (previous day)
Saturday

When her 'friend' Akmal had asked her if she was interested in earning some 'easy money' she had been all ears. And when he told her all about the man in room 457 at the Med Palace, where she worked as a chambermaid and then what was required of her, she had jumped at the chance, without any hesitation or thought to the possible consequences for either the 'mark' or herself. As far as she was concerned, it was indeed easy money, and having checked out the intended target; he was tall, blonde and 'fit', with nice eyes and an engaging, friendly smile. She also thought that he had a very nice bum, so what was not to like? And she was being paid.

Yes, she was really looking forward to her work.

Chapter 30

January 22, 2018
Monday

Sam awoke the next day to cloudy, overcast conditions, which perfectly matched his mood. He had also missed breakfast as he had no real appetite, preferring instead to make himself some cereal and have a cup of tea sitting out on the balcony, as, despite the conspicuous amount of cloud, it was still pleasantly warm. As he sat there reflecting on the events that had occurred since his arrival on the island, and particularly those of the previous day, his thoughts naturally and inexorably drifted back to his experiences in Benidorm only months previously, prompting him to think, *'There's no fucking way I'm going through that shit again. Why me, what have I done to deserve this?'* and then realised that he knew the answer to that question.

However, it also made him wonder whether other forces were at work and whether the two situations were connected in some way and if so, how? As he pondered these questions, his thoughts were interrupted by a loud knock on the door, which sounded very ominous. On answering it he was surprised to find two people, a man and a woman, proffering police ID. They were accompanied by another male, who identified himself as 'Senor Hernandez, the hotel manager', who, the Guardia Civil officers advised, had made a room available for the purpose of them being able to speak with him privately. The officers advised Sam that they would explain everything to him whilst also asking him to confirm his name and requesting his passport as proof of his identity. Sam knew that he had no option other than to comply with their request, whilst at the same time wondering, '*What the fuck is happening?*'

On arriving at the room which had been provided, the male officer introduced himself saying, 'Mr Meredith, I am Detective Inspector Delgado,' and then gesturing towards his female colleague, whom he introduced as 'Detective Inspector Herrera' who looked at Sam with no expression, and advised him that whilst he was not being charged at that stage, added that serious allegations had been made against him. When Sam asked, quite indignantly, what the allegations were, he was told that he would be advised 'all in good time' and was asked for his co-operation and to accompany the officers to the police headquarters to be interviewed, where he would also be given the further details of the allegations and allowed to respond accordingly. He was also offered the services of a lawyer, which he, rather impetuously declined. On arriving at police Headquarters Sam was taken to a room by the officers, which had the usual table and four chairs around it, and some recording equipment on top of it. Detective Inspector Delgado motioned for him to sit down at the table and asked him if he wanted anything to drink.

Sam responded in the affirmative, asking for some water, having learned from previous experience and anticipating that his mouth would likely dry up at some point during the anticipated interrogation.

'*Here we go again*', he thought, shaking his head disbelievingly.

***

With the pleasantries over with and Sam having indicated his willingness and readiness to proceed, Inspector Delgado pressed a button on the recording device on the table and said, 'Please state your name for the purposes of the recording,' which Sam responded to accordingly. After a further series of routine questions, Sam was asked if he had any questions of his own, which he responded, quite impetuously to, with; 'What the fuck is this all about?' only this time out loud. He was subsequently advised, in almost perfect English, that 'what it was all about' was that allegations of indecent exposure had been made against him by a chambermaid in the hotel.

Sam could hardly believe what he was hearing, and, if truth be told he was having great difficulty in taking the situation seriously, which he then realised was not endearing him to the officials, at which point he also realised the need to take it very seriously indeed. Accordingly, he then asked for legal representation and that the British Consulate be contacted, whilst also vehemently protesting his innocence.

After a short break that allowed for representatives from both the agencies to be contacted and in place, Sam gave them and the police his side of the story, whilst strongly insisting that the chambermaid was a 'liar'. When asked by the female officer why the chambermaid would lie about such a thing, Sam initially said; 'I have no idea,' before then hesitatingly speculating that it might be a case of; 'Hell hath no fury like a women scorned', whilst explaining the circumstances surrounding his statement.

Unfortunately, this did not appear to endear him to the female official, and, if he was being honest, Sam himself didn't really believe that was what it was either, because it felt like there was something more to it, but he didn't know what.

Regarding his more immediate predicament, Sam wondered whether he was dealing with a Spanish version of 'Good Cop Bad Cop,' as whilst Inspector Delgado couldn't exactly be described as sympathetic, he, as far as Sam was concerned, appeared much more reasonable than his female counterpart, who Sam thought was a real *'piece of work'*. It was his perception that she obviously did not feel the need to be pleasant or polite, whilst her unapologetically cynical and seemingly judgmental attitude and approach made him feel that she had already decided that he was guilty of something. She also reminded him of a woman that he had worked with some years previously when he was employed by the Department of Health and Social Security.

She was a manager in personnel, before it evolved into Human Resources (HR) and if ever somebody was in the wrong job it was her. Her reputation preceded her; she had been moved from one office to another due to a litany of complaints and allegations of bullying and unreasonable behaviour.

She had reportedly left a trail of destruction in her wake which required considerable surgery and rebuilding in all her previous workplaces. However, in Sam's view, the worst crime was perpetrated by the senior managers who consistently failed to address the issues and protect staff from her egotistic, irrational and manipulative behaviour. During the relatively short time that he worked with her he came to understand why she had garnered such a reputation and, in his opinion, it was clearly well earned; whilst in her managerial position she had contrived to create a climate of division and fear in the workplace. She did this by deliberately favouring some workers whilst actively isolating and targeting others.

Following Sam witnessing and being made aware of several

such incidents and processes occurring in the workplace, he eventually raised concerns with senior management, but to no avail. Eventually and perhaps inevitably, some staff, with no practical support or guidance in place, went off sick, some long term, being advised by their doctor that they needed a significant break from the pressures of the job.

Some were prescribed anti-depressants by their doctor – people who would never previously have considered resorting to such a thing. The bully, meanwhile, continued to present as totally unable and unwilling to accept any kind of criticism or tolerate any other point of view which differed from her own, no matter how well reasoned. Furthermore, and even more concerning, her reaction to this was invariably both vindictive and unreasonable, and this wasn't just Sam's view; it was everyone's. Also, following her finding out about him having raised concerns her attitude towards him changed dramatically, changing from sour tolerance to out and out hostility.

However, Sam had stood up to her predictable attempts to both intimidate and gaslight him, and shortly after she left to take up a post elsewhere, which is also apparently a familiar course of action or escape route used by bullies in the event of them being confronted by any challenge or exposure.

Sam was glad to see the back of her when she left, and he was in absolutely no doubt that the feeling was mutual. He was also in no doubt that she would almost certainly still be making somebody's life a misery, because her own was so desperate and sad. He left himself not long after, due to his disenchantment with the dysfunctional and ineffective management in place, with the mutual antipathy and disregard between them being all too apparent.

After the questioning was over, which, it appeared to Sam,

115

was clearly not to Inspector Herrera's satisfaction, he was allowed to remain in the room where he was questioned, 'Whilst further enquiries were carried out' rather than being locked in a cell.

He was also provided with coffee- or something approaching it- and some biscuits.

As he sat there in his informal and unofficial confinement Sam recalled with some amusement, his previous idle musings regarding the language used to describe holidays as suggesting people were being held prisoner in some sort of captivity. Many a thing said in jest indeed. Whilst Sam was hoping that his current confinement was only a temporary state of affairs, it also provided him with plenty of time to think about his predicament. And the more he thought about it- and the events and 'coincidences' surrounding it, the more he was convinced that he had been set up by someone—he just didn't know who or why.

But he was going to make it his business to find out.

Chapter 31

22 January 2018
Monday

After further investigation, the hotel's electronic keycard records revealed that the maid, after entering Sam's room and then being asked to return later, had re-entered the room a second time within minutes, when Sam was in the shower, before leaving again and then returning as Sam came out of the bathroom. So, she would have known that he was in the shower and could have easily timed it so that she was there outside the bathroom door when he walked out. Her version of events was that she had entered the room to clean it, having knocked first but received no response. She claimed that Sam then came out of the bathroom with a towel wrapped around him which, on seeing her, he removed before lying down on the bed, whilst asking her to join him. She claimed that she then ran from the room very distressed.

The hotel management, after interviewing the maid, contacted the police, at which point questions were asked as to why, if she was so distressed, did she leave it so long after the event to report it to her superiors? And which, unfortunately, for her, she could not answer to their satisfaction. She was also unable to explain why she entered the room a second time within minutes of being told that it was not convenient. And, when questioned further, her account of what she alleged had happened did not add up and had changed from her initial report, leading to the police believing that her explanation could not be trusted. The situation raised more concerns about her behaviour than Sam's, who was later released, the authorities informing him that there was no case to answer. The chambermaid was held in custody whilst further enquiries and interviews were carried out before eventually being released on bail, having been charged, with Attempting to Pervert the Course of Justice and Wasting Police Time.

Before Sam left the premises, Inspector Delgado advised him that while making routine enquiries about him they became aware of his involvement with the police investigation into two murders in Benidorm the previous year. He also advised that he had consulted with both Inspector Costales and Inspector Powrie, the main investigating officials, regarding the circumstances to obtain more comprehensive details and information in line with routine fact finding. Sam's heart skipped a beat as he began to wonder where this was leading. However, his fears were assuaged as he was informed by Inspector Delgado that his counterpart had spoken very positively about the co-operation and assistance, he had afforded them in their investigation and the important role that he had provided in securing arrests. He then added, 'You seem to have eventful holidays, Mr Meredith,' with a half-smile and offering his hand in a farewell, which Sam shook, saying; 'I can assure you it's not intentional Inspector'.

The inspector advised Sam that they had his contact details and, in the event of them needing to speak to him again, which was mainly dependent upon the outcome of the now ongoing investigation into Sam's accuser, they would be in touch. He also confirmed that they would contact the hotel manager to bring him up to date regarding the situation and offered to provide Sam with transport back there. However, he declined, saying, 'I don't need the attention and indignity of arriving in a police car.' Whilst the Inspector attempted to reassure him, saying; 'I think we can manage to provide an unmarked vehicle to protect your privacy Mr Meredith,' Sam responded with, 'it's okay Inspector, I think I need a walk anyway'. Unfortunately, on leaving the police station Sam immediately regretted his decision, on realising two things: firstly, it was significantly darker than it had been when he had arrived and, second; he had absolutely no idea where he was. So, he just kept walking, hoping that it was in the right direction.

As he gradually regained his bearings by scanning the skyline for familiar structures and illuminated hotel names, and on realising that he was still quite a bit away from his hotel, Sam saw and hailed a taxi, which thankfully stopped. As he stepped into the taxi, Sam realised another two things; firstly, that he had missed the best part of the day, which he was really pissed off at, and secondly; he was absolutely ravenous. So, rather than heading back to the hotel he decided to head for somewhere to have food. Sam asked the taxi driver, who, he subsequently discovered, was Italian, to take him to a café or somewhere near his hotel. The taxi driver nodded and asked, 'Do you like pasta?' And on receiving a confirmatory response from Sam, took him to a small bistro on Avenida Antonio Dominguez, named Café Epoca, which, he discovered, was a small Italian family business, which made the most delicious homemade pasta, in large amounts, for very little cost. And the beer was cheap too-job done!

As he sat enjoying his beer, Sam's head was full of questions with very little answers, why would the chambermaid deliberately tell lies and accuse him of such behaviour? And why wait until the next day to make a complaint? Was it really, as he had, perhaps unwisely, suggested, simply a case of;' "Hell hath no fury like a woman scorned." Had she sat and mulled over it and become more and more resentful? Or… had she been asked …or perhaps even made to do it…. but why? He still could not think of any possible reason why or who could have any reason to. He was starting to get that same uneasy feeling that he had had in Benidorm when he… 'Benidorm' he heard himself say out loud, and again wondering if the two things were connected. And then he realised that there was only one connection, or at least one obvious one - Akmal- and he needed a word.

Sam finished his drink and headed along Avenida Antonio Dominguez towards Avenida Santiago Puig and turned right at the end towards the junction at the Hotel Zentral Center.
As he approached his destination, he saw that Akmal was indeed standing in the same place where he had seen him before. And he was talking to the chambermaid.

Chapter 32

22 January 2018
Monday

" Well, well, well, my, my, my and well, well, well all over again", as Worzel Gummidge used to say,' said Sam, quite playfully, before asking; 'What do we have here then?' clearly enjoying the moment and adding: 'Isn't this cosy? and interesting, very interesting indeed. So, what's the reason for this little *tete a tete* eh? Just two old pals meeting up for a chat, is it? And is this a private criminal conspiracy or can anyone join in?' said Sam, as he approached Akmal and the chambermaid. The latter, on seeing him started to walk away, but Sam grabbed her arm saying, 'Oh, don't rush off on my account Senorita, or should I say Senora,' said Sam, being intentionally sarcastic and cutting, before continuing with; 'We should catch up, chew the fat, you could tell me some stories, because you're very good at that. Had a lot of practice, have you? I think you've done this before by the looks of it. I'm surprised they let you out to be honest'.

'Let go of my arm,' she screamed, pulling it away very melodramatically.
'Or what, eh? What will you do? Tell the police that I assaulted you? Akmal here could be your witness. And then he can also tell them about how you two know one another and all about the little scheme that you cooked up together eh? I imagine that you're out on bail, so I don't think that you really need any more grief at the

121

moment. Eh, what do you think Sparky?' said Sam, looking at Akmal.

However, before Akmal could answer, the maid, said;' I don't need to listen to this shit' and stormed off, leaving him to face the music.

'A friend in need indeed, eh,' said Sam, 'you certainly can pick them.' Initially, Akmal just stared at Sam, saying nothing, but then seemed to find inspiration from somewhere, and threatened to reveal to the police that it had been Sam who had brokered the deal with him in Benidorm to have Rab Lindsay killed (failing to mention, of course, that he had already divulged that information and more to his brother). And who, unknown to him, had already shared it with people that he shouldn't have.

Sam, however, was not going to be threatened (even if it did cause him some degree of anxiety) reminding Akmal that it would be one person's word against another and that there was absolutely no evidence against him, whilst also pointing out that the police probably still wanted to talk to *him,* not Sam, about the situation in Benidorm.

Sam then also pointed out that Akmal would only be incriminating himself regarding the current situation and that once his relationship with the chambermaid became known, it was only a matter of time before things fell into place. 'Then the police would then want to know details of why and who else was involved,' as did Sam, who continued; 'And I imagine that will not go down well with certain people' said Sam, as menacingly as he could manage, '... to have the police poking their noses into their business-again. Your credit must be getting pretty low in that regard, I would think, Sparky.'

Akmal was thinking on his feet, which it had to be said, was not his forte, but which led him to believe, quite reasonably, in his opinion, that, if push came to shove, he could claim that his recent actions were simply revenge against Sam for their 'altercation' in Benidorm, which the police there would be only too well aware of and able to corroborate. However, he also realised that Sam was correct in his assessment; it was attention and hassle that neither he nor his masters wanted or could afford, whilst also acknowledging to himself, albeit reluctantly, that his current credit with his bosses was indeed decidedly low. So, after evaluating the situation and his available options further he eventually admitted to Sam that he had been ordered to set him up. However, he was adamant that he did not know why and could not give him any further information.

'You mean, you won't, or more likely can't, because you're too frightened. That's it isn't it Sparky? you're scared shitless, aren't you? You look scared to me; scared to piss your bosses off any more than you already have. Well, you should be fucking scared, you and your little partner in crime, because you have both confirmed what I suspected; what I don't know yet is why. But I will find out, one way or another, even if it means involving the Police, which, despite your empty threats, you really don't want to do you? Either that or I will just have to beat it out of you again' said Sam, as menacingly as he could manage, before walking away and leaving Akmal to consider his threat.

Chapter 33

22 January 2018
Monday

After Sam departed, Akmal remained preoccupied for quite some time with his threats. However, he wasn't worried about the threat of violence, as he now believed, rightly or wrongly, that he could deal with any physical threat that Sam posed, if he was prepared and didn't allow him to catch him off guard. But he was annoyed with himself for allowing his association with the chambermaid in making false allegations against Sam, to be discovered. Also, he was only too aware of his already precarious position with his employers, given his past track record. He had apparently only survived his unfortunate involvement in the previous debacle in Benidorm because he had agreed to be moved away and out of the line of fire, thereby removing the likelihood of him attracting any more undue attention to himself or his corrupt and ruthless paymasters.

However, whereas up until now he had been reliably silent regarding the events in Benidorm, unfortunately, for whatever reason, he had chosen to forget or simply ignore the importance of continuing to discharge that responsibility, by recklessly discussing very sensitive details. And, unfortunately, the person whom he had shared it with had shown equal carelessness and disregard by also casually shouting his mouth off to the wrong people, thereby creating an extremely unfortunate situation for other people, and consequently, for them both.

Not that it really mattered, as what he hadn't factored into the equation was that after his participation in the whole murky business was completed, he, and possibly his brother, simply by association, were pretty much what could be termed as 'loose ends' And unfortunately for Akmal, the people whose bidding he had been instructed to carry out, with no questions asked, were not the kind of people who could afford loose ends, because loose ends lead to risks, and he suspected that there had been more than enough of them already for their liking.

And he was right, because the view being taken by the people who mattered was that it was clear that he was most definitely a security risk who could no longer be trusted or relied upon to act in the best interests of the organisation. Indeed, if truth be told, he had been on borrowed time for a while and now, despite reassurances that he was not under any kind of threat, his head was also now being demanded as collateral payback for his involvement in facilitating the contract carried out on Rab Lindsay. He was now, in effect, a bargaining tool as part of a negotiation between the warring factions in Glasgow, with a view to bringing the longstanding gang feud to an end.

Whilst it was true that Akmal didn't know the reasons behind what he had been instructed to do, or rather what he had asked the chambermaid to do, he had begun to wonder if it was in any way related to or a consequence of his conversation with his brother, it was just too much of a coincidence—yet another one.

He had called his brother, but he wasn't answering his 'phone and hadn't returned his calls and Akmal had speculated that he might be avoiding him and any awkward questions about whether he might have divulged certain sensitive information, following their last conversation. At least, he hoped that was the only reason, becoming more and more concerned the longer time passed with no word from his sibling.

Chapter 34

22 January 2018
Monday

Following further exploration into and scrutiny of the chambermaid's background by the authorities, a less than respectable past was revealed. Police records had recorded that she had previously been imprisoned for a period of twelve months, almost three years before, because of her making false and vindictive claims to police in London, when she told them that she was regularly subject to regular beatings beaten by her boyfriend.

Eve Pascal, thirty-eight years old, real name, Melissa Tadic, was born in Noosa in Queensland, Australia, to Croatian parents and had previously worked as a nail technician in London, where she had met Luke Bradley, a Landscape Gardener, from Auckland, New Zealand at a Thai cookery display, and they subsequently had a relationship lasting two years.

However, when he informed her that he was ending the relationship, she informed him that that she would 'ruin his life', if he left her.

She also told him that she was pregnant (which she wasn't) and that she would contact the police to report him for domestic assault if he ended their relationship. When he subsequently did so she had carried out her threats, contacting the police to make the malicious and vindictive claims, alleging that she was subject to regular physical abuse and that he had raped her. He was subsequently arrested, and a restraining order granted by a judge against him. However, after she was examined by a specialist doctor, it was established that, whilst she had some marks on her arms, there was nothing to suggest that she had been physically or sexually assaulted. It was also discovered that she wasn't pregnant. Following her being arrested and her vindictive threats being revealed at a subsequent trial, the jury decided that she had lied and had also attempted to pervert the course of justice. Consequently, she was sentenced to two years imprisonment, being released after serving half her sentence.

Unbelievably, after her release, she proceeded to stalk and harass her ex-boyfriend, who had since married his new girlfriend. She also went online and posted negative comments about his marriage and made extremely offensive comments about his wife, whilst also claiming to still be in an intimate relationship with him. However, police were able to trace the IP address to her mobile number, at which point a search warrant was obtained and her mobile phone inspected, confirming her guilt.

On appearing at Court, she pleaded guilty to Stalking and another charge of Attempt to Pervert the Course of Justice and was sentenced to a further twelve months imprisonment. On being released nine months later she decided that she needed to get away and travelled to Tenerife to look for work, which she found as a Chambermaid, failing to mention any of her previous criminal history or convictions whilst also using a false name.

Over the past year she had met, become friendly and then intimate with Akmal Samir, who, in the last couple of days, following instructions from his bosses, had contacted her to request her co-operation in making the malicious allegations against Sam, who was conveniently staying at the same hotel where she was working.

However, she had not revealed this information to the police when interviewed, being terrified of the consequences, and it was only Sam who knew this, following his 'chat' with Akmal. Regarding the malicious allegations against Sam, she had been only too happy to oblige and hadn't thought twice about it, particularly as she was being paid a handsome sum for her co-operation. Initially she was supposed to have sex with him and then accuse him of rape, however, when that didn't work out as planned, she resorted to the accusation of indecent exposure, the idea stemming from the incident earlier in the day.

This had also met with the approval of her paymasters, as they didn't just want Sam killed – the plan being that this would happen when he was in custody–they also wanted him disgraced, humiliated and shamed.

Unfortunately, when this backfired spectacularly, leading to her being questioned by the police and then charged, there was a need to reconsider the planned strategy, including the already factored in contingency/back up plan.

As Rabbie Burns had lamented, "The best laid plans…"

Chapter 35

23 January 2018
Tuesday

Sam was awakened the next morning by his phone ringing persistently but when he tried to reach it before it stopped ringing, in his semi-conscious, drowsy state, he only succeeded in knocking it off the bedside table on to the floor, when it stopped ringing abruptly. Initially he was worried that it had broken on the hard tiled floor but on subsequent inspection he found that the protective casing had done what it was intended for and absorbed the impact. He got up and headed to the bathroom, performing his basic ablutions and gradually waking himself up, before inspecting his phone to discover that the missed call was from Emily. His phone then pinged loudly, indicating that he had received a voice message, which was also from Emily, suggesting that they meet up.

He hadn't contacted her, as promised due to being somewhat preoccupied and distracted by his encounter with Tenerife's finest and he wondered what she would think if he told her what had transpired. He could still hardly believe it himself. Then he again found himself questioning whether he should tell her about it at all, as it might lead to her asking too many questions.

And would she believe his version of events, or would she judge him, particularly given her trust issues with men? He decided that he couldn't think about it anymore on an empty stomach and got up and headed down to breakfast for some much-needed fuel and energy, resolving that he would call Emily after he had eaten. It was only after he had eaten that Sam realised that what had been quite a grey day had now become a very hot, sunny day and that there were already a lot of people at the pool. He decided that relaxing in the sun was just what the situation required and headed back to his room to fetch a towel and his Kindle, when the manager approached him, asking to speak to him in private.

Christ what is it now? thought Sam, as he followed the Manager to his office, where he had initially been interviewed by the police and wondered if he was heading for more of the same. Were they going to tell him that they had charged the chambermaid and that they needed him to make a statement or perhaps even give evidence?

Or, even more concerning, was it to do with what had happened in Benidorm? recalling that Inspector Delgado had mentioned that they had already spoken to Inspectors Costales and Powrie from the Costa Blanca and Glasgow, respectively.

As it turned out he needn't have worried, because the manager only wanted to speak to him to apologise for the situation, advising that he was extremely sorry for all that Sam had gone through because of the chambermaid's malicious and unfounded allegations and that she had been dismissed. It occurred to Sam that he was probably more worried about the prospect of him taking legal action against them, which hadn't occurred to him until now.

And which he had no intention of doing, even though he was still really pissed off at having effectively lost a day of his holiday. All he really wanted to do was to make up for lost time and get out in the sun, which he was presently being prevented from doing.

However, his spirits lifted when the manager told him that they were offering him an upgrade to an executive room in the Mark Anthony Hotel for the remainder of his holiday and also a further free week for up to four people there, or any other resort of his choice at a time of his choosing, with the option of adding it on to his current holiday if he so wished, to compensate him for the all inconvenience he had suffered.

Sam had not expected to be offered any kind of compensation, not even remotely, apart from maybe a couple of bottles of wine in the fridge but certainly not to the extent of what he just had been gifted. Accordingly, and not surprisingly, he advised the manager that he was more than happy to accept his kind gesture, whilst informing that if it was all right with him he would prefer to leave the move to the next day, as he was heading directly to the pool at the Cleopatra, where he planned to chill out for the rest of the day, finding the pool at the Palace too busy and loud.

The manager smiled and said that he understood, whilst advising that the pool at the Mark Anthony was also very quiet and nice, but nevertheless advising Sam that he was free to move at his own convenience and that they would also take care of moving his luggage. He also asked him whether he preferred red or white wine. Sam informed him that he liked both.

Chapter 36

23 January 2018
Tuesday

The pool at the Cleopatra Princess was relatively busy, but Sam managed to find an empty bed in the sun and practically equidistant from the pool and the pool bar, where he and his Kindle settled for the day, dipping into the glorious pool whenever he felt the heat getting too much for him to bear. Around noon, he thought about heading to La Palapa Beach Bar, but felt so content and settled that he decided to have his lunch at the pool bar instead. However, as he headed there with his reading material, he noticed that it was busy too and feeling that he was unlikely to get a table turned to walk away when he heard someone shout his name. On turning back, he saw Jill sitting at a table and waving at him, whilst gesturing that he was welcome to join her by pulling out a chair from the table.

'Sam, over here, come and join me,' she called, smiling at him.

Sam found himself both surprised and relieved to find that Jill was still apparently feeling friendly and welcoming towards him.

But then he realised that that was one of the things that was bothering him. 'Why should she be?' he asked himself. I wouldn't blame her if she never wanted to see or speak to me again. I think if I had been in her shoes, I would probably have just ignored me. And yet here she was being as pleasant and accommodating as ever. *It just didn't ring true*, he thought, whilst smiling back and joining her at the table anyway.

'I just saw you out of the corner of my eye and thought I would say hello, but It's okay if you have other plans' Jill said, smiling. 'I just thought I would offer, as you seemed to be looking for a table.'

'No, it's fine,' Sam answered, 'I don't have anywhere else to be and yes I was looking for a table.'

He had started to tell her about his escapade with the Chambermaid and his subsequent good fortune with his move to the Mark Anthony Hotel but, for some reason that he couldn't explain to himself, decided against it. A woman got up from the table next to them, smiling at Sam as she passed them, followed by the waitress arriving and asking if they wanted any food or drinks. Sam ordered a beer and looked at Jill by way of an enquiry, and she said that she would have a white wine and that she was paying.

'I think I can manage to buy you a drink,' said Sam and asked the waitress for a menu, saying to Jill, 'and I'm going to have some food too, what about you, my treat'?

'Don't be silly, we can just go Dutch again,' she said, as the waitress appeared with their drinks and a menu. 'Have you been here long'? she asked.

'Only a couple of hours said Sam, I'm just over there,' he said, gesturing towards where his sun bed was. The Med Palace pool was too busy for me. What about you?' he asked.

'A little longer, since just after breakfast,' she replied. 'But I never saw you arriving, I must've been too engrossed in my book,' she spoke.

Sam was thinking that she didn't have a book with her and

that she must've left it at her sun bed, wherever it was, as she hadn't given any indication.

'I think we better order' said Jill, looking at the menu to see what was on offer, at which point Sam noticed that the Manager had appeared. He smiled at Sam as he passed, before heading to the bar to speak to the waitress. Sam decided upon a club sandwich and Jill had a salad, both of which were delicious, as they had shared and tasted each other's food. After checking with Jill, he ordered more drinks, with Jill again repeating her offer to go Dutch.

However when they had finished and Sam asked for the bill the waitress advised him that; 'There is no charge, the manager say it is free for you senor,' looking towards the bar area where the manager was, who waved at looked at Sam and shook his head and made a sweeping gesture with his hands and then a thumbs up, confirming the waitress's message.

Sam smiled back, returning the thumbs up, whilst trying to look as surprised as Jill, who looked him and said, 'How nice was that?' and asking Sam, 'Do you know him?' Sam again briefly considered confiding in her about his encounter with the local plod but again thought better of it, instead answering, 'What? No... well yes, I know he's the manager because I had to speak to him about a problem with my room... eh... room booking, which he sorted out,' he lied, adding, 'So maybe it's by way of a complimentary gesture,' hoping that he sounded convincing.

'Maybe he likes you,' she said, smiling and then winking. 'If you know what I mean?' and looking at Sam for his reaction. However, before he could respond, she added, 'Or maybe he thinks that you fancy him?' with an expression that made it clear that she expected a response. *Great now she thinks I'm gay* thought Sam. And no bloody wonder who can blame her? I mean why the hell wouldn't she, given my recent performance? He momentarily toyed with the idea of going along with such a pretext, thinking that it might suit his purposes, whilst also preserving her feminine pride and ego. However, his testosterone, heterosexual instinct and male pride kicked in as he heard himself say, 'Don't be ridiculous' and then couldn't resist adding, 'He's not my type,' and then burst out laughing.

However, Jill wasn't laughing and clearly didn't know if he was being serious or not. 'Oh, for God's sake, you don't really think I'm gay, do you?' he said, still smiling.

'I don't know, are you?' she asked, looking into his eyes.

'Do you want me to prove I'm not'? asked Sam, looking at her disbelievingly and then regretting his rather impetuous response. However, before she could answer, her mobile phone rang. Jill looked at the number displayed on the phone and then at Sam, before saying; 'I must take this sorry,' and then headed off to do exactly that in private, saying over her shoulder' and don't think I'm letting you off the hook', and still not smiling. Sam wondered what it was that was so important, but she had returned within a matter of minutes looking relaxed and smiling.

'Everything all right?' he enquired, sounding concerned.

'Yes, all good, nothing serious, just work,' she replied, at which point Sam realised that he had no idea what she did for a job because she had never told him, and he had never asked.

As he was toying with the idea of doing just that she reached over the table, taking Sam's hands in hers and saying; Now where were we?'

Oh, yes, you were offering to prove something to me, if I'm not wrong?', all the while looking into his eyes, whilst caressing his hands and then moving them towards her breasts, which felt firm and supple. Sam looked back at her, whilst making no

135

attempt to move his hands away, and realising that this time she had him cornered and that there was no way out and that he might as well enjoy it.

'Sounds like a plan,' he said, as he tended to do, before adding, 'Can't wait', and trying to look as if he meant it.

Jill also liked the idea of him having a point to prove, and the thought of him seeing it as a challenge excited her so much. And she planned to play her part in ensuring his enthusiastic participation.

'Give me ten minutes,' she said standing up, throwing 10 euros on the table, saying, 'For the tip,' and telling him her room number.

Sam watched her go and then gave the waitress the tip, before returning to his sun bed to collect his stuff, realising that if Jill really was any kind of a threat to him then he had completely sold himself down the river by thinking with his bollocks rather than his brain. As he was having this debate with himself his phone rang and it was Jill telling him that she was sitting naked on the balcony, thinking about them being together and getting quite excited at the prospect and telling him to look up. And sure enough there she was, now standing, clearly topless and looking quite animated, her movements synchronized with her breathless words on the phone.

'I need you here with me now Sam, please don't keep me waiting 'she said, ending the call. Sam could feel himself getting aroused and had to use his towel to hide the obvious consequence of this, as he got up from his sun bed to head to her room.

On arriving at the door number that, she had given him, he stopped, knocked and then waited. 'It's open, come in and lock the door after you,' he heard Jill say, which he did. On entering he saw that she was still on the balcony, still naked, apart from a wrap around her waist, hanging loosely on her hips. She was standing facing him with a glass of wine in her hand. 'Why don't you pour yourself a glass of wine and join me?' she said, which he did.

As Sam sat down beside her on the balcony she began putting after sun cream on her upper body and breasts, which were very sun kissed. She then turned round and asked him if he would rub some on her back, which he did. And, as he did, the feel of her was again producing a predictable response in his loins, particularly when she moved her hands down to his all too evident bulge and started caressing him, very sensuously and expertly. He had to adjust himself to prevent him sustaining an injury to his nether regions, such was the extent of his reaction to her foreplay.

Noticing this she smiled and said, 'Why don't we free him from his discomfort and give him some room?' and then pulling his shorts down and taking his swollen appendage in her hand and easing it out his shorts, as she crouched down between his legs. Sam moaned involuntarily as he felt her caresses and the soft wetness of her mouth envelop and then manipulate his manhood, before teasing him with her body and her tongue. 'Oh fuck', he groaned, grabbing her hair in his hands and tugging it back gently, so that he could see her pleasuring him, which she responded to by issuing her own moans of pleasure.
Suddenly they heard noise and the sound of voices, which seemed to come from one of the other balconies, either beside or below it seemed, which caused Jill to giggle and Sam to smile and say, 'Maybe we should go inside?'

'Yes, I think we should, I want to see and feel all of you Sam,' she said, standing up and kissing him on the mouth and then carrying both glasses of wine into the room. Sam righted himself and followed her closing the door and the curtains behind

137

him. Jill had removed her wrap and sat naked on the sofa awaiting his attention.

'You are a very sensual woman,' said Sam. Her reply made him smile, 'I kiss better than I cook,' she said, smiling mischievously, before adding; 'And I'm a good cook,' Sam joined her on the sofa and kissed her strongly and passionately on the mouth, which she responded to by moving him into a seated position and then straddling him and easing him inside her, which elicited long moans of pleasure from both of them. There was a mirror on the wall opposite the sofa allowing him to gaze unhindered at the visage of her beautiful back profile as she began moving slowly up and down and then backwards and forward, finding a rhythm that they both spontaneously embraced.

Their movement gradually became more rapid and urgent, eventually culminating in both yielding to their respective climaxes with loud gasps and screams of fulfilment. Jill collapsed into Sam's arms with a sensual moan and a sigh, her body glistening with sweat from their exertions. Sam also felt spent, and they just lay there in each other's arms as their breathing subsided and until they had both recovered sufficiently.

They then carried their wine to the bed and just lay there drinking and talking, with both alcohol and conversation flowing freely. However, when they eventually ran out of both they returned to their other mutual area of interest- each other.

Jill then positioned herself so that they were able view their entwined bodies in the mirrored wardrobes. Sam couldn't help thinking that he was getting the better deal, as Jill 's firm and lithe body was a sight to behold. 'I see you like to watch, so do I', said Jill, taking his hand and pulling him from the bed towards the sofa again.

'Come on, my turn, sit down 'she said, straddling him again but this time in the reverse position so that she was facing the wall mirror, which he initially thought was a bit narcissistic. However, he wasn't complaining, as he was just glad that it was her body that was on show more than his. She then positioned herself on top of Sam but lying back with her arm round his neck so that he also had an unhindered view of proceedings. Jill seemed completely lost in the moment, totally uninhibited and abandoned in her enjoyment, with the resultant sounds and movements quickly becoming louder and more frantic, respectively. Sam found himself responding and reciprocating accordingly, as they again both headed towards their individual climaxes.

On returning to bed, they both drifted into a gentle slumber, borne of satisfaction and fulfilment, totally spent and satisfied and not waking up until the next day, when they made love again. However, this time Sam was the initiator and the main driver of proceedings, which Jill was more than happy with.

She had been pleasantly surprised and reassured by his response to her 'challenge' both the night before and in the morning.

He had seemed to welcome her dominant approach, not finding it intimidating or threatening to his masculinity and accordingly had responded enthusiastically and creatively, allowing her to demonstrate her own enjoyment, which she had done in a completely non-self-conscious fashion. Then when he had taken the initiative, he hadn't been frantic or hurried in any way; on the contrary he had been confident, assured and adventurous, with a finesse that made her feel extremely relaxed. And consequently, her enjoyment was assured. She thought that he made love like he had nothing to prove but everything to gain, and not just for himself either, her own satisfaction being testament to that. She also knew that she wanted to experience it again, as soon and as often as possible, before the situation arrived at its unfortunate but inevitable conclusion.

Chapter 37

24 January 2020
Wednesday

The tall, swarthy man sat on the balcony of his hotel room and scrutinised the information that had been delivered to him anonymously from an untraceable source, providing details of his next 'project'. And that's the way he liked to view it; a 'project', to be completed on time and with no complications or loose ends, a routine business transaction. Because as far as he was concerned that's what it was—no emotion involved, and no payment in kind, or any other currency other than pure, hard cash - by whatever means it reached his bank account. Anything else just complicated things- and he didn't like complications; 'I like things simple. I'm a simple man with simple tastes' is his much-repeated mantra. All well and good, however, his 'simple' tastes include Renaissance and Impressionist art, Cordon Bleu food in Michelin Star restaurants, prostitutes, guns, and gambling—and not just in casinos or for money.

For as long as he could remember, at least in his adult life, he had always been a creature of the night, never really feeling comfortable during the daytime; it felt like an inconvenience, an obstacle that had to be negotiated in order to get to the place where he came alive and thrived, the dark of the evening and the night, which made him calm, creative and lethal. And that was where he lived now.

His eyes are as dead and lifeless as many of his unfortunate victims or 'marks'—dark emotionless holes which reveal and offer nothing in terms of his feelings, thoughts or intent. Consequently, he is also a very good poker player. And, if eyes are indeed the 'windows of the soul' then his is a very dark and desolate, 'soulless' place. He is being paid £30,000 for his current job, half now and half after the job is done, with the 'mark' being some middle-aged guy who worked at a newspaper. He was not aware of the reason for the hit, and he had no interest in knowing.

It was not necessary or important to him, all he needed to know was the guy's details: routine, movements and location, which on this occasion, just happened to be in Tenerife, where he also has a contact, although it is unlikely that they will be over the moon to hear from him after such a long time. However, that wasn't really a concern, as he was confident of their co-operation- and then he would move on to his next project, which *was* personal very personal indeed.

Chapter 38

She was raised by a respectable and wealthy family, also having had the benefit of a private education; Jill Gilchrist was, by her own admission, a loved and privileged child, with a bright future. However, in her mid 30's, on a holiday to Egypt, she became involved in something that would change her life forever; a meeting with a seemingly respectable Englishman had culminated in her becoming involved in something that she would never have imagined in her wildest dreams. His name was Oliver (call me Ollie) and after several conversations over meals and drinks, he managed to convince her that he had found a way to earn easy money. He told her that he had contacts in Cairo, who supplied him with both cannabis and cocaine, which he sent to America by mail to friends, in religious artifacts, mainly hollow iron statues of the Egyptian gods, Osiris and Isis, sealed with cement and then painted over. The contacts would then sell the drugs and send him half of the profits.

He explained to Jill that courier companies didn't ask for ID to post parcels, which meant that it was easy to provide false details and consequently the chances of being caught were almost non- existent; or at least that was what Ollie led her to believe, and that was what decided it for her. And indeed, it did prove to be very lucrative for a long time, with her regular trips to Egypt raising no concern. However, following one of the parcels arousing suspicion and being intercepted, the scam was discovered, as was Jill's involvement, following her contacting the courier service to make enquiries about the missing mail delivery. She was charged with drug smuggling and following a trial, she was found guilty and sentenced to five years imprisonment

Initially, she was kept in a basement cell in a police station in central Cairo, which was approximately five by nine metres. She shared the cell with thirty other prisoners, and there was not even sufficient space on the floor to sleep. Prisoners had to provide their own blankets with which to cover the tiled floor, and there was no place to wash them or hang them out to dry.

Finally, she was moved to a large prison in the southern suburbs of Cairo, where she shared a 'large cell' with eighty other prisoners, which was comprised of nearly forty concrete bunk beds, with no space set aside for eating or other activities and prisoners ate their food either between the beds or in the washroom area. There were no blankets or anything else provided to help keep prisoners warm at night when the temperature often fell to around just 1 or 2 degrees above zero. There were showers but you had to pay cigarettes or money to the *Kabeer* to access them, and there was running water only at certain times of the day. There was also no soap provided unless you had something to trade, which, if you were female, normally involved some form of sexual favours for the guards, both male and female. That had been her life for five years basically day to day survival, whatever it took.

And she *had* survived, whereas others hadn't; and when she was interviewed by the press on her return home about her experience in custody, she expressed the view that; 'Prison brutalises and hardens you, otherwise you wouldn't survive. It steals your soul; even the guards in prison had been brutalised by the system to the point where they had no soul and no conscience, otherwise they couldn't have done the things they did to people'. She refused to go into any more details but added that 'There were others who suffered much more than I did'.

She was forty years of age when she was finally released, but, with a criminal record and no skills or significant employment history, she had found it very hard to find work. She also realised that she had neither the energy, business acumen nor the resources to think about setting up in business again.

Consequently, she found herself turning to some of the 'contacts' that she had become involved with during her time as a drug smuggler. Despite the trauma, squalor and abuse that she had endured in jail, Jill was still an attractive woman and she had also managed to keep her mind and body intact. She was subsequently offered work, initially as an 'escort', in the seamy underworld of Tenerife, later graduating to being involved in blackmail and extortion scams. Whilst she never again got involved in trafficking drugs, although she continued to use, she instead became involved in trafficking and recruiting girls, and men, into sex work and illegal low paid jobs, in Tenerife and other locations, including Newcastle, Edinburgh, Stirling, Aberdeen and Glasgow.

In recent years, however, having settled in Tenerife, she had gradually and purposefully made it known that she planned to get out of the 'business', bemoaning the fact that she was 'getting too old for it' and that it was now a 'young person's profession'. However, the truth of it was that she was finding it increasingly stressful and taxing on her mental health.

She had seen others around her either come to grief or be tracked down by the authorities, bringing back the very real terror of imprisonment, which, she continually attempted to minimise or rationalise, to allow her to continue in her 'work'.

She had also managed to get herself off drugs and had been clean for just over a year. And so far, thankfully, she had not come up against any opposition or resistance to her declared intentions to 'retire', or at least not overtly. Her hope therefore was that she would be regarded as having 'served her time' and her masters, to their satisfaction to the extent that she deserved the chance to have a new life and that there would be no unexpected consequences for her. But she should have known better.

Chapter 39

24 January 2018
Wednesday

Sam lay back on the very comfortable lounger on the large balcony of his luxurious hotel room at the Mark Anthony hotel, with its' own personal plunge pool and with a view to die for over El Camison and Las Vistas beaches. As he relaxed with a particularly delicious Rioja, courtesy of the manager, looking out to sea, he reflected on the blissfully enjoyable events of the previous evening. Initially, he had found himself thinking that maybe he had been wrong about Jill, given that he had just enjoyed a night of mind-blowing sex and nothing terrible had happened to ruin the moment. *At least not yet*, he thought. They had parted with a passionate kiss, promising to be in touch with each other and meet up again soon. She joked that she might even surprise him by turning up at his room unannounced and saying, 'Room 457 isn't it'? He was just about to tell her that he was moving to the Mark Anthony hotel and all about the circumstances surrounding it when something again stopped him from doing so. He wasn't exactly sure what it was that had led to his hesitancy and resistance, however, on subsequent reflection, he realised that he couldn't ever remember telling her that he was staying at the Mediterranean Palace.

Then he reasoned that, as she knew that he wasn't staying at the Cleopatra Place, she had probably just assumed that was where he was staying, rather than at the more exclusive and up-market 'sister' hotel and neighbour that was the Mark Anthony. But he was certain that he hadn't ever told her his room number. He had been just about to ask her how she knew when he thought better of it, again for reasons that he wasn't entirely sure about– that same feeling of unease and sense of distrust kicking in once more; *Emily wasn't the only one who has trust issues,* he thought ruefully. Maybe he had more in common with her than he realised.

And then his phone rang. On picking it up, he saw, almost unbelievably, that it was Emily, whom he had still not contacted and which he felt bad about. So, on that occasion, he answered it, whilst trying to sound as casual as possible.

'Hi Emily,' he said.

'Hello stranger how are you?' she asked, equally as casually.

'I'm fine, Emily, nice to hear from you and sorry I haven't been in touch but...'

'No need to apologise, Sam, I just didn't want to leave it without saying something, either hello, or goodbye, whatever it is to be, but definitely to say thank you.'

'What for?' asked Sam, not sure what she was referring to.

'Just for being so sensitive and understanding,' said Emily...

'Oh, don't be silly, I just hope you're okay... or feeling better about things... or less bad, I mean...' he added, suddenly feeling very awkward.

'I know what you mean Sam, and yes, I do... I am... feeling better, thanks to you. So, I thought I would show my appreciation by offering to take you out for more food and drink. And I promise to be on my best behaviour'. Sam felt like shit because he hadn't called her back and here, she was being so nice, and apologising - again. He also felt guilty, for reasons that he couldn't quite fathom, then immediately realised that it was most likely because of his all too recent intimacy with Jill. But why do I feel guilty? he asked himself. He didn't owe Emily anything,

147

did he? But then he immediately also realised that he wouldn't want her to know about his dalliance with Jill, but, again, he wasn't sure why he felt that way.

He almost felt as if he had been unfaithful. Was it because he felt sorry for her, because of her apparent vulnerability and everything that had happened to her? Or was it because he felt that what had happened with Jill should have happened with Emily instead?

Did he wish it had? And if it had, would he have spurned Jill- again? He was so lost in his thoughts that he had completely forgotten what Emily had said, until she spoke again, jolting him from his ruminations.

'I'm sorry Sam, I never even thought to ask if you had other plans, it's okay if you want to…

'I'm sorry,' said Sam, realising his ignorance and apologising accordingly, 'Don't be silly Emily, and there's no need to apologise, but I do have other plans for tonight…

'Oh, oh, right, well, that's ok, we can just leave it then if …'

'I'm going to watch a football match' said Sam, wondering if she thought that he had another assignation. 'My team; Celtic are playing Partick Thistle in the League Cup, and I don't think football is your cup of tea really, is it? What about tomorrow night? If you can make it, that is? And you don't need to pay, we can do Dutch aga….'

'I want to Sam,' said Emily, interrupting, and I would be very happy if you would let me,' and then adding, 'Please?' probably accompanied by that lovely, warm smile'. She also offered to watch the football with him, but he believed that she was only being polite and accommodating and accordingly he let her off the hook.

'Tomorrow sounds like a plan,' said Sam.

148

Chapter 40

24 January 2018
Wednesday

Sam ate dinner at Sugar and Spice again as he had really enjoyed the food on the previous occasion that he had eaten there and because of its very convenient location, as he had decided to watch the game at the Gaelic Corner, which was practically diagonally opposite. After another enjoyable meal, Sam headed to the pub, which was already quite busy when he arrived, and the lounge, or conservatory space, had a nice, welcoming atmosphere, as did the bar, so he stayed to listen to a band playing in the bar after the game, which Celtic had won 3-1.

As he sat at the bar, he found himself thinking about Emily and wishing that he had arranged to meet her, as he suddenly and unexpectedly realised that he was missing her.

Even more unexpectedly, he began to think about the possibility that maybe they could continue to see each other after the holiday before bringing himself back down to earth with the sad acceptance of the fact that he was undeniably shit at relationships, as evidenced by the not too distant and still painful demise of his marriage.

Sam then mentally admonished himself, realising that he was indulging in some less than admirable self-pity, whilst also acknowledging that since the demise of his last, or rather, *only,* relationship since the breakup of his marriage, he had not been even remotely interested in negotiating *anything* serious. In fact, he had almost systematically avoided even thinking about it, also reluctantly acknowledging that it was most likely to avoid further disappointment or rejection. His dramatically consistent failure in that regard was, he found himself conceding, because he found the commitment and responsibility too much to deal with, for whatever reason.

'I am just too set in my ways,' he heard himself say out loud and immediately looked round to check if anyone had heard him, however, the place was too busy and loud for anyone to notice. He realised, nevertheless that he was right in his assertion; he *was* so used to things being a certain way, to the extent that he felt that it was unreasonable to expect him to change now. Accordingly, he felt that the odds were stacked against him doing anything other than messing up again. Despite that admission, however, he was still toying with the idea of phoning Emily, just to hear her voice. As he nervously fidgeted with the phone in his pocket, it pinged loudly and on looking at the screen he saw that it was a text from Jill, asking how and where he was. As he read the text, he experienced conflicting emotions; firstly, he realised that he was wishing that it was Emily texting him and not Jill, and secondly, he couldn't decide whether to answer it or not. What if she wanted to meet up with him?

Or even ask him to go to her hotel, being only too aware that he wasn't up for either scenario, but again, not quite sure why. '*Right*' he thought,

mentally chiding himself, '*Let's get this into some kind of perspective.*' He accordingly acknowledged to himself that they had enjoyed great sex and each other's company to the extent that he had also felt disappointed when he had initially thought that they were parting ways on their previous meeting. And now he was also feeling bad - no, make that guilty- almost in the way he did with Emily, after what happened between him and Jill. 'You really are in a mess,' he again said out loud, whilst at the same time acknowledging that he had created the situation for himself, because of his weak character and inability to make a decision. But, again, as before, he told himself that it was more than that, but he still couldn't explain to himself exactly what it was. Then, deciding to put it out of his mind, again, he instead found himself reflecting on Jill's comments about coming to his room, still certain that he had not given her his room number at any point.

It really doesn't matter anymore anyway, he realised, as, even if she really had just turned up unannounced, she would have been at the wrong room in fact not just the wrong room but a completely different hotel – albeit part of the same complex – and she couldn't know that. Unless... no, she couldn't possibly know that, how could she? he told himself, because he knew for certain that he hadn't told her that he had been moved because of the situation with the chambermaid. So, if it turned out that she did know, then there had to be some other explanation; but what? Was she stalking him and if so, why?

Then another thought occurred to him, '*Was she part of whatever Akmal and the chambermaid were mixed up in? Does she know about what happened in Benidorm?* And then he managed to catch himself, thinking, '*Listen to yourself, for God's sake, accusing the woman of all sorts. She hasn't done anything to merit that, calm the fuck down will you.*'

Whatever the truth of it was, he had decided that he wasn't going to text her back and would just simply tell her that he hadn't heard the phone pinging as his battery had died. He also needed time to further evaluate the situation and knew that the still noisy and vibrant atmosphere of the bar wasn't conducive to him being able to do that clearly and effectively, so he made the decision to head back to the hotel.

It was still relatively early, in the context of such a busy resort and the streets were busy and populated as he made his way back to the Mare Nostrum resort along Avenida Rafael Puig Luvina. As he approached Emily's hotel en route, he tried unsuccessfully to work out which room was hers to see if her light was on and thought about phoning her again. Then, he had the strangest feeling that he was being followed, resulting in him stopping and looking behind him to check.

However, he saw no one or anything that concerned him, and accordingly, told himself that he was imagining things. And then, all of a sudden, he was back at his hotel, where it was his intention to try and come up with some answers.

Chapter 41

24 January 2018
Wednesday

At the exact same moment as the Celtic game had kicked off against Partick Thistle, Farouk arrived for his shift at the 'nightclub' in Glasgow and was immediately summoned into the office by his boss, who told him in no uncertain terms that he had 'Caused a lot of problems for a lot of people. And, not just anybody either, but the fucking wrong people'- he blazed, through gritted teeth and almost foaming at the mouth, continued, 'as a result of you being a stupid fucking loud mouth and talking about stuff that nobody should know about,' He then added, angrily, that 'Unfortunately, one of your loudmouth friends then told somebody else until it eventually reached the last person it needed to reach. I'm sure you know who I mean?', he said, staring at Farouk with clear rage and disbelief in his voice. Farouk said nothing, mainly because he didn't think he would be able to speak.

He was having difficulty breathing but was trying to control it so as not to make it obvious. 'And, surprise, surprise, he isn't too fucking happy about it, let me tell you', said his boss, before adding, 'however, what he is really getting… what was it he said? … ah, yes, his 'arse in a fankle about' and is now trying to hold us to ransom for, is that, according to his 'reliable sources', two of *our* people, one of whom claims to have been directly involved, have now confirmed what had previously only been rumours, which is that this organisation were involved in setting up what happened to his brother in Benidorm. And - big fucking surprise - he wants something done about it, or else things are going to get even worse than they already are, which, surprise, surprise' he said loudly and forcibly, for effect... our 'organisation' is really fucking pissed off about–and my boss in particular, because he is the one who is going to be in the firing line.

So', he continued, looking into Farouk's eyes and pointing aggressively into his face, 'Somebody is going to have to pay, and it looks like that somebody is going to have to be your crazy fucking brother, who couldn't even manage to do what was asked of him to make up for his mistakes.'

Farouk felt his whole body begin to tremble and found himself again having difficulty breathing, which his boss noticed and possibly misconstruing it for anger, or an indication of discontent, or possibly an imminent protest, immediately blasted; 'Unless you would rather it was you? Maybe it should be, after all it was you who was shooting your mouth off? What were you doing, trying to impress your idiotic friends?'

Farouk still said nothing, mainly because he was still trying to steady his breathing, but also because he knew that what his boss was saying was accurate that because of his drunken, careless and reckless behaviour, he had again succeeded in bringing unwanted attention upon both him and the 'organisation.'

And he also knew that his boss and his bosses had no option but to literally 'bite the bullet' and agree to whatever was being asked of them as payback for the 'organisation's' involvement in the killing of Rab Lindsay in Benidorm. And, because if they didn't there would be consequences- most likely in the form of an escalation of the long-standing gang war, probably in the form of more arson attacks on their businesses, which were already nearly at breaking point because of the existing and ongoing conflict.

'Go on get out of my fucking sight,' Farouk's boss snarled angrily at him, gesturing dismissively towards the door. 'And don't speak to anybody, just try to keep your fucking mouth shut for once − or I'll shut it for you − for good. You don't have any more chances left, you or your fucking idiot of a brother.'

Farouk slinked backwards and apologetically out of the office, suitably chastened. He hoped that none of his co-workers would speak to him, as he still didn't think that he would be able to talk. But he really needed to speak to his brother-like yesterday.

Chapter 42

24 January 2018
Wednesday

Sam had just entered his hotel room, when his mobile phone rang, causing him to jump.' Fuck, it must be Jill', he thought, 'She's obviously not taking no for an answer'. But then, when he looked, he saw that it was Emily calling him. 'Hello Sam?' Emily said, although it seemed more of a question.

'Hello, Emily, yes, it's me Sam. Is everything okay?'

'Hello Sam, yes everything's fine, why do you ask?'

'No reason, I just wasn't expecting you to call, that's all,' said Sam.

'I was just thinking about you, and I thought I would call and see how you were. Where are you?' she asked.

'I'm at my hotel, I have just come in actually...

'Oh right, I thought you might still be out... sorry if I interrupted you...

'No don't be silly, I stayed to watch a band after the football but then decided to call it a night, had my fill of drink for one night and...

'Did your team win?... sorry I did it again...,' she said apologising again.

'You're fine,' said Sam, but at the same time thinking that she sounded nervous, at which point he answered her question;

'Yes, they did as a matter of fact; and the band were very

good too but it was just a bit too loud. Does that make me sound really old?' he asked.

'Not at all, but I know what you mean,' said Emily and then the line went silent for a bit before Emily spoke again, saying, 'I missed you tonight Sam and I just wanted to hear your voice, are you annoyed at me for saying that?' she asked.

'Not at all,' said Sam, adding, 'I was actually going to call you because I was missing you too.'

'I am so happy to hear you say that Sam, and I wished you had called me,' she said, sounding relieved.

'I passed your hotel earlier, and I tried to work out which room was yours to see if your light was on, but I failed miserably.'

'Oh, I wished you hadn't told me that Sam, I'm missing you even more now because if I had called you just a little earlier you could've come up and we could have had a cuddle.'

'Yes, that would have been nice,' he said, now really wishing he had called, and then philosophically stating, 'But hey, never mind we'll see each other soon.'

Then, on instinctively looking at his watch and seeing that it was almost eleven, he said, 'It's almost Thursday already, not long to go now.' I'll call you tomorrow, and we can make arrangements.

'Ok Sam, looking forward to it, goodnight, and sweet dreams.'

'That would make a pleasant change,' thought Sam, but he didn't say that. Instead, he just said, 'you too Emily, goodnight.'

Chapter 43

24 January 2018
Wednesday

Akmal was at his usual post, handing out leaflets and accosting passersby on Avenida Arquitecto Gomez Cuesta. He still hadn't heard from his absent and unresponsive brother, and now he really was becoming concerned. Also, he was now almost certain that this silence was, in some way, related to his previous discussion with Farouk, even if he wasn't sure what it was that made him feel that way-just a feeling. Also, in the absence of being able to communicate with Farouk, his mind was working overtime about what could possibly be the reasons for his younger sibling's failure to respond. He was just about to call and leave another message, having decided that if he didn't get a reply he was going to head to Glasgow, with or without his respective bosses' permission, when, as is the way with these situations, his phone rang, practically scaring the shit out of him.

Proof, as if it were he needed, that he was a nervous wreck—so much so that he answered his phone without even looking to see who it was.

'Hello,' Akmal, is that you?' said the voice on the other end of the phone. Akmal had never been as relieved to hear his brother's voice-or as angry.

'Farouk? Where have you been? Why have you not answer my calls? I have call you hundreds of times,' said Akmal, exaggerating wildly, before calming down and just feeling relieved that his brother was still breathing,

'I'm sorry, bro,' said Farouk, apologising, whilst claiming that he had dropped his phone and broken it, and it had to go in to be repaired.

'Are you okay, everything is all right, yes? asked Akmal. The line went silent for what seemed like an age, when in fact, it was only a few seconds, before Farouk finally spoke.

'I have to tell you something,' he said, hesitantly, anticipating his brother's likely disapproval and ire, before proceeding to tell him about his own drunken, careless 'blabbing' and the possible serious fall out of it all, for both. He informed his brother that he had been made aware, in no uncertain terms, by his masters, who were extremely angry, that his 'loose talk' had caused them severe grief and inconvenience and repeating his boss's dictum that 'somebody was going to have to pay.'

After listening to his brother describe his situation in more detail, and then angrily telling him what he thought of him, Akmal realised that he himself had been equally as careless in confiding in him in the first place, given his sibling's tendency towards reckless, irresponsible behaviour. He also realised that both he and his brother's actions had only served to give added credence and value to the previously unsubstantiated allegations and rumours concerning his and the organisation's involvement in the death of Rab Lindsay.

Not to mention that of Sam Meredith, the man whom he had initially found himself in conflict with, in the Costa Blanca the previous year, again because of his own impulsive, unthinking actions and with whom he had since become inextricably linked. And ironically, his recent contact with that very same person had now brought him to the attention of the last people that he wanted to be involved with. Even more concerning, and what he didn't yet know, was that he was now the subject of negotiations between the warring factions in Glasgow's underworld. What goes around comes around.

Chapter 44

25 January 2018
Thursday

Sam woke up with a start, sweating and shaking with anxiety, having just had the nightmare again, only this time Kim, his estranged wife, was in the car with him. He went to the fridge for a drink of water but then suddenly had to run to the toilet to throw up, which, strangely, also calmed him down. After dousing himself in cold water, he took his bottle of water and headed out on to the balcony, only to find, to his surprise, that it was still dark. He checked his watch, which informed him, to his surprise, that it was only just after four a.m., then he remembered reading an article, god knows where, some years before, which had claimed that most people tend to have nightmares around that time of day/night, particularly if they have been experiencing difficulties, feeling anxious and/or preoccupied with issues in their lives.

It had also stated that in the event of them waking up around that time, that they were likely to be feeling extremely vulnerable, anxious and distressed. *Well, they got that right*, thought Sam.

He then found himself, inexplicably, needing to know that Kim was okay. He knew that it made no sense, that it was just a dream, but he found himself needing to hear her voice and to be reassured that she was still alive. He also realised that he was now shaking uncontrollably, before running to the toilet and throwing up again. On cleaning himself up, gathering his thoughts and calming down, Sam realised that he couldn't call Kim at that time in the morning but resolved to call or text her at some point in the day, just to make contact. Whilst they had both promised to keep in touch after the drama and the significant emotional fall out of the events in Benidorm, inevitably and perhaps predictably, neither of them had managed to live up to their stated good intentions—the road to hell, as they say.

For his part, Sam wasn't entirely sure why he hadn't stayed in touch, as he had been sincere in his expressed sentiment at the time, being also aware that he did genuinely still care about Kim. However, for some reason he hadn't lived up to his promise, but then, neither had she, he thought, and, of course, he wondered why. And then he stopped himself from thinking about it because he knew why. And he had no desire to dwell on his limitations and failure as a husband, or even as a friend, particularly now. However, he found that he was unable to put his concerns out of his mind and even though he went back to bed, he couldn't find sleep. Consequently, he gave up and then got up around seven a.m. and went to breakfast soon after, even though he wasn't in the slightest bit hungry and ate very little.

Sam spent the rest of the day at the pool, with his kindle and his thoughts, with the latter effectively preventing him from concentrating on the former. He had sent Kim a text asking how she was whilst informing her of his whereabouts, but not the details of the recent developments or his current predicament. *She probably wouldn't believe it anyway, or maybe she would,* he speculated, given past events, as recently as November of the previous year. He could just imagine her response; *'Can you not go anywhere Sam, without getting into trouble?'* But that was the thing; she hadn't responded, and he didn't know what she would think, or more importantly, how she was. He had therefore decided that if he didn't hear from her within the next twenty-four hours, he would call her.

Sam put his kindle away and reflected upon the events of the previous year in Benidorm that were coming back to haunt him and indeed now appeared to have followed him to Tenerife; his involvement with Trish Roy, the woman who had tried to blame him for the murder of Heather Lindsay and then to use that to try to blackmail him into murdering Heather's estranged husband; Audrey McPherson, the woman who he had met at the hotel where they were both staying and with whom he had had a brief but memorable assignation. And of course, Akmal, who, he was certain, held the answer to how and why recent events had unfolded, even although he had steadfastly claimed not to know any more than what he had already admitted to that being his involvement in recruiting the chambermaid to set him up to be accused of rape. The question was still who and why? Akmal was adamant that he didn't have the answer to that. But if he didn't know who did?

And was there still a threat present here in Tenerife? If it did indeed relate to what happened in Benidorm then it needed to be connected to Rab Lindsay in some way, or someone associated with him, he reasoned. He was not aware of anyone connected to either Trish Roy or Audrey McPherson who posed a threat to him and so therefore, if that was indeed the case then Akmal, or his masters must have spoken to someone who had some kind of connection to Rab Lindsay, but who? He was absolutely determined that he would find out. In the meantime, however, he was looking forward to meeting up with Emily later that evening, and as the sun headed behind a large puffy cloud, he headed to his room to prepare himself accordingly.

Chapter 45

25 January
Thursday

They met at the Magic Bar and had a couple of drinks watching the world go by and chatting easily, before heading to the Monkey Bar for dinner and some more drinks, prior to heading down to a bar nearby to Emily's hotel (her choice) to watch a band, but left due to it being too noisy, as they couldn't hear themselves talk. So, they found somewhere quieter nearby and sat outside, as it was still quite balmy. As they were chatting, Sam was seriously considering telling her about the events of the past couple of days-but he didn't, thinking better of it, as he still didn't think the time was right because of the concerns he had about what she would think.

Maybe later, he thought.

He also hadn't told her that he had been to the singles night at the Cleopatra Princess, but he did tell her the story of the singles night in Perth, which she found very amusing and entertaining. *She had a beautiful smile and a quite marvellous, dirty laugh,* thought Sam, remembering a saying from his youth, which went something like; *If you make a woman laugh, you're half way there* (to wherever *there* is) and it certainly seemed to be having a positive effect on the evening and Emily's mood and demeanour, as she was clearly becoming more relaxed and affectionate as the night wore on.

'It's all changed now, what with singles clubs, and internet dating,' continued Emily, in response to Sam's tale. 'And the young ones have things like, em... what's it called...Tinder? ... I think that's what it's called. It seems to be the way to go nowadays. And I suppose it is a good thing for some people, but I couldn't be doing with it myself, it's not my cup of tea at all, too old in the tooth for that. And you don't know who you're meeting, it could be anybody.'

There's that trust thing again thought Sam, and then thought that she might have a point.

However, he decided to lighten the mood again, 'Do you remember when they used to have things called Personal Ads?' As he looked at him askance, he felt the need to explain; 'People used to put them in newspapers as a way of attracting partners and some of them were very funny and creative. I was always going to make one up for myself, but I never got round to it. Just for a laugh, I mean,' he added quickly.

'Oh, of course,' said Emily, and then smiling at Sam and saying, 'Why don't you try and make one up now?'

'What? now now?, said Sam, wishing that he had kept his big mouth shut, and then asking; 'You mean right away, just like that?'

'Now you sound like Tommy Cooper,' she said, which made Sam laugh.

And then, of course, he did the voice-very badly-and then apologised profusely.

'Well?'

'What?'

'I'm waiting,' said Emily, the thing, the...

'Personal Ad,' said Sam, laughing, and then adding, 'you're serious?

165

'Well, you started it,' said Emily, laughing.

'Ok, let's think,' he said, screwing his eyes and chewing his bottom lip in mock concentration.

'Well, you can think about it, I'm off to powder my nose, I expect a result when I return,' said Emily, rising from the table and asking the waiter the location of the 'ladies,' whilst also ordering another drink.

'No pressure,' said Sam. As he watched her go, he thought that she looked quite lovely, dressed simply in a rust-coloured cotton dress, which complimented her glorious red hair, which surprisingly gave him pause for thought. And, as he sat searching for further inspiration and creativity, his concentration was distracted by a flicker of light, which he caught out of the corner of his eye, and looking round he saw it was the flame of a match which a man at a nearby table had used to light a cigarette. However, after catching a whiff of a very distinctive odour, he realised that it was in fact a cigar, at which point the waiter appeared with the drinks order.

"Gracias Senor," said Sam, as he paid the waiter and looked up to see Emily appear behind him. 'Timing,' she said, raising her glass.

"The secret of comedy," said Sam.

"Speaking of which, have you found inspiration?" she asked, looking at Sam expectantly.

'Yes, you have inspired me Emily, well you and that man at the table over there,' said Sam, gesturing with his head, before realising that there was no longer anyone there.

'What man?' said Emily, looking confused.

'Never mind,' said Sam.

'Never mind what?' said Emily, confused,' I thought you were going to amaze and amuse me with your creative powers?'.

'I am, well I'm going to give it a try at least. Okay here it is, for what it's worth,' he said, clearing his throat; '*AMOROUS ARSONIST; HAS A BURNING DESIRE TO FORM A LOVE MATCH WITH A NEW FLAME- STRIKING REDHEADS ONLY'*.

Sam looked at Emily, who, was very quiet for what seemed like an age, before she suddenly burst out laughing incredulously and spontaneously applauding, saying; 'That's brilliant'.

'I thang you,' said Sam spreading his arms and bowing extravagantly, 'Even if it was a bit of a delayed reaction, but better late than never.'

'I was so taken aback by your genius,' said Emily, before asking, 'Did you really just make that up?'

'What? you dare to impugn my integrity and talent, said Sam melodramatically, in a mock French accent, which made Emily laugh out loud. 'To be honest, I'm as surprised as you, but yes, I really did. As I said, you inspire me, Emily.'

'And you make me laugh Sam,' said Emily, raising her glass and saying cheers, before leaning over and kissing him softly on the mouth.

Meanwhile, the tall, swarthy, cigar smoking man who had both inspired and intrigued Sam in equal measure was sitting on his balcony reflecting that the woman being there, whoever she was, had prevented him from carrying out his mission, but that nevertheless it had been a useful reconnaissance exercise.

And there was still plenty of time to take care of business before he headed home to take care of his next contract, which he was very much looking forward to.

Chapter 46

25 January 2018
Thursday

They went to Emily's hotel, but this time there was no angst, hesitation, or soul searching. Everything had already been said that needed to be, as openly and as honestly as each of their respective situations allowed. On entering her hotel room, they both lost their clothes simultaneously in an almost perfectly choreographed movement of mutual sexual excitement and abandon, demonstrating their shared intent and passion for each other. As they stood naked together, they touched and then kissed, tasting each other in, a long and sensuous embrace. 'Hold me, Sam,' said Emily, and he did, taking her in his arms, lovingly and gently, like she was a piece of fine crystal or porcelain, conscious of her emotional vulnerability and fragility.

Emily, perhaps sensing his hesitancy and uncertainty, looked at him, saying, 'It's all right Sam, I won't break or snap, you don't need to be gentle with me. I want you so much, and I have hoped that this would happen with somebody for some time now. I want your desire, and I want to feel your passion. I want to know that you want me; I just want you to make me feel like a real woman again.'

Sam responded by lifting her and placing her on the bed. As he looked at her, her hair spread out over the pillow, he thought that she looked beautiful, and he kissed her again, his body responding to her smell, her taste and the feel of her beneath him. On feeling the extent of his arousal against her body, Emily found his manhood with her hand and then her mouth, causing him to moan with pleasure. Sam, feeling his arousal mounting and not wanting to be selfish and think solely of his own satisfaction, pulled her up towards him, kissing her again before gently easing her on top of him, and then it was her turn to moan as she felt him entering her.

Their bodies moved slowly and rhythmically together, with Sam enjoying watching Emily atop him, grabbing her hips and kissing her breasts as she gradually gathered and increased both her momentum and excitement, before finally surrendering to a blissful climax with a loud moan and collapsing on to Sam, clearly fulfilled.

Sam just lay there smelling Emily's hair, which was spread over his face, and not even bothering to disturb or remove it and enjoying feeling her breathing and weight on him, such as it was, until she moved, seemingly having recovered and easing herself tenderly from his embrace. She looked at him and said, 'Thank you, Sam, that was absolutely beautiful, but you didn't finish.'

'Not a problem,' he replied, 'And it was beautiful for me too.'

Emily kissed him softly and snuggled into him, moving her hand down to his groin area, producing an immediate response from Sam, who felt a lovely sensation run through his whole body.

'I think we have unfinished business by the looks of it. It's your turn now to have your fun,' said Emily, pulling him on top of her, saying, 'I want to give you the pleasure that you deserve Sam,' and guiding him inside her and kissing him passionately. Sam felt himself grow inside her as their bodies merged in a movement of almost balletic grace, each consuming the other in their shared, mutual excitement, passion and unrestrained lust. He felt Emily respond to his increasingly urgent movement and returned his animal thrusts, wrapping her legs round him, which brought him to the point of no return, announcing his arrival with an almost bestial grunt and the universally recognised expletive associated with sexual fulfilment.

After they had both recovered from their respective exertions Sam and Emily both just lay breathing in each other and enjoying their new intimacy and the raw satisfaction of it, speaking no words but smiling at and touching each other endlessly.

Whilst Sam regarded their encounter as a less frenetic and adventurous affair than his experience with Jill, he had also found it to be much more fulfilling and potentially nascent, but he wasn't altogether sure why. But his last thought before sleep took him was that he did know that he wanted more.

Chapter 47

He has connections and history with senior crime figures involved in protection rackets, prostitution, extortion, blackmail, drugs, and murder, to mention just a few. Max Holland is a serving undercover policeman in the Serious Crime Squad; he has been involved with and infiltrated criminal organisations dealing in people and sex trafficking. He has also assumed the role of a contract killer and taken part in armed robberies and terrorist activities to fight organised crime. Unfortunately, such a dangerous occupation leaves him at serious risk of exposure to people who are likely to want revenge for being duped and infiltrated by him, invariably resulting in them being convicted and often also imprisoned. The crime bosses are also likely to be under threat from or want to save face with other people in the criminal fraternity whom they may also have inadvertently compromised and rendered vulnerable to prosecution, as a result of their misguided trust in Max; enemies or competitors who are looking to or might have already orchestrated their own form of payback, possibly involving the person's family.

Currently, there is more than one contract out on him, and he is aware that a particular crime boss that he had crossed is actively encouraging completion of said transaction as a matter of some urgency. He is also aware of who has been charged with the responsibility of carrying out the contract, and his plan is to deal with him before he can complete the transaction, preferably whilst he is distracted with other business, which he knows he will be soon.

Max has also been made aware, via well-established covert channels of communication that his prospective executioner has also taken on another contract which, Max, as an agent of the law, is also obliged to prevent, if possible, and which will require him to travel to Tenerife to do so. And that would suit Max just fine, as once he has taken care of business, he will be able to enjoy some well-earned R and R in the sun with his chosen companion because, against all odds and his better judgement, he has met and formed a relationship with someone with whom he wants to spend the rest of his life with.

The only problem is that he hasn't told her yet. And he also needs to make sure that she will be safe. He cannot allow anything to happen to her. Not after what had happened to his father and family when he was a child.

Chapter 48

25 January 2018
Thursday

Max Holland was glad that the streets in Las Americas were as busy as they were, as it made it easier for him to blend in and avoid being noticed or discovered by his would-be executioner without having to resort to an actual disguise, because he would obviously recognise him in the event of him revealing himself. He had found it extremely difficult maintaining his vigil of both his quarry and their intended victim, resulting in him having to enlist support in accomplishing this. And the contribution of his accomplice had proved to be invaluable in monitoring the whereabouts of the assassin's other quarry, which by association, also afforded invaluable intelligence concerning the likely location of the assassin himself. Max's hope and intention was that this knowledge could be employed to positive effect, by, hopefully, preventing the successful completion of both the outstanding contracts by the assassin and thereby also contributing significantly towards him extending his own lifespan.

***

She had been contacted by people who she had hoped she would never see or hear from again, which had caused her considerable anxiety, stress, and trepidation, wondering what they wanted from her and what the personal cost would be. She had long dreaded the thought of this moment arriving, having hoped that she would be allowed to live the rest of her life, such as it was, in peace and free from such an eventuality. Whilst, after considerable, and emotional dialogue - she was assured that she was not under any threat or risk of harm, she took faint comfort and reassurance from this, being only too aware of the kind of people that she was dealing with and what they were capable of. However, she agreed to listen to what was being proposed and, accordingly, required of her. Not that she had had much choice in the matter.

As it was explained to her, it was straightforward; all she had to do initially was to maintain surveillance prior to initiating contact and then, using her still impressive attributes and feminine wiles, lure and then charm the unsuspecting victim into a compromising and vulnerable situation before taking the appropriate action.

And, after due consideration, she decided that she could do whatever it took, and that compared to things that she had done in the past, it was relatively easy money. It also meant that she would be able to enjoy an all-expenses paid break in a four-star hotel in Las Americas, as opposed to her normal modest, one-bedroom accommodation in nearby Costa Adeje. She was provided with the necessary information by her contacts and afforded every co-operation to ensure the maximum opportunity to secure interest and then hopefully, compliance.

She had felt confident and assured about what she needed to do to achieve the desired outcome and had carried out her duties exactly as directed.

Unfortunately, things had not exactly gone as planned due to circumstances beyond her control, resulting in the need to resort to a contingency, which had then also ended in failure. Whilst she had eventually managed to seduce and manoeuvre her prey into position, she had then received a call on her mobile phone, which informed her of the unfortunate situation with the chambermaid and her subsequent arrest. Accordingly, she was advised that given the resultant and very inconvenient police involvement, it was considered that an allegation of rape may not be a wise move and would probably only arouse further suspicion and possibly even investigation, which was the last thing that was needed. She also then realised that this created a whole different situation, as there was no expectation that she become involved in any form of entrapment, or indeed for her to engage in any form of sexual contact with the 'mark', unless she wanted to. In which case it would be her choice, which was a whole different ball game.

And after very little deliberation, she had come to a decision, which was that given that she had teased him relentlessly to prove his masculinity and attempted to seduce him to the point where he probably expected that something would happen between them, she could hardly back out, could she? And if truth be told, she didn't really want to.

Chapter 49

26 January 2018
Friday

Sam and Emily woke to a room awash with sunlight, as they had neglected to close over the blackout curtains. Sam was reassured that Emily seemed happy to be waking up with him by her warm embrace, and he made a conscious effort to make sure that she knew he felt the same. He held her close and showered her body with soft, sensitive kisses, re-igniting both their passions again and leading to even deeper, harder kissing. Emily then started making her way down Sam's body caressing, teasing, and kissing him until he felt he that he was about to explode, which he eventually did, emitting a sound that he didn't believe could have come from him. As Emily looked up at him, he stroked her hair gently, unable to speak, simply emitting more breathless noises that confirmed his state of ecstasy, before again drifting off into blissful oblivion.

When he woke, Emily was fully dressed and had made coffee for them both, which he rose and drank with her on the balcony after he had washed and freshened up. They had been greeted by another beautiful, hot and sunny day, with not a cloud in the sky.

'What time is it,' asked Sam, realising that he had left his watch in Emily's bathroom.

'It's… nine thirty, she said after going into the room and

checking her watch, which was still sitting on the bedside table where she had put it the night before. 'I'm probably too late for breakfast, I think,' she said, 'I can't remember if it's nine thirty or ten, and anyway, I wouldn't go and leave you on your own. And to be honest, I'm not that hungry anyway. And if you are, I'm sorry, but unfortunately, I don't even have any bread to make toast. I do have some more coffee, but no tea. I did have but I've run out as I only brought a few teabags from home.'

'Another coffee will be fine,' said Sam, then adding, 'Maybe we could go somewhere nice for lunch?'

Emily seemed to hesitate, before saying, 'I had planned to go looking for some presents for my family and friends. I mean you're welcome to join me, but I can't imagine you would want to be dragged around a load of shops,' handing him the coffee that she had made for him.

'No... I mean, yes, you're right, I hate shopping, and to be honest, I was hoping to go and watch the Manchester United FA Cup game after we had lunch. Not very romantic, I know, and I am happy to miss it as...'

'No, no that's fine,' said Emily, I don't mind playing second fiddle to football again, she said, before smiling and saying, 'I'm kidding, maybe we could meet up tomorrow, unless there's football on then too...

'Yes, unfortunately there is,' he said with a grimace. 'My team, Celtic, are playing again, but it's in the afternoon, so we could meet up tomorrow night if you like as I'm not planning on having a lot to drink and I'll have plenty of time to get organised.

'Yes, I'd like that, Sam,' said Emily, smiling.

'Great,' said Sam, 'do you have any preference? Where we eat, I mean?'

'No, no, wherever you decide is fine with me, where do you

want to meet? asked Emily.

'Why don't we meet in the bar at my hotel at seven? Is that okay, or earlier if you like?'

'No, that's fine Sam, I'll look forward to it,' she said, kissing him and tasting the coffee that she had just made for him, which he drank the remainder of from his mug before heading off.

On returning to his hotel room, Sam showered and then, feeling at a bit of a loose end, went for a walk along the beach. It was a glorious day, so he decided to head back to the hotel, buying some more provisions on the way to have as snacks and lunches. On arriving back at the hotel, he headed to the pool where he remained with his kindle until lunch time, which consisted of a beer and a burger at the pool bar, which thankfully on that occasion stayed on the plate as he couldn't be bothered moving. He enjoyed a few more hours of beautiful sunshine at the poolside, not planning to leave until early evening, weather permitting. He had downloaded the latest novels by two of his favourite Scottish authors, Ian Rankin and Val McDermid on to his kindle and was almost a third of the way through the former, finding the plot intriguing and, as usual, speculating about the likely outcome.

Sam's background was marketing rather than journalism, but he believed that he had it in him to write a novel, or rather he wanted to believe it; *they say that everybody has a book in them,* he told himself, almost as a justification for his aspirations. He had always been creative and blessed with a vivid imagination; he remembered with equal amounts of bemusement and annoyance that when he was growing up, people, e.g. family, teachers, would say things like; 'He has a fertile imagination' or 'he reads a lot' like it was a bad thing. From a young boy to a teenager, he had read everything: books, magazines newspapers, and particularly American comics, which would buy from a stall in the Barrowlands, more commonly referred to as the 'Barras', a sprawling indoor and outdoor market in the east end of Glasgow, where his father had a stall at weekends. He recalled the place and time with considerable affection, in particular a tearoom which sold the most delicious Welsh Rarebit, which he had never tasted the like of since.

Sam enjoyed cooking, but despite his best efforts, he had never even remotely come close to recreating the taste of the dish, as he remembered it.

After reading his comics Sam would then return and exchange them for others, which he would also swap with friends. He no longer had them of course, having got rid of the last of them many years ago, in his mid-teens, realising with some regret that had he kept them they would be worth a small fortune.

He recalled his avid reading of stories about both Marvel and DC superheroes. However, in addition to the main superhero content of the comics, they also contained factual, often historic or scientific articles and stories, which he would read, memorise and then stand up and orate in front of his classmates at the prompting of his then primary teacher, whom he loved and who told him that she believed that he had a "photographic memory." It had also helped to improve his confidence and ability to speak in front of others.

She also encouraged his reading of comics, telling him that it didn't matter what you read so long as you read something. His love of all things American had also grown exponentially, with his avid reading of the Marvel and DC comics initiating him, totally willingly, into the wonderfully mesmerizing lives lived by

179

his 'Yankee' counterparts, if the stories were to be believed. It was, he thought, a much more exciting place. Even the place names and locations were significantly more dynamic and had a tremendously exciting and lyrical nature about them names like Tuscaloosa, Nebraska, Philadelphia, Tulsa, Chicago and Chattanooga; the list was endless; places that you could write songs about, and they did, constantly. Sam laughed out loud as he began to mentally imagine how the songs would sound if they were substituted with the names of Scottish towns somehow 'Twenty-four hours from Forfar.' 'A Rainy Night in Airdrie' didn't have the same glamour to them. Whereas, on the other hand, in his considered opinion. "Is that the Auchtermuchty Choo Choo?" most definitely had a bit of a ring to it.

It had also brought back memories of the times when, as a young boy, he would visit an elderly aunt whose garden looked on to a railway line where steam trains used to regularly pass by, recalling how he used to sit on her garden wall and wave to the drivers as they passed. There were also coal deposits located over the wall, which he recalled with disbelief and amusement, he had regularly plundered, mainly because people used to regularly steal coal from her coal bunker, which was outside and locked with a padlock. However, it was easily disabled and after replacing it several times they eventually decided that there was no point. And latterly, there had also been another unfortunate situation to contend with; she lived in an upstairs flat and the coal merchant, or 'coalman' who visited weekly would open the door at the foot of the stairs, which had been left open for that express purpose, and shout "coal." Unfortunately, she would never hear him due to being extremely deaf, despite having a hearing aid fitted, which she wouldn't ever buy batteries for and which, ironically, emitted the loudest, most excruciating, high pitched noise.

He also recalled that it was there that he learned how to light a coal fire on a cold winter morning using a fireguard and a newspaper, although you had to be vigilant to avoid the whole thing going up in flames. As a boy, he had regarded the house as a magical place, smiling as he remembered she also had a budgie that used to sit on his head as he walked about the place. She also made the best soup that he had ever tasted, ranking alongside the revered Welsh Rarebit for taste and quality.

She was also a 'hawker' who went from door to door selling used clothes, most of which were obtained at 'jumble sales' which were like a 'bring and buy' sale or 'rummage', sale; an event at which second hand goods are sold, usually organised by an institution such as a local Boys' Brigade Company or Scout group, or church, as a fundraising or charitable effort. He supposed that the American equivalent would be a 'garage; or 'yard' sale.

On reflection, they were, he supposed, the forerunners of today's charity shops, smiling as he recollected an image of her in action at these events; She was an absolute whirlwind as she plundered her booty to watch her 'rummaging' through the goods was a sight to behold and she was also not averse to pilfering stuff from other people's bundles.

As well as the stories in American comics that he used all his pocket money on, there was also the new American films and television programmes, which were full of young people swimming in the creek, riding freight trains and exploring all sorts of dangerous locations, invariably resulting in all sorts of exciting discoveries.

He then suddenly found himself remembering idyllic days from his own childhood that he had almost certainly

181

undervalued–days when he and his pals would disappear for hours on end, doing things that would give parents nowadays nightmares, e.g. jumping from roof to roof of half-demolished 'pre – fab' houses, climbing industrial chimneys, digging 'dens' in old coal 'bings' and building rafts to sail on the local reservoir, only going home when they felt hungry–which, in fairness, was round about normal tea time.

It wasn't as if they were expected to survive Bear Grylls style on nature's meagre provisions. He also recalled a very rare and idyllic 'berry picking' holiday in Blairgowrie, when he saw Peregrine Falcons close up, caught and ate rabbits, found Sand Martens nests in a quarry, and watched kittens being born under a caravan. It was a never to be forgotten and totally magical experience, which, the more he thought about it was much preferable to snakes, spiders, coyotes, earthquakes, and twisters.

Sam had no real clear, concrete idea, what he would write about, as he had never really done anything about it in terms of planning or organizing himself and his thoughts and ideas in that regard. However, it had suddenly occurred to him that he had had enough incident, and excitement in his life in both previous and the current year to fill several volumes, and that if he couldn't make anything of that, then he would never be a writer. He just wasn't sure that he could do it without incriminating himself, not realising that somebody had already beaten him to it.

Chapter 50

26 January 2018
Friday

Sam, after having spent the majority of the day lying at the pool, had showered, changed, and grabbed something to eat at the Café Epoca and was now sitting outside in the still glorious, warm sunshine at Leonardo's bar, watching Alexis Sanchez play a hand in two goals as his Manchester United debut ended in a comfortable 4-0 FA Cup fourth-round victory at League Two strugglers Yeovil Town.

As he sat in the sun, he reflected that, notwithstanding Kim's often expressed concerns about his 'obsession' with football, he regarded it as one of the few things that made going on holiday on your own, as a single man, tolerable, particularly in a resort like Las Americas and especially during the day if the weather was bad, when sightseeing and sunbathing were not really a realistic option.

So, unless you wanted to just sit in the bar in the hotel or elsewhere and get shit faced which no longer appealed to him, there really wasn't anything else to do other than read a book or watch television in your room. Then he smiled as he recalled his experience with Beverley and realised that there was something else to do after all, which he had also demonstrated all too recently in his liaison with Jill.

Unfortunately, that only served to remind him, as he sipped at his third beer of the day, that he had not contacted her, which led to him feeling, for whatever reason, that he really should, whilst also being surprised that she had not contacted him. Sam finished his beer and headed back to his hotel; he had just entered his room when his mobile phone rang, causing him to jump again, confirming his persisting fragile and nervous state of mind. *I hope it's not Emily, or more likely Jill.* he thought, realising that he was not mentally prepared to deal with either eventuality at that moment in time. Accordingly, he had made his mind up to ignore it. However, when he looked, he saw that it was Kim calling him. He nearly dropped the phone in his anxiety to answer it. 'Hello' said Sam, 'Kim, are you there?' he asked, concerned that she had maybe hung up.

'Sam, is that you? Can you hear me?' said Kim, sounding quite agitated.

'Kim, hello, yes, it's me, Sam, are you okay?' he asked, realising that he sounded quite dramatic and trying to calm down.

'Yes, I'm fine Sam, why are you asking that? Why wouldn't I be? Is something wrong? Are you okay? And where are you? Are you still in Spain?

'Yes, yes, I'm in Tenerife, Las Americas, I'm on holiday, I...

'I'm sorry, I never noticed your message until today and when I got it, I wondered why you were calling me. It sounded as if you were worried about something....

Sam started to tell her about what had happened but then hesitated and instead said, 'I'm sorry that I never kept in touch Kim, I meant to but it just...'

'You contacted me to say sorry for not contacting me?'

'No, that's not what I... well... yes, in a way because I said that I would and...

'We both did Sam, but sometimes people don't for lots of different reasons... but it's okay, I'm not angry with you or anything. Is that the only reason you called?

Sam realised just how ridiculous what he was about to say would sound, but he didn't know what else to say. So he just said it;

'I... I had a dream... about you, about us, we were in a ...

'You called me because you had a dream about me? And what do you mean by us... you're not making any sense Sam.'

So told her about the dream and how it had affected him and why he needed to speak to her, to which she replied, 'But it was only a dream Sam, you must've known that?'

And then he told her that it wasn't only a dream; that it had happened on his way back from that traumatic 'holiday' in Benidorm the previous year, minus the more harrowing and fatal conclusion obviously. He also told her that the dream was a recurring event, but that had been the first time that she had been in it. And, he hoped, the last.

'Oh my God Sam, no wonder it affected you the way it did. Why didn't you tell me about it at the time Sam? Maybe it would have helped to talk about it? Have you spoken to anyone else about it?'

Sam told her that he had only told her and that this was the first time that he had spoken about it out loud. He informed her that he hadn't told her about it before because of all the issues she was preoccupied with because of the fallout from what had happened in Benidorm and how that had affected her.

As soon as he said that he also realised that they had not spoken about her situation since then either and he was about to ask her how she was coping in that regard when she said, 'You really should talk to someone Sam, and I don't mean me, maybe somebody professional, particularly if you're still having nightmares after all this time.' He didn't tell her that that wasn't the only thing that he was having nightmares about, instead just saying; 'Maybe I will,' whilst knowing that he had absolutely no intention of doing so. There was no way that he was going to sit down and start opening up to a total stranger about his personal trauma because he knew that it would lead into discussion about other aspects of his life and in particular the emotions and feelings connected to his actions in Benidorm, which still regularly caused him considerable anxiety and permeated his everyday thoughts. And he certainly wasn't ready to come clean about that to anyone; not now and maybe not ever; so, he very deftly took the focus away from himself by asking her;

'So how are you coping? Have you spoken to anyone about your own issues?' referring to the personal and intimate revelation that she had divulged and confided in him about, which she had never told anyone else about.

As she didn't respond Sam filled the loud silence by saying; 'You know, what we talked about regarding...

'I know what we talked about Sam,' she said tersely and dismissively and no I won't be discussing that with anyone.

And remember I told you that you can't speak to anyone about it either. Sam was tempted to point out to her that whilst she was happy to recommend that he should consider seeking some form of counselling, she had roundly dismissed the same suggestion for herself totally out of hand.

However, he decided that discretion was perhaps the better part of valour and instead responded with, 'Don't worry, 'I have no intention of speaking to anyone about it, you can trust me in that regard, and you should know that, Kim.'

'I know Sam, I'm sorry, I didn't mean to offend you, it's just that I don't want…'

'I know Kim, it's okay, you don't need to explain yourself, I know how you feel and it's fine.'

'Thanks Sam,' said Kim and then, after a short silence, added 'and I'm glad you called and that we talked. And if you ever need to talk about anything you can call me anytime, that's what friends are for Sam.

'I'd like that,' said Sam, 'and I'm glad we talked too.' Maybe it would be good to stay in touch after all. Maybe we should try a wee bit harder to make time.' But he still couldn't bring himself to tell her about the recent troubling events and developments, simply giving his farewells and good wishes. However, the conversation had had a calming, reassuring effect on him and he slept soundly with no more troubling dreams, which was very welcome.

Chapter 51

27 January 2018
Saturday

Sam had awakened early to another glorious day and had gone to breakfast at the hotel, after which he lay at the pool for a few hours before deciding to have lunch at the pool bar before showering, changing, and heading out, as planned. He was now sat in front of a huge plasma screen watching Celtic play Hibernian in sub-zero temperatures in Glasgow, whilst he himself was fortunate enough to be basking in glorious, warm sunshine, outside at Leonardo's bar in Las Americas. He was also blissfully unaware of the tall, swarthy man observing him from The Traveller's Rest, the bar immediately adjacent to Leonardo's, where Sam had once assisted the staff to repair the shutter to their storeroom after their resident 'handyman' had failed miserably in his own clumsy and ill-judged, efforts and, in the process, almost taking Sam's head off with a lethal weapon in the shape of long pole with a hook on the end of it.

The manageress, who was English, had apologised profusely ('So sorry, my love') and remonstrated loudly with her errant employee, who had slinked of cowed and duly admonished.

She then subsequently expressed her gratitude for Sam's successful intervention by allowing him to drink free all day. Sam had expressed his gratitude by kindly accepting her generous hospitality.

As the tall swarthy man maintained his vigil of Sam sitting, drinking and watching football, from his carefully chosen position in The Traveller's Rest, he felt safe in the knowledge that his quarry had absolutely no idea of his presence or his purpose, which on this day was solely to observe and assess his prey. However, as he sat smugly congratulating himself on his covert vigil, he was totally unaware that he himself was the object of someone else's surveillance—someone who was observing him equally as forensically and professionally, from just a short distance away.

Sam's concentration on the game was momentarily distracted by something, but he couldn't work out what it was. Until he suddenly realised exactly what it was, it was a smell, a very distinctive smell, the unmistakeable smell of cigar smoke; the same smell he remembered from the bar he had visited with Emily on Thursday. He looked around and searched his immediate surroundings until he saw the person who was smoking it; there was a man sitting on his own at the bar opposite. He thought that it looked like it was the same man, but he couldn't be sure.

He was certainly tall, swarthy and rangy, like the other man had been, but he was wearing sunglasses and had a beard, which he couldn't recall the other man as having. Or maybe he had; he had only seen him fleetingly after all and it was at night, and he had also had a few drinks, so his recollection was probably not that clear. *Anyway, what does it matter?* he thought, and then; *I better stop bloody staring at him, before he takes exception and decides to say or do something about it, because he doesn't look like the kind of guy that you want to get on the wrong side of.* And was he just imagining it or was the guy staring at him? It was hard to tell, because he was wearing sunglasses. Sam looked away and redirected his attention towards the football match but found himself instinctively looking back to see if he was still looking in his direction. However, when he did, the man had gone, disappearing in much the same way as he had done on the previous occasion, which Sam had a strange feeling about given recent events. However, he was jolted from his thoughts by a loud roar followed by spontaneous applause from the other customers watching the football as Celtic scored, drawing his attention back to proceedings on the huge plasma screen.

As Sam made his way back from Leonardo's, having watched his team secure a 1-0 victory, he began to think about the man with the cigar again, to the extent that he nearly walked in front of a car, prevented only by a loud blast from its horn by the irate driver. Then he nearly bumped into a couple and their two kids, as he stumbled onto the pavement, before issuing humble apologies. As he regained his composure, he realised, that he was approaching Emily's hotel.

And then, on focusing his gaze in that direction, realised that he was actually looking at Emily standing outside. And she was talking to Akmal.

Chapter 52

27 November 2018
Saturday

The man sat on his balcony and reflected on the day's events; why had his intended victim stared at him so intently? Was it possible that he knew who he was or was he just being paranoid and imagining things? He wasn't normally given to such concerns and thoughts of uncertainty, but he had not been expecting the difficulties that he had encountered in what he had previously regarded as a straightforward, routine piece of business. Also, whilst he would normally still have been stalking his prey on the still well-populated streets of Las Americas, there had been another development which had caused him to reconsider this situation; after leaving his surveillance position in the Traveller's Rest, following the staring contest with the 'mark', he was almost certain that he had seen his next target walking along Avenida Rafael Puig but had then lost sight of him.

Initially, he had thought that he was imagining things, but subsequent inquiries via certain sources had confirmed that his next intended victim was indeed in Tenerife and not back in Britain, as first thought, which changed things. Unfortunately, that was all the information he was able to access, and therefore he could only speculate as to the reasons for his unexpected presence in the resort; was he here on 'business' and did it involve him? And if so then he needed to be concerned, as it probably meant that he was here with a view to terminating him before he was able carry out the contract. Or was he simply here on holiday and it was just a coincidence? The problem was that he didn't believe in coincidences. Also, as he had made his way along the Avenida Rafael Puig the previous evening, he had had a definite sense that he was being followed, without having seen any real evidence to support this. However, this latest information made him think that maybe he was right and that he needed to be more careful and alert to the possibility of a threat.

And if that was indeed the case, then he decided that he wasn't going to sit around and wait for something to happen and that a more direct course of action was called for. He still had two contracts to carry out. So, he made a phone call.

***

She needed to feel that men desired and wanted her, for whatever reason; she knew it was a flaw in her character, but there was nothing she could do about it, it was just a fact of life; it was who she was. She had long since accepted that she needed that kind of validation, even although she had no intention of granting the poor fawning and adoring unfortunates' fulfilment of their desires. She reflected that over the years she had never had any trouble attracting men—good men, whom, she now acknowledged, she had mostly rejected, for reasons that she never really understood. However, she did know that she had needed to have them believe that she was too good for them, which she enjoyed, whilst not ever believing or convincing herself of that same fact, mainly because of the path that her life had taken.

She had long since stopped being concerned with her looks or appearance and found that she was incredibly bored with men, who invariably and predictably, told her that she was "beautiful." Accordingly, and perhaps unsurprisingly, she had always found herself attracted to the less honourable and more morally reproachable breed of men, who invariably treated her with disdain and little respect; however, every now and then she would meet someone who she made an exception to the rule. She enjoyed being with Sam, someone that she liked and was attracted to; she hadn't really expected to or even wanted to 'like' him, but she eventually had to admit to herself that she liked being in his company - it made her feel normal and respectable again. She also liked tall, blonde men (well fair, with some grey, which she also found quite attractive). Also, his rejection of her initial advances, even if they had been completely staged and bogus at that point, had only made her want him even more. And even more surprising, she had found herself wondering if there could be a possibility of her and Sam getting together after the holiday, particularly following her initial instructions being changed, and she had hoped, cancelled altogether. But who was she kidding? She knew that the assassin wasn't going to go away unless the contract was cancelled, which wasn't likely. And even if it was, she knew it wouldn't work or last. *It never does'*, she thought, '*and, if he ever found out about my past... or indeed present*, she realised. *Well, that would definitely put paid to any prospect of any kind of relationship. There I go again*, she thought, *Getting carried away on a flight of fancy – no, fantasy - because that's what it is.*

The more that she thought about it the more that she believed that there was no chance of that happening. Her past would continue to determine her future and ensure that there was no chance of it being anything like she had imagined all those years ago before she took that fateful decision to become involved in drug trafficking.

And, consequently, she had no husband and children or even family to speak of anymore, as she had either lost touch or they had disowned her. So, she resolved that she was just going to enjoy being with Sam as much as she could, which would be for as long as he wanted to be with her, and if that meant until the rest of the holiday then so be it- she deserved nothing more, particularly given what she had done. Then she received a phone call that confirmed that that she would never be free of her past.

Chapter 53

27 January 2018
Saturday

Sam had been completely taken aback at seeing Akmal and Emily together happily chatting away, clearly oblivious to his presence. However, despite his surprise and shock, after due consideration, he decided that rather than confront them, he would keep his powder dry and return another time to have words with Akmal. His main concern now was: what on earth did he have to do with Emily? Was she involved with him in some way and were they both involved in what had happened to him earlier? Whilst at first this seemed totally inconceivable to Sam, the more he thought about it, the more that the parallels with the situation he had encountered with Trish in Benidorm became apparent; *the similarities were inescapable*, thought Sam, if also completely and utterly irrational.

Sam had positioned himself in a doorway hidden from sight until Akmal had left, heading in the direction of his normal post on Avenida Arquitecto Gomez Cuesta, whilst Emily was now heading away from the hotel along Avenida Rafael Puig Lluvina before turning down Calle Mexico towards the shore. Sam, without planning or consciously deciding to do so, then realised that he had started to follow her, almost on automatic pilot, but at a safe distance where she would not notice him. After walking a short distance Emily suddenly stopped at a small café before sitting down at a table and then placing an order with the waiter. Sam watched as the waiter came back and placed a coffee in front of her. He then waited and watched until she was joined by another man, who also gestured to the waiter that he wanted the same, before reaching over and kissing Emily on the cheek, which she reciprocated. Sam was completely taken aback and felt almost lightheaded with a sick, shaky feeling in his stomach. He had not expected this and nor had he expected to feel like that.

Sam watched Emily and her companion for another fifteen minutes, but when they then ordered some drinks, he decided to end his vigil and head back to his hotel. It was now five fifteen and he had arranged to meet Emily at the bar in the Mark Anthony for drinks around seven p.m., prior to heading out to have dinner somewhere nearby. She was, not surprisingly, quite confused when he had called her to make her aware of the change in arrangements, saying, 'I thought that you told me that you were staying at the Mediterranean Palace? Have you moved hotel or were you deliberately giving me false information in case I decided to pay you a visit?' However, Sam reassured her that that was not the case whilst informing her that he would tell her all about it when they met. *And you can tell me all about your cosy chats with Akmal and you're other "coffee mate." I can hardly wait to hear what she has to say about both,* thought Sam, but then asked himself *Do I really want to know?*
He had also not expected his phone to ring at that moment in time, but it did, causing him to nearly jump out his skin again, before pressing' answer 'without first checking who it was.

'Hello, Sam?' said the voice, at which point he realised that it was Jill.

'Hello Jill, how are you?' he asked, hoping that there was no trace of the tension that he was feeling in his voice.'

'I'm well,' she replied, 'Just missing the love of a good man. How are you?'

'I'm okay, sorry I haven't been in touch, but I ran into some friends who are also here on holiday that I hadn't seen in ages,' he lied, so effortlessly it shocked him. 'And' he added, 'we had a lot of catching up to do, particularly as I am going home the day after tomorrow.'

'That's nice for you, Sam, so are you spoken for tonight or do you have any time for little ol' me?' she said, for some reason, in a mock southern belle accent, for some reason, then adding; 'My bed feels empty without you in it.'

'To be honest I was planning on having a night off as I've been hitting the old drink a bit and need to dry out a bit and recharge my batteries, so was just going to watch a bit of telly and the footie highlights if I can stay awake long enough,' Sam replied, again lying easily, whilst not feeling particularly good about it.

'Sorry to hear you're a bit tender Sam, I could keep you company if you want, I don't mind a bit of football'.
'Thanks Jill, that's so nice of you, but really there's no point as I don't think I'll be very good company. But we could meet up tomorrow if you like, for lunch maybe? I know a nice little place where we can go,' he said, possibly thinking about Cafe Epoca.

'Okay, but I can't pretend that I'm not disappointed about tonight, she replied. 'We could have christened *your* bed, but if it's not to be...

'Nice thought Jill and on any other night I would be more than up for it, but really, there's no point because you would only be disappointed again. But I promise I'll call you tomorrow and we can take it from there.

Okay Sam, I look forward to it, sweet dreams, of me I hope.'

197

Sam didn't know what to say, so he just said, 'Goodnight Jill, but he found himself feeling bad about his treatment of her. However, he told himself that she would be fine, as she always seemed to be-which was exactly what bothered him and wondering why? She was a very attractive woman who had every right to expect better. And he wondered whether that was what she found attractive about him. He had been thinking that he had known women like Jill previously in his life, women who needed to know that men desired them. However, such women, whilst eminently desirable were, he knew, unlikely to be fulfilled by or attracted to lovelorn idiots, who were so obviously entranced and besotted by their charms, ironically being attracted to men who had either rejected or treated them with little or no respect.

It reminded Sam of his youth and the things that some young men, including some of his friends and perhaps even he himself would say when confronted with obviously attractive women. In the event of somebody stating the glaringly obvious and saying something like, 'She's absolutely gorgeous,' someone else would invariably counter it with the cynical rider of, 'Aye but she knows it' which only served to reveal that person's resentment at the fact that not only was she beautiful but she also clearly possessed a degree of self-awareness. And that just wasn't on; beauty and confidence, oh no! And being in possession of both those attributes, accordingly, she was accordingly very unlikely to be impressed or interested in anyone like them. So, roughly translated it meant, 'I have absolutely no chance of her or anyone else that gorgeous and smart ever being even remotely interested in me'.

As he reflected on recent events, Sam realised that Jill had told him very little about her life, nor had he told her anything of any consequence about his and accordingly they really knew very little about each other. Not that it bothered him, it was just the way it was, but it made him wonder why they had both independently chosen to do that, or more accurately, not to do, consciously or otherwise. As he pondered the situation, Sam acknowledged to himself that his sense of mistrust and caution, borne of previous encounters and mistakes had undoubtedly contributed to his hesitancy. He wondered whether it was it the same factors that had led to Jill's reluctance, but for some reason, he couldn't help feeling that her reasons were possibly far more complex or sinister.

Chapter 54

7 January 2018
Saturday

As he sat in the bar at the Mark Anthony with a beer awaiting Emily's arrival, he sensed a frisson of activity, gradually increasing to an air of unsettled agitation, around the foyer and reception area and in the bar and pool area, which was still relatively busy for that time of day, probably due to the lingering warmth and brightness of the sun. However, there was now most definitely an air of burgeoning commotion apparent, with a discernible sense of people becoming alarmed, talking loudly and excitedly, and behaving as if something terrible had happened, which apparently it had. And, what had actually happened (this eventually being established after an extended period of time, with people coming and going and talking in whispers and exaggeratedly hushed voices) was that somebody, a male, had been assaulted, strangled, by another man, in his room at the Mediterranean Palace, and would have been killed if it hadn't been for his wife coming out of the shower and screaming the place down, and then attacking the assailant with red hot hair tongs, causing him to flee before he could be apprehended.

As Sam was digesting and processing the information from a variety of sources, Emily arrived, her curiosity piqued by the apparent flourishing excitement and desperate to know the cause of it all. Whilst she directly asked Sam what had happened, he was apparently oblivious to her questioning and seemed to be in his own world, totally lost in concentration. Then suddenly, he seemed to snap out of it and began asking people if they knew what the room number was and on getting no confirmation, then headed to the reception to make the same enquiries.

Whilst initially, the staff were very hesitant and reluctant to have that dialogue with him, advising that they didn't have that information to hand and even if they did, they could not divulge it without consulting senior management, or words to that effect, to protect the people concerned. However, Sam informed them that he knew people staying in the Med Palace and that his enquiry was borne of concern. He then stated that he did not want to know the identity of the guests but only the room number to set his mind at ease. He also pointed out that clearly the news of the incident had spread and would soon become common knowledge. At that, the apparently Spanish receptionist, who spoke fluent English, told him to wait and she would check before disappearing behind a partition and then emerging a few minutes later with a piece of paper with a number written on it, which she handed to Sam, whilst asking that he not share it with anyone else at that point in time. Sam thanked her and gave her his assurance that he wouldn't. Then he looked at the number of the room, which was 457.

Chapter 55

27 January 2018
Saturday

As Sam was digesting and processing the information relating to the dramatic events, Emily approached him to ask him if he was okay and what was going on, as he had gone as white as a sheet. However, at that moment, Senor Hernandez, the manager he had dealt with at the Mediterranean Palace walked into the foyer accompanied by Police Inspectors Delgado and Herrera. On seeing Sam and realising from his expression that he was both aware of and understood the gravity of what had happened and the possible implications for himself, Inspector Delgado very sensitively approached him and politely requested that he speak with them. Then, realising that Emily was with him, Inspector Herrera, looked questioningly at her and then Sam before saying to him, 'Maybe it is better to speak alone?'

Sam, on considering the situation for a few moments, decided that given his concerns about Emily and her connection with Akmal, he wasn't quite ready for her to know everything until he got some answers from her, so he agreed with Inspector Herrera that he would comply with their request for discretion and confidentiality.

However, he also wasn't ready to tell them about his own suspicions either and resolved to keep them to himself for the time being. He apologised to Emily for having to leave her on her own, who indicated her understanding of the situation (whilst not really understanding anything at all) and advised Sam that she would wait in the bar for him, clearly being desperate to know just what the hell was going on.

***

The 'man' also needed to know what the hell had gone wrong. He had acted on the information provided by his accomplice, who, it had been arranged and agreed, would take whatever action was necessary to ensure that the 'mark' would be in the room, even if meant being there with him. Unfortunately, things had not gone to plan and that had not been possible, for reasons that he did not fully understand and didn't really care about. He had been provided with the room number and assured that the target would be there all night. So, he had gone to room 457 in the Mediterranean Palace, as instructed, and had stood outside the hotel room and knocked on it—because his accomplice was not there to ensure that it was either open or to open it for him - holding the garrotte behind his back. He had heard the unmistakable sound of a shower running, prior to the door being opened by a male who had on a Terry towelling bathrobe and was still drying his hair with a towel. As speed and efficiency were of the essence he had needed to act quickly and had not had time to really scrutinise his appearance; he was of similar height and build and he had simply assumed that he was the intended target. Why wouldn't he? He had been given an assurance that it was his room. So, when the man had smiled and asked, 'Yes?' of him, he had also smiled a friendly smile prior to then simultaneously barging into him and knocking him against the bathroom door, to his immediate left and then attempting to position the garrotte around his neck. Unfortunately, or rather fortunately, for the surprised victim, the bathroom door was then opened from the inside by a woman who, on witnessing the shocking scenario had attacked him with some sort of hot metal instrument and then screamed the place down, attracting the attention of other guests who had begun banging on the door, which had closed behind him. This had then alerted cleaning staff who were working nearby, who had then accessed the room. He had sustained some nasty burns on his hands but had managed to get out before anyone realised what had happened and before anyone else had arrived. He had subsequently discovered, from reports from various sources, that the person he had attacked was in fact the wrong person, and the woman who had attacked him was his wife. Without a doubt the whole thing was a monumental fuckup which had serious implications for his professional reputation and credibility.

He could just imagine his other target having a good old laugh at his expense when he found out. Well, he would make sure that it was short lived. And somebody was going to pay for the humiliation he had suffered—big time.

Chapter 56

27 January 2018
Saturday

Something was bothering Sam, gnawing away at him, like a memory that he couldn't retrieve, like some kind of ephemeral, fleeting thought that was annoyingly just out of reach. And he was also convinced that whatever it was, it was the thing that connected everything and made sense of it all. He decided that he needed time on his own to try and drag it from his "photographic memory" and hopefully then he would be able to work it all out. So, he poured himself a drink and sat down and tried to clear his mind, which wasn't an easy thing to do, particularly with all the ongoing thoughts and concerns that were weighing heavily on his mind. Nevertheless, he tried to do so and concentrate on the main issues and people, and what could possibly connect them.

In Sam's mind, Akmal was still the clear, if not only, link with the events in Benidorm, apart from Trish Roy, who, he understood, was still being held in custody awaiting trial in regard to the murder of Rab Lindsay, the crime which she was still claiming to have paid him to commit, despite there being absolutely no evidence to that effect—apart from the word of a dishonest, corrupt Algerian pimp.
And *he* wasn't talking. Or was he, and if so, to whom? And then there were the inexplicable parallels with Trish Roy's situation

in Benidorm and the recent developments involving Emily.

Then Sam remembered what it was that he had been trying to recall from the back of his mind; it was something that Trish Roy had said to him in Benidorm when he had been questioning her concerning her own knowledge of Rab Lindsay and his late wife, Heather, who Sam had also spent time with during that fateful 'holiday.' Trish Roy had told him that Rab Lindsay had a brother who was 'even more corrupt' than his late sibling was and who also had interests and involvement in nail bars and car washes in Glasgow, both of which exploited foreign, mainly North African and Asian illegal labour.

And who did Sam know that was currently working in a car wash?

Akmal had indicated that he was in regular contact with his brother Farouk, claiming to speak with his sibling on an almost daily basis. Was it possible that Akmal had told Farouk that he was in Tenerife and even more importantly, had he discussed with him what had happened between them in Benidorm? Then he began to wonder if it was possible that the latter had then told someone something that he shouldn't have?' And, if that someone had blabbed to someone else etc, then anything was possible. *And if that was the case,* thought Sam, then he needed to speak to him. He also realised, that if there was any value in his theory then Akmal was most probably in as much, if not even more danger than he was, from all sides.

Sam was aware, as were many people in Glasgow, and not just those involved with the media, of an historic gangland dispute which had long blighted the Glasgow landscape and which, in recent years, had seen a return to violent clashes and destructive attacks on businesses. This conflict had long been referred to as the 'Car Wash Wars' which, as far as Sam was aware, were still an ongoing cause for concern for Glasgow's finest. He went online on his mobile phone to research the situation further and gain an update, to discover that it was still very much an ongoing issue between certain criminal factions, without, it seemed, any sign of resolution in sight. He couldn't help but see the unavoidable parallels with the 'Ice Cream Wars 'of the 1980's, when the ice cream vans were used as a front for illegal activity in the East End of Glasgow and as a means of laundering illegal cash.

Both situations had also culminated in turf wars between the respective gangs and serious arson attacks, with the car wash fires resulting in the death of six people. Unsurprisingly, no names had ever been mentioned by the media, possibly due to the fear of litigation. However, all the available information and evidence seemed to confirm that the ongoing conflict was involved a long-standing dispute and intense rivalry between two well-known crime clans, competing for control and power, with neither side willing to give an inch, despite the reported considerable damage and casualties for both sides. Also, whilst the two warring factions were reportedly of Scottish and African/Asian origin, respectively, this was not a conflict rooted in racism, as has previously been the case regarding gang wars in the South Side of the city. No, this was pure and simply about power, control and money.

Sam also realised that if he had indeed worked out the connection, then Akmal, despite his protestations to the contrary, would also certainly have been made aware of the situation, and the resultant implications, from his contact with his brother.

Whilst Sam hadn't made sense of it all yet, what he did know, unfortunately for him, was that the people involved, on both sides, were known to be very dangerous and ruthless individuals, regarding both their business and personal dealings. Accordingly, Sam was now in no doubt that the recent events and developments in Tenerife were clearly an extension of all this and, even more concerning, a demonstration of intentions, much more personal in nature -very personal indeed.

Chapter 57

27 January 2018
Saturday

She hadn't expected things to turn out this way; she was on holiday in Tenerife by herself when she had received the telephone call from her friend and ex colleague—whom she had previously talked to about her holiday plans – asking a favour of her. After listening to and considering what was being asked of her, she had reluctantly agreed to help her old friend–to come out of retirement, albeit temporarily, on the condition that it was a one-off, irrespective of the outcome. And whilst those terms had been accepted and she had embraced her duties accordingly, she could never have factored in how she would find herself feeling about her 'charge' within a very short period of being with him. So much so that it had led to her going 'off track' and abandoning her normal long-held rules and maxims, as she found herself becoming more and more attracted to him. She knew it was wrong, but she had been unable to help herself.

She enjoyed being with him, and when she wasn't with him, she wanted to be with him. The one undoubted positive resulting from the situation was that she now had very personal motivation to keep him alive and was even more determined to do so. And hopefully, once it was all over, he would understand, and maybe they could have a new start and be open and honest with each other. She had felt so bad about deceiving him that it had affected her to the extent that she found herself wanting to tell him everything, but she couldn't, at least not yet, not until he had served his purpose.

Chapter 58

27 January 2018
Saturday

If Inspectors Delgado and Herrera knew anything about the motivation or reasons for the attack, they weren't letting on, instead asking Sam if he knew of any reason why anyone would want to kill him. Unfortunately for them, Sam was playing things equally as close to his chest, so, in effect what they had was a stalemate. The elephant in the room had already been openly acknowledged, in the sense that there was a tacit acceptance from everyone concerned that the attack had not, been intended for the unfortunate and completely innocent victim and occupant of room 457 at the Mediterranean Palace. Rather, the more informed and reasoned conclusion was that it was most likely that the intended victim was the previous resident, who, fortuitously and fortunately for him, had subsequently been accommodated elsewhere, obviously without the prospective assassin's knowledge or the person who had provided them with the erroneous information. Which begged the obvious question; who had believed that he was still in that room and in that hotel? The answer was equally as obvious.

Clearly, the fact that Sam had since told Emily that he had moved out of room 457 at the Mediterranean Palace into the Mark Anthony and then arranged to meet her in the bar at the latter, ruled her out, although he realised that it was still possible that she had already made arrangements with someone prior to that. And she could also have quite easily informed any conspirator of the new circumstances in time for him to abandon his plans and make other arrangements. In addition, the fact that she had kept their appointment also indicated that she expected to see him there, whilst she also seemed genuinely surprised and totally in the dark about the dramatically unfolding situation that she had encountered on arrival. Either that or she was a particularly gifted actress. He already knew that she was a very good liar after all given her claim that she had intended to spend the day shopping for gift for friends instead of meeting with Akmal and some mystery man. That was a conversation that he still needed to have with her.

But that wasn't the only conversation he needed to have; he needed answers, and he wasn't going to get them sitting in a room with two police inspectors, who were giving nothing away. So, he decided to take the bull by the horns and stood up, saying, 'Well, if there's nothing else, I have a very attractive woman waiting for me and I have kept her waiting for long enough thank you very much.'

'You might also have a killer waiting for you, Mr Meredith,' said Inspector Herrera, showing uncharacteristic concern for his welfare.

'Once they come to terms with what just happened, or rather didn't, here tonight, they will try again. I think it is unlikely they will give up because of one little mistake.'.

'And most likely they will have a point to prove too,', added Inspector Delgado.

And maybe I've got one too, thought Sam, but he kept it to himself, instead saying, 'Well I'll just have to take that chance then, won't I?' trying to sound dismissive and unconcerned, which could not have been further from the truth. As if confirming this, he then asked, 'Unless you're offering me protection?' As neither of the police officials answered him, Sam, after a short pause and an ironic smile, headed out of the room. And of course, someone was directed to follow him.

Chapter 59

27 January 2018
Saturday

Emily was still sitting in the bar waiting on Sam, when he arrived back there, standing up when he entered with an air of expectancy that he would provide her with information about what was going on, apart from what she had already gleaned from staff, social media and various other guests in the hotel. However, Sam walked right past her and headed to the bar saying, 'I need a drink,' which he collected, again for no charge, and brought back to the table. However, on sitting down, he immediately realised the thoughtless and inconsiderate nature of his actions, and accordingly apologised profusely to Emily whilst ordering her a drink, adding, 'To be honest, I'm surprised that you're still here, I wouldn't have blamed you if you had thought;

'Sod this for a game of soldiers and headed off to somewhere and someone more hospitable.'

'It's okay Sam, I can see that you're preoccupied and affected by what's been happening, which is perfectly understandable. Also, I was concerned about you, and I wanted to know what was happening. So can you please tell me what is going on?' As Sam was considering his response, the waitress arrived with Emily's drink, which gave him pause for thought and time to consider his answer. So, after ordering another drink for himself, he decided that given his concerns and reservations about her motivation and interest in him, he wouldn't be telling her anything until he got some answers from her regarding her own recent movements and activities. Accordingly, he turned to her and said pointedly; 'I could ask you the same question Emily'.

'What?'... what do you mean Sam?' she asked, looking shocked at both the question and his tone. So, Sam told her that he had seen her with Akmal and then stating further; 'That lowlife is probably the cause of everything bad that has happened to me since I arrived here.'

'Which is what Sam?' she asked? whilst informing him that the only reason that she had been talking to Akmal was that he worked at her hotel during the day as a porter and odd job man and she had bumped into him outside the hotel as she was leaving. Sam again found himself thinking that the similarities with Akmal's involvement with Trish Roy in Benidorm were now even more startling and unavoidable, which made him feel even more unsettled. However, he was determined to stay focused on the main issues at hand and replied; 'That would be as you were leaving to meet the other man that you had lunch with?'

'You followed me?' she asked indignantly.

'Wouldn't you have done the same, under the circumstances?' asked Sam, looking at Emily expectantly for her response, obviously feeling that he was making a valid point. However, Emily just stared at him and said nothing, seemingly choosing to regard the question as rhetorical.

'Was it your ex-husband?' said Sam, ignoring her disregard of his question, and then adding, 'Or should that be ex-partner'?

'What do you mean?' Emily asked, looking shocked and taken aback.

'I mean... you said that you never married...you said

that…that you then found out that he was still married to his ex-wife. Is that not what you told me? What did you think I meant?' asked Sam, looking and sounding perplexed.

'Nothing, I mean yes… yes, that's what I meant, sorry I wasn't thinking straight' she said, but thought Sam, at the same time looking and sounding relieved.

'Well?' said Sam, obviously expecting a response.

'What?' asked Emily, looking puzzled.

'Was it your ex…partner?'

'Oh, no… no,' said Emily seemingly remembering the question suddenly and still seeming to be quite flummoxed.

'Well, who was it then?' asked Sam, and then, seeming to realise that he was being very aggressively confrontational, said; 'I'm sorry Emily, sorry, it's none of my business, I just thought that we…

'No, it's all right Sam, I…I understand, and you're right, I would probably feel the same, I suppose. And I'm sorry too, but honestly, he's just a friend, nothing more. And then, looking at Sam, who gave her a look that suggested that he wasn't convinced in the slightest, said, 'Look, it's …complicated. So please don't ask me anything else, please, I beg you Sam.
I wanted to tell you before, but I couldn't, but hopefully I will be able to soon. I need you to trust me and believe me when I say that. Can we just go for a drink or something to eat? I want to be with you tonight, Sam, please don't push me away. Sam didn't know what to think apart from, as before; *Here we fucking go again. Why do these things always happen to me? Why can't I just have straightforward situations with no complications?* And did he really believe that her meeting with Akmal was as innocent as she claimed?' So, he asked her if she knew about his other job, to which she replied, 'Yes, he told me that he works in a nightclub, but he told me that he might be leaving both jobs to head back home to Algeria to deal with family issues.'

'Did he indeed? Family issues, eh? Well, I'm going to need a word with the little reprobate before he goes anywhere and there's someone else, I need to see first, so I need to go.

I'll walk you back to your hotel first if you want?' offered Sam, which Emily accepted sheepishly, and asking him 'Where will you find him'? do you know which nightclub he works in?' Sam smiled a wry smile as he replied;

'Yes, and it's not a nightclub he works in, it's a brothel. And he's not heading back home for family reasons' said Sam, finding himself becoming quite irate and intolerant, and then wondering whether it was wrongly directed at Emily. Also, his toothache had returned.

'What do you mean Sam?' said Emily, clearly confused.

'I mean' said Sam, 'that he's running for his life'.

And now so am I, he thought, at which point he decided to do something about it.

Sam's thoughts about Akmal and his own experiences in Benidorm had given him cause for reflection and an idea, which he owed, ironically, to his previous involvement and collaboration with Benidorm's finest. He stood up and walked straight towards the tall, suited man standing at the end of the bar and said; Habla Ingles? to which he replied, 'Si senor'.

'In that case call Inspector Delgado or Inspector Herrera and tell them that I want to talk to them'.

Chapter 60

27 January 2018
Saturday

She was sitting in her hotel room, drinking more than was good for her and smoking too, which she hadn't done for years, but she didn't care; she needed it to help her cope; to deal with the feelings she was experiencing because of her actions. However, she was under no illusions, she knew that ultimately the alcohol would only lead to her feeling a whole lot worse, and not just physically either; she knew that the more she drank, the more it would compound the feelings of guilt, failure, self-loathing and depression that she had to contend with on a daily basis.

As she reflected on the day's developments, Jill just couldn't understand what had gone wrong; she had definitely provided the correct room number, as requested; the target himself had confirmed it to her the last time they met.

And he had also told her that he was going to be there all night. So, what had happened for the situation to change so quickly? Perhaps he had simply forgotten to tell her that he had moved room, she thought or maybe even hotel, and wondered where he was now? However, after consideration, she decided that she was glad that she didn't know as it meant that she couldn't tell anybody.

Then she also began to wonder whether he had known about her all along? i.e.; that she was a lying, cheating whore who would do anything for money. Initially, on learning about the dramatic events which had taken place in room 457 of the Med Palace, she had concluded that Sam must have lied to her when she had called him earlier in the evening and that he had been spending the night with the other woman that she knew he had been seeing. But that was before she found out that it was a completely different person who had been attacked and that the room was in fact now occupied by both, he and his wife, who, by her actions, had reportedly saved her husband from certain death.

Then she realised that the same could be said of Sam Meredith, in that he had, by whatever combination of circumstances, fortuitous or premeditated, been granted an unlikely extension to his extremely precarious existence. But she knew that was all it was, a temporary respite from what was an inevitable outcome. The people concerned clearly weren't about to give up easily however, following several failed attempts at both destroying and ending Sam Meredith's life. After the initial attempt at seduction had ended so disappointingly, the debacle of the chambermaid's ill-fated encounter had then required a change of plan, bringing a halt to the originally intended intervention, due to security and disclosure concerns. Whilst her subsequent seduction had proved more successful, it had only been for her own satisfaction and pleasure, with no ulterior motive or intention involved. She had then subsequently found herself harbouring totally unrealistic and forlorn hopes that that might mean the end of the contract and maybe the start of something else for her and Sam.

But she didn't have to wait long to be disabused of that notion and for her worst fears to be confirmed when she was contacted by the subsequently enlisted assassin, requesting her co-operation in hastening Sam's demise. However, whilst she had obviously screwed up, in one sense she was glad things had turned out the way that they had, for Sam's sake. However, following the debacle she knew that it would now be a matter of pride for the failed executioner, and, unfortunately, for Sam, only a matter of time. Her real concern, however, was that her actions, albeit unintentionally, had resulted in the very visible and public humiliation of a very dangerous and vindictive individual, meaning that it was inevitable that he would soon come looking for her too.

She was jolted from her thoughts by a loud knock on her room door, and on opening it, she found herself looking at the last person she expected or wanted to see and tried but failed to hide it.

He could tell instantly that she had been drinking- a lot. She was also smoking, which he had never previously seen her do.

Looking over her shoulder Sam could see a large bottle of gin with very little left in it. And then, noticing her surprised reaction to his presence, asked 'What's the matter, surprised to see me, Jill?' expecting someone else, were we?' as he pushed past her into the room. 'To be honest, I wasn't sure if you would be here or not, all things considered.

I thought that you might have scampered off to pick up your fee from whoever it is you're working for,' said Sam.

'What do you mean? Who? I'm not working for anyone Sam, said Jill, appearing confused and annoyed. 'I don't know what you're talking about.'

'Aye Right! You must think I'm a real fucking idiot,' said Sam.

'You were the only person who knew my room number, or thought you did; you even told me what you thought it was.

So, you quite clearly believed that I was still in room 457 in the Mediterranean Palace and believed that I would be there tonight, all night, after speaking to me. Didn't you?' he barked at her. 'After unsuccessfully trying to lure me into spending the night with you, which would have made it so much easier wouldn't it?'

'I really haven't a clue what you mean,' said Jill, trying hard to look innocent but not quite pulling it off.

'You really are a piece of work, aren't you?' said Sam, disbelievingly. 'But there's absolutely no point in denying it and keeping up this pretext because it all fits and makes perfect sense. You obviously gave somebody my room number, or what you *thought* was my room number and told them that I would be home so that they could do what they had been asked… sorry…told… no… probably *paid* to do- which is looking seriously like killing me.'

'But' he continued, 'the question is why?' although it was a question that he probably knew the answer to.

And then, warming to his task and not waiting for a reply, he continued, 'Unfortunately he attacked a perfectly innocent person who would be dead if it hadn't been for his wife's quick thinking apparently. It's not really going to plan, is it?' Jill said nothing, and was having difficulty looking Sam in the eye, instead staring down at the floor and not lifting her head.

'Look, I haven't informed the police about what I think-yet- but I will if you don't tell me what the fuck is going on, and you can take your chances with them.'

'Maybe I will,' said Jill indignantly.

'What? Really? In Spain? Are you serious?' said Sam, quite incredulously, but then realised that she was indeed very serious.

'Well at least they might be able to protect me,' said Jill, quite angrily but emotionally.

'Protect you from what? Who?' asked Sam.

'Myself,' said Jill, before bursting into tears.

Chapter 61

27 January 2018
Saturday

Jill eventually confessed everything to Sam, telling him all about her checkered past from her time spent in prison for drug trafficking to her subsequent involvement with major crime figures, prostitution and people trafficking, and finally, how she had ended up becoming involved in the abortive attempt to accuse him of rape. She also maintained that she was happy when it had been called off and that that was not why she had had sex with him. However, she claimed not to know why someone wanted him dead, whilst also maintaining that she had had no option but to do what had been asked of her, because they were 'very dangerous people' who knew things about her past and who 'are very difficult to say no to when they come calling'. Notwithstanding all of that, however, she also admitted, when asked outright, that she was being paid the sum of 10,000 Euros, whilst not being able to look him in the eye when she said it.

However, she also advised, when questioned by Sam, that the man who had tried to kill Sam was a contract killer, whilst still claiming that she didn't know his name and stating that was just fine with her as she didn't want to know, because he was a violent, vengeful maniac, who would kill her without as much as a moment's hesitation. Sam was about to ask how she knew all that but didn't know his name when she lost it completely, bursting into tears and becoming hysterical, saying that he would already be looking for her. When asked why, she then admitted to him that he had been correct in his analysis and that she was indeed responsible for the debacle that had taken place in his old hotel room earlier in the day. When Sam asked her if she knew the name of the man who had hired and paid both her and the professional killer, initially she did not reply or confirm it one way or another, before simply reiterating that they were 'Ruthless people, who you don't want to be pissed off with you' and then adding, 'As you yourself are currently discovering Sam, whatever it is you have done'.

Sam chose to ignore her comment and found it hard to believe that she didn't know about the events in Benidorm, specifically those culminating in the death of Rab Lindsay and suspected that she might just be playing dumb. So, he decided to enlighten her, whilst not admitting to anything, but noticing a flicker of recognition when he said the gangster's name. Encouraged by this, he then came right out and asked her if the person who had recruited them both was Rab Lindsay's brother Terry, at which point, she again dissolved into tears, which Sam interpreted as confirmation. However, she was still refusing to make any definitive comment, seemingly being terrified of the possible consequences. 'Are you serious about talking to the police?' asked Sam

'What? why?' asked Jill, looking puzzled.

'Now's your chance, and believe me, it's your best chance,' said Sam, at which point Inspectors Delgado and Herrera entered the room, as Sam left it, handing the latter a small microphone that had been concealed in his shirt pocket, on his way out.

'Don't do anything silly Senor,' Inspector Delgado shouted after him, at the same time gesturing to another officer to follow him.

'Too late for that,' said Sam.

Chapter 62

27 January 2018
Saturday

After he had left Jill, Sam had made his way to Akmal's usual station on the corner of Avenida Arquitecto Gomez Cuesta and Avenida Santiago Puig across from the Hotel Columbus. However, there was no sign of him, or anyone else for that matter, and whilst Sam doubted that sex and sleaze were having a night off, in the absence of anyone else being available to make enquiries of regarding Akmal's whereabouts, he decided to call it a night. Then, realising that he was absolutely starving, as he hadn't eaten for hours, he decided to head to the Cafe Epoca in the hope that it was still open, which it was, and thankfully still serving. He ordered a beer and some crab and chilli pasta, the latter arriving just in time to address the rather loud grumbling noises that his stomach was making to the amusement of the waitress.

After devouring his pasta like a wild animal, along with some delicious Focaccia, salad, and two glasses of Rioja, Sam headed back to his hotel, whilst looking very warily all about him as he went. However, he was pretty sure that he was still being followed by at least one of Tenerife's finest, even if he had not actually been able to see anyone—which, of course, was the point of covert surveillance after all. He reckoned that Inspectors Delgado and Herrera probably had everybody working flat out following the situation at the Med Palace. It reminded him of the scene depicted in so many American films and TV programmes, where the official in charge of the investigation says earnestly to his team 'Okay, listen up people, the next 24/48 hours are crucial, nobody leaves here until we crack this case.' Sam was always amazed that nobody ever said anything in protest, like, 'Are you having a laugh? I'm on to a promise,' or 'Aye, that'll be right, I've got the supermarket to go to, weans to pick up and dinners to make. And who's going to walk the dog, you?' No, I didn't think so, see you tomorrow, I'm off.'

He arrived back at his hotel safely in no time at all and went straight to bed, with the food and drink appearing to have done the trick, because, as preoccupied as he was with the ongoing situation, he was asleep as soon as his head hit the pillow, dreaming of being back home safe in Glasgow; but for how long?

Chapter 63

27 January 2018
Saturday

Max Holland had followed Sam after he left the Mark Anthony until he arrived at his respective destinations, and then he had maintained a vigil nearby, watching for any sign of the assassin. But it was to no avail, as he was nowhere to be seen, which led him to conclude that he was clearly keeping a low profile following recent events, little realising that this was due to him being made aware of his own presence on the island. Whatever the reason was, Max knew that it wouldn't last, because he knew the man who accepted the contracts to kill both himself and Sam Meredith; his name was Ivan Lasenko and he knew that he wasn't about to give up, particularly after such a monumental fuck up, and the damage that would do to his reputation.

He had trained with him over twenty years ago when they were both in the same programme for undercover agents and had even worked together on a few jobs, the last and most telling being a particularly risky and dangerous operation, the purpose of which was to infiltrate a people trafficking organisation operating in Glasgow, Edinburgh and Stirling.

Whilst they had been briefed and prepared extensively, it had been a disaster an absolute shambles of an operation, with his fellow agent being lucky to get out of the whole sorry mess with his life, due to a security leak, which he had subsequently, and wrongly, blamed on Max, having convinced himself that he had sold him out for a payoff. However, the truth, which Lasenko would never acknowledge, but clearly resent, was that Max, in complete contrast to himself, was unfailingly professional, disciplined and trustworthy and highly unlikely to be susceptible to corruption. And, with the benefit of subsequently acquired intelligence, it was discovered that the disastrous outcome was more than likely due to his colleague's relationship with a mysterious woman, who neither Max, nor anyone else, for that matter, had ever met.

There were no photographs of them together, but it was also felt likely that she would have changed her appearance since then. Also, Lasenko, who acknowledged that they had had an intimate relationship, was reluctant to provide any more information regarding her identity, maintaining that she was not in any way responsible, most likely to protect himself from blame and ridicule. Despite his unwillingness to accept the likely reality of the situation, the smart money was on her being a 'plant' or perhaps, more accurately, a 'honeytrap' who had seduced and duped her unsuspecting victim into divulging information which ensured that the operation failed, before then disappearing altogether. The belief was that the main purpose of her involvement was to find out how much was known about their operation and whether it was safe to continue to operate their illegal trafficking operations.

It also meant that Lasenko's identity had likely been discovered and that therefore, by association, so had Max's and consequently the operation was blown. Unfortunately, Lasenko's refusal to accept it and then predictably behave in trademark cavalier fashion almost got him killed in a confrontation with the enemy before eventually making his escape, mainly, it must be said, following intervention from Max, who had anticipated his errant colleague's maverick actions. Not that the wretched, humiliated Lasenko would ever acknowledge it, refusing to accept that he had been duped and to take any responsibility for the debacle of the failed mission, preferring to lay the blame at Max's door. That was over fifteen years ago but the memory was still fresh in Max's mind, and he had no doubt that the details were still forensically imprinted on his former errant colleague's mind too, or rather his warped version of it.

There was also the small matter of Lasenko's subsequent involvement in a failed assassination, which he had become involved in soon after him leaving the force and going 'rogue'– and which Max, whilst working undercover, unknown to Lasenko, had been involved in sabotaging, whilst posing as him, albeit very briefly. All things considered Lasenko wasn't short of reasons to resent and hold a grudge against his ex-partner in crime, so to speak.

Posing as Lasenko hadn't been that difficult for Max, as he was familiar with his accent and mannerisms, whilst they were also very much alike physically; both were tall, Max being 6 feet one, and the latter being just an inch taller. Both were also dark skinned with brown hair and brown eyes.

But that was where the resemblance ended; whilst Lasenko was brash and arrogant in nature and presentation, Max was relatively mild mannered. However, the calm presentation belied a steely, determined nature, he was also regarded as someone to rely and depend upon, whereas Lasenko was regarded as something of a 'loose cannon'; impulsive, volatile and prone to violent behaviour. Max also knew that he was nothing if not vindictive and that, whilst recognising the current contract on his own head as being a strictly business transaction, he also knew that there was also no doubting the very personal nature of his nemesis's motivation and desire for revenge.

Chapter 64

27 January 2018
Saturday

Terry Lindsay was not a happy man; he was not a happy man because nothing had gone according to plan in fact, it was an absolute bloody shamble. The plan had been to lure the person who had reportedly been involved in brokering his brother's death – allegedly "in cahoots" with the brother of the Algerian who had carelessly and drunkenly divulged the crucial information—into a compromising situation, thereby causing him great personal shame and disgrace and hopefully leading to him being imprisoned. The Algerian, as part of the restitution for his recklessness, had subsequently been tasked with arranging this, with the rest hopefully taking care of itself. At least that had been the plan. However, it had never really got off the ground, whilst the subsequent and hastily arranged contingency plan had ended in an even bigger fuck up with police involvement of the wrong kind and more unwanted attention.

The intention had been that the scheming, conniving bastard would be the one on the receiving end of the police intervention—in the form of a rape charge—awaiting a trial that would not be required, as he would have been dealt with decisively in custody before it ever took place. He had also tried to re-negotiate with the Algerian's bosses-those same bosses who had sanctioned the execution of his brother to try and secure their agreement to terminate Sam Meredith, as part of a trade-off. However, this was rejected out of hand, with the powers that be advising that; 'He's your enemy, not ours'. What they did agree to though, at Terry Lindsay's insistence—along with regular free access to any of the girls at the 'nightclub', where he already visited on a regular basis—was for the 'Algerian scum named Akmal', to be silenced, once and for all, with them sharing the view that he had become a liability and that was the best outcome for all concerned. Terry Lindsay, however, not content with that outcome, had also demanded the identity of the contract killer who had carried out his brother's execution, which the other firm eventually agreed to, on the condition that it brought an end to the longstanding gang feud and violent power struggle being played out in the streets of Glasgow. On being given assurances and a guarantee to that effect by Terry Lindsay, he was provided with the necessary information. And the name he had been given was a name he recognised and knew to be an alias; he was also aware that it was on several other crime boss's hit lists. However, he was going to make it his business to absolutely ensure that it was he who was given accreditation for his execution within the criminal fraternity, thereby serving both as a warning and as revenge for his brother's murder.

Following the subsequent debacle however, it was decided to urgently engage the services of a professional contract killer to deal with both matters clinically and decisively. At least that had been the hope, but, inexplicably, that too had ended in a mess, with increased public scrutiny, possible exposure, and more importantly, risk to himself.

Chapter 65

28 January 2018
Sunday

Sam woke up in his own room to his own thoughts, which, whilst troubling, had, thankfully, not kept him awake, and he had managed to enjoy a half-decent night's sleep. He had, however been awakened by his phone beeping several times and then ringing and when he eventually managed to open his eyes, the room was in darkness as he had closed the blackout curtains. Accordingly, he had no idea what time it was, as his watch was in the bathroom and his phone was charging at the other end of the room. However, the noise coming from the pool outside indicated that it was already quite busy, although he couldn't hear any music playing or tannoy announcements from unbearably cheerful 'reps' about the day's planned activities, like water polo or pool aerobics, which, Sam reasoned, suggested that it was still quite early.

His curiosity piqued, he rose and opened the curtains to a blast of brilliant sunlight, which swamped the room like a searchlight, bathing it and him in glorious warmth. Sam stepped outside to a sky so blue and bright that it looked like it had been freshly painted, with little wispy flecks of cloud added for artistic effect.

The sun blazed loudly and defiantly in the proud sky and seemed to be almost trying to remind Sam that he was supposed to be on holiday and that whilst it was doing its level best to provide preferred, almost ideal weather conditions to heighten his enjoyment, Sam was failing to keep to his part of the arrangement. He checked his 'phone to find that the call was from Stuart, one of the reporters at his newspaper, who was also a friend and fellow musician. He had also left a voice message and sent a text (a belt and braces job, so he was obviously very keen to ensure that Sam got the message) asking if he could provide any details or 'on the spot' information about the incident in the hotel, which, despite the hotel's efforts to keep it under wraps for the time being, had clearly been leaked to the press and then published, however accurately.

Sam decided that he would reply at some point, just saying that he didn't know any more than was reported, once he had read what was in the newspaper. Then he noticed that one of the texts was from Kim, advising that she had read about the incident in the press and also asking, 'jokingly' if he was all right and "if he was up to his old tricks' and ''Can you not go anywhere without becoming involved in high drama?" just as he had predicted. He texted her back saying that he was fine and adding a 'laughing out loud' emoji in order to keep the mood light and hoped that would do the trick.

Sam headed to the bathroom and had a shower, after which he dressed and put on his watch, which told him that it was eight forty-five a.m.

He thought that he might as well head to breakfast, before then pausing and wondering if it was safe to do so, and then deciding that he wasn't going to be cowed into being afraid to go anywhere, which was either very brave or very stupid. But he believed that to be scared was to concede defeat, and he wasn't ready to do that just yet.

Sam picked up his mobile phone on his way out, only to see that there was a missed call from Emily whilst he had been in the shower, and he decided that he would call her after breakfast, as he wasn't up to talking to her on an empty stomach. His toothache was also still a persistent reality, and he resolved to pick something up from a pharmacy after breakfast, to help ease the pain. Despite his oral discomfort, Sam enjoyed a full breakfast, which he devoured with relish, being pleasantly surprised by how hungry he was, particularly as he had eaten late the previous night.

As he was leaving the restaurant, completely nourished but armed with some fresh fruit for later, he received a text from Emily, saying that there she wanted to meet with him as soon as possible before they parted, which sounded ominous. Then he remembered that he had still not explained to her the reasons and circumstances behind his move from the Med Palace to the Mark Anthony. He decided that there was no reason not to tell her, as he now knew for sure that she was not responsible for or involved in any way with the recent events and current developments. However, he was also keen to hear her explanation for her recent meeting with Akmal and the mystery man. So, he called her, and they arranged to meet at her hotel room, with her saying that she was so glad to hear from him and that she had things to tell him.

Despite her previous innocent protestations to the contrary to Sam, Emily was aware of he and Akmal's previous history, as well as the latter's recent involvement with the chambermaid, the reasons for which she now also knew were clearly linked to he and Sam's 'alleged' involvement in the death of one Rab Lindsay. And she now also knew that the latter's brother was responsible for sanctioning and financing the contracts on both Sam and one other person, who, ironically, was Sam's best hope

233

of survival. She had not judged Sam regarding his reported involvement in the death of Rab Lindsay in the same way that she had not judged the other person regarding his role in the same unforgiving scenario. She just wished it was all over so that she could finally tell Sam how she felt and could only hope that he had the same feelings for her. She needed to know how he felt one way or another, and if it turned out that he felt the same, she could not wait to share her happiness with her friend and colleague.

On arriving at Emily's hotel room, Sam was greeted warmly with a smile and a kiss, and on entering the room was surprised to see that she had prepared a small buffet lunch for them which she was taking out to the balcony. 'Go on out and have a seat and I'll bring out some wine, I bought both red and white,' she said smiling and then appeared carrying a bottle of each. 'Do you want to be mother and pour?' adding, 'I'll have white please,' and then joining him. Sam obliged, whilst also pouring a glass of red for himself and disregarding all common sense and previous experience, lifted a handful of 'cacahuetes' and tipped them into his mouth.

'This is lovely,' said Emily as she raised her glass towards him and said 'Cheers.' And despite his reservations, Sam couldn't help but agree and reciprocated accordingly.

They sat on the balcony in the sun, facing each other, both seemingly relaxed and happy to be with each other, when Emily looked at Sam and asked, 'What are you thinking about Sam?'

There it is, the dreaded question again, was what he was thinking, but surprisingly, he didn't say that instead, he replied 'Just admiring the view,' gesturing towards the splendid vista of Las Americas from her seventh-floor room.' 'And there was me thinking you were paying me a compliment,' she said, smiling.

'I could pay you loads of compliments if you want, and they would all be sincere,' said Sam, hoping that he didn't sound too corny.

'I'm only teasing you,' said Emily, kissing him softly on his cheek. And so, they both sat there, eating, drinking and chatting about everything but the important stuff, with Sam taking the philosophical view that they would get round to it eventually. But they never did, because at that very same moment, the tall swarthy man was in a room in the opposite side of the hotel looking through a sight of a L115A3 Long Range Rifle, a bolt-action weapon with an effective range out to 1.2 km, which employs a Schmidt & Bender 5-25x56 PM II 25x magnification day scope. It was also fitted with a silencer and was aimed directly at Sam.

Moments later, Sam grimaced in pain and let out a yell, holding his face before bending down to pick up what was left of his tooth, which had completely broken off as he had crunched into some nuts.

At the same time, a bullet fired from the room opposite missed his head by inches when he moved before embedding itself in the wall behind Emily, producing a puff of smoke. It also produced a cascade of blood from her neck as it pierced her carotid artery, whilst the second one put a hole in her head, killing her instantly.

Chapter 66

28 January 2018
Sunday

Sam, unable to believe or process what had just happened, grabbed Emily and dragged her to the floor of the balcony, where he spoke softly and reassuringly to her for almost five minutes, although it was most probably complete gibberish due to him being in a state of shock, before then finally noticing that he was covered in her blood, as was the balcony, as it continued to run freely, like a tap had been turned on. Minutes later, a manager arrived, because of the occupants of the room below contacting reception to advise that blood was dripping on to their balcony. The police and medical staff arrived soon after and Sam, who was quite clearly still in shock, was provided with medical attention and treatment. He suddenly realised that the pain in his mouth had completely disappeared.

Several years previously, Sam had watched his wife die from cancer, but thankfully she was spared a cruel, long-drawn-out death as the cancer had spread rapidly and devastatingly throughout her body, ending her life over just a period of months from diagnosis to death. Nevertheless, it had taken him and his family a considerable period to deal with if not actually recover from the shock, although they had most definitely never recovered from the loss. However, he had never witnessed somebody so close to him being killed as suddenly and clinically in such an immediate and stark manner, nor at such close quarters. Whilst he had found the experience incredibly traumatising it had also brought his own actions in Benidorm the previous year into a sharper focus than he would have liked, causing him to think about the reality of the consequences of them in a way that he had not previously considered. Indeed, he was now occasioned to think that had he done so, it is likely that he would not have been able to proceed with his momentous decision at the time.

He had even begun to wonder if this nightmarish experience was a cruel, ghoulish retribution for what happened in Benidorm and specifically concerning the murder of Rab Lindsay, which, like Emily's death, had been a 'hit' carried out by a contract killer.

After he had been given all clear from the medics, Sam was escorted back to his hotel by the police, who offered to move him elsewhere for the remainder of his holiday, whilst indicating that it might have to be an extended one, depending on how things developed. Sam listened in disbelief, with a feeling of Deja Vu and again, almost bewildered by the inescapable parallels with the situation he had faced in Benidorm. However, he stated that he wasn't moving anywhere else, regardless of the consequences, which the police reluctantly accepted, whilst advising him to be careful and to contact them in the event of anything suspicious or untoward taking place. They also informed him that they would be monitoring him from a distance.

Sam went to his room, poured himself a drink, and, reassured by the police's guarantee of surveillance/protection and the general belief that it was unlikely that the killer would make another attempt on his life so soon, he sat out on the balcony in the still of the evening of one of the worst days of his life to date. He had originally planned to grab something to eat somewhere in the Safari Centre before heading to one of the bars to watch either the Barcelona or Manchester City game, depending upon what was being shown and where. However, he found that he was not hungry in the slightest and had no interest in football either. As he sat there sipping a beer in a state of bewilderment, he found himself thinking for the first time about what kind of person became a contract killer? He imagined it would need to be someone who is able to feel completely detached from their murderous behaviour, and the consequences of same for their victims and their families, who regard it as nothing more than part of a professional remit, or, in other words, strictly business.

As he began to feel a bit less anxious and more settled, Sam went online to explore the subject further online, which led him, strangely, and interestingly, to the Annual Social Science Public Lecture of 2014, which had taken place four years previously on Wednesday 28 May. It had been held at the University of Brighton and was delivered by Professor David Wilson, Professor of Criminology from Birmingham City University. Professor Wilson talked about his research on contract killing and the British 'hitman', noting that whilst they are often the subject of Hollywood films, little is understood about the role of professional, contracted killers in Britain.

Professor Wilson's research had also previously revealed that the number of killers outweighed victims because of something that was not well known, i.e.: that often several accomplices were involved.

One man, John Childs, carried out six murders in the 1970s; his targets included a ten-year-old boy, who was killed because he witnessed the shooting of his father, as Max Holland had, the difference being that the latter was fortunate to survive the traumatic experience, at least in a physical sense.

Professor Wilson's research also contradicted certain myths about contract killers, for instance, the idea that killings are carried out in dark isolated spots by organised gangs. In fact, contract killings tend to be much more mundane, with 'hitmen' murdering their victims openly in a street near the victim's home while they are going about daily errands. A paper was subsequently published entitled, 'The British Hitman, 1974-2013', which detailed how a 'hitman' must 'objectify [the target] as someone who deserves to be killed for money, which relies on being able to boil murder down to an economic transaction'.

It states further that, 'They have to condition themselves to continue with daily life after [the murder]'. Sam was able to acknowledge and recognise if not completely understand and sympathise with the likely emotional difficulty such people could experience in dealing with the consequences of their actions. He also unexpectedly found himself recognising parallels in the mindset of 'hitmen' with people who can perpetrate casual violence, with no thought to the consequences of their actions.

Casual violence terrified Sam, having been the victim of it some years previously, and which he remembered with terrifying clarity like it had happened yesterday; he had just finished a 'gig' with the band at Blackfriars pub in the Merchant City and was walking to the taxi rank with the bassist and his girlfriend when they were accosted by three suspect looking individuals who clearly had only one thing on their mind, which unfortunately involved mindless violence directed towards anybody who happened to be in the wrong place at the wrong time, which, on this occasion, just happened to be them. Sam had very quickly realised that there was no way they were going to avoid some sort of confrontation, given the hostile and aggressive nature of the interaction and told his band mate to 'leg it with his girlfriend, which he had. Sam then ran in the opposite direction and, of course, they followed him all three of them. He remembered being caught and dragged to the ground as they issued oaths towards him; a complete stranger who had done nothing to them, and 'do him now'. He somehow managed to get a vicious kick and a punch at one of them which only served to enrage them further, eliciting shocked and angry cursing and even more determination to cause him harm. He remembered screaming for help several times in an increasingly desperate and loud voice, unfortunately to no avail, as none arrived. However, it may have been what made them stop either that or they were happy with their night's work. He never felt a thing other than a dampness at the side of his face, which when he touched it with his hand, realised was due to blood flowing from a wound just below his ear.

At that point his band mate and his girlfriend re-appeared, whose shock at his appearance didn't help reassure him about the seriousness of the injury. In the end, they headed back to Blackfriars where the staff called the police and an ambulance before cleaning his face and wound before applying ice to it.

The ambulance arrived quickly and took him to Glasgow Royal Infirmary Accident and Emergency (A& E), where he was stitched up and given due sympathy and reassurance that his injury wasn't too serious in contrast to some others in attendance at A&E on that evening, where, apparently, business was booming, even by their particularly prolific standards. Indeed, the newspapers, local and national, subsequently reported a bumper weekend for violence in the city, with an unprecedented number of violent crimes and totally unprovoked attacks reported against totally innocent victims. It was almost like it had been planned beforehand, abhorrent as it seemed. Strangely, Sam's enduring memories related not to his own predicament but the other sights and scenarios on offer at A& E on that particular night a particularly lifeless and desperately unhappy-looking woman with a black eye and beside her, what appeared to be her equally as unhappy husband, nursing bruised knuckles.

Sam remembered hoping that he had sustained them defending her rather than the unacceptable but perhaps more predictable alternative.

The doctor who had attended to Sam's wound had also drawn his attention to another sorry looking individual, who was seated atop a trolley, obviously severely under the influence of something, to the extent that he had no idea whether it was New York or New Year, with a face leaking blood from multiple, significant lacerations and resembling a map of the Amazon basin. 'Wait till *he* sobers up,' said the medic, which he assumed was possibly meant as some form of reassurance to Sam concerning his own situation. However, as Sam was to discover in the months, and indeed, years to come, the physical scar was the least of Sam's concern, and his ordeal was far from over. The psychological effects were much more pervasive and far reaching and over a period after his ordeal, he became increasingly anxious and fearful of leaving the house, worrying, irrationally, but nevertheless genuinely, about the prospect of a repeat performance. Glasgow city centre became a place to fear, a no-go area, to be avoided at all costs. And it was, for a long time, to his friends, and band mates', annoyance, although generally they were understanding and supportive of his feelings.

Sam had also had to look at police identikit pictures of well-known offenders and recidivists with a history of violence, which, with his "photographic memory", proved to be productive with the police officials looking at each other knowingly at his choices and describing them as a 'real couple of lowlifes.' Whilst the resultant physical and mental scars gradually healed Sam found himself unable to relax for a long time when out, even with others and he studiously avoided secluded and/or dark streets for a long time after, which was probably only common sense anyway in normal circumstances.

If there was any kind of positive outcome to be garnered from such a dreadful situation, it was, strangely enough, that it also resulted in him developing an almost sixth sense regarding any impending danger.

He recalled one evening when he and some friends were walking down Jamaica Street, heading to the Arches when his attention and suspicions were triggered by the behaviour of a dodgy looking individual a short distance ahead of them. Possibly in an attempt to impress his low life cohorts, or the girls they were with, the low life deliberately took a step backwards, with a view to colliding with Sam, to maliciously generate conflict. However, Sam, by virtue of his new 'Spidey Sense', saw it coming a mile away and simply slowed down and walked through the gap in front of the reprobate. It was a move Lionel Messi would have been proud of and the look of bewilderment on the face of his would-be assailant was priceless. But Sam didn't look back and just kept on walking, whilst telling his friends to do the same, which they did, sensing the earnest and serious nature of his demeanour and words. As the years passed, thankfully there were no further such episodes to contend with, but really his concern was not for himself, but his kids growing up.

As a result of his experiences, Sam found himself pondering the notion that there was similarities in the pathology of people who carry out contract kills and those that perpetrate casual acts of violence, even if the motivation which fuels them is quite different; whilst one is a means to an end and a professional occupation the other is a mindless act borne of deep unhappiness and a damaged psyche. And he didn't believe that there was any reasoning with either.

As he sat there reflecting upon recent events leading up to Emily's fatal shooting, he realised that he would never get to hear her explanation for her meeting with the tall dark stranger that day, when he had also seen her with Akmal and then followed her. Then he suddenly had the craziest and most unexpected thought, which he tried but failed miserably to stifle or ignore; *were they both involved in conspiring to kill me? Is that why they were meeting in secret? Was she supposed to set me up and then it all went pear shaped and he ended up killing her instead of me? Is that what happened?* Sam asked himself, gradually becoming more and more agitated.

Was the meeting and the lunch on the balcony just a set up? Had she arranged it for the sole purpose of him being killed by the guy she had met? The more he thought about it, the more reasonable it seemed, *It's the ideal situation,* thought Sam, but then, at the same time told himself that he was crazy to be even thinking that way; that he had no reason to suspect Emily of anything like that. I'm overreacting because of the emotional effect of her death is all, he told himself, trying to be rational. And she had made it clear on the phone that whatever it was that she couldn't tell him before, she was going to tell him when they met up. 'Or was that also part of the bait and the plan?' he heard himself say out loud and realised that he didn't know what to believe any more.

Chapter 67

28 January 2021
Sunday

Max Holland was sitting in his hotel room, trying to come to terms with the unexpected and tragic recent events, but not quite managing it. Despite being battle-hardened from having been involved in everything from terrorism to contract killing in the course of his undercover work, he was finding it extremely difficult to accept and process his colleague's brutal and sudden end. Whilst he realised and rationalised that nothing could have prepared him for such a terrible event, he couldn't remember having felt as affected by anything for a very long time. But that wasn't his only emotion, he was angry−very angry, enough to want to do something about it. The reason for his anger related to the fact that he had finally decided to tell her how much he loved her, and in fact had decided to ask her to marry him.

At least that had been his intention before he came to realise- and be completely taken aback by−how much she had become attracted to Sam Meredith in such a short period of time, perhaps even to the extent that it had got her killed. Or was he just looking for another reason, excuse or someone else to put the blame on, rather than accept that if she had not come out of retirement as a favour to him, none of it would have happened and, more importantly, she would still be alive.

Chapter 68

28 January 2018
Sunday

Farouk had been unable to contact his brother since the last time they spoke, as he wasn't answering his phone, which was either dead or possibly deliberately switched off. He had also contacted his hotel to be told that he no longer worked there, having advised that he needed to go back to Algeria for family reasons. Farouk thanked them for their information whilst smiling ruefully to himself, given that he was Akaml's only remaining family member, both their parents and sister having been killed by a bomb blast in Algiers in 2010 during the period of the 'Arab Spring' conflicts. The woman on the 'phone also informed him that, as Akmal hadn't been unable to say when, or indeed if, he was likely to be back, they had required to fill his post and accordingly had already hired someone else.

Farouk could not believe that his brother would not contact him but nevertheless also found himself thinking, *Surely he was not getting him back for his own previous failure to keep in touch?* particularly given the seriousness of the situation that they now found themselves in.

Akmal sat on the flight to Glasgow, which he had booked following the telephone call from his brother, after realising that unfortunately, his own and Farouk's irresponsible, reckless behaviour had effectively sealed his fate, and it was clearly no longer safe for him to be in Tenerife. He knew that he had to get away as soon as possible before he met the same fate as the person whose death he had brokered in Benidorm. And the more he thought about it the more convinced he was that it was only a matter of time before Farouk met the same fate, given Terry Lindsay's ruthless reputation. He hadn't called his brother from Tenerife as he knew that he could be tracked on Google via his mobile phone number using something called 'dorking', even although, he didn't understand the process and accordingly, how to counteract it. And, as far as he was aware, it was also illegal.

However, he planned to call him as soon as it was safe to do so, having managed to successfully negotiate his escape from the island and from the threat against his life for the time being at least. He didn't think that the powers that be would ever think that he would head to Glasgow, and he really didn't want them to find out.

He had told his employers at the hotel that it was his intention to head back to Algeria, and he planned to do just that, but not quite yet. He was full of anger and resentment, but he was also completely focused and determined to be proactive and take the initiative, rather than just sit back and wait to be found and then ruthlessly taken out. So instead, he had decided to get his retaliation in first with a pre-emptive strike that nobody would be expecting.

But he had also finally learned from his experience and mistakes of the past, and he had no intention of behaving reactively and going off half cocked, without thinking things through. No, this time he had a plan. And to carry it out, he needed to go to Glasgow to meet up with his brother to make the necessary arrangements. It was also a much more agreeable and pleasant route back to Algeria that way.

Chapter 69

29 January 2018

Monday Sam had a disturbed sleep but still slept until nine a.m., when he woke up to another hot, sunny day and decided that he would head down to breakfast. On arriving at the dining room and advising, when asked, that he was on his own, he was ushered to a small table with two chairs by one of the hotel staff, who asked if he wanted coffee or tea and then headed off to fetch Sam's choice. Sam then went to the breakfast buffet selection to fetch some cereal, toast and orange juice. However, when he returned to his table, there was a couple sitting at it, who did not respond very kindly to his assertion that he had been sitting there, with the woman becoming very hostile and belligerent, saying that they 'were there first' and the table was empty when they arrived. *Jesus, what is it with people and other people's seats in this bloody place,* thought Sam. Sam tried to explain that he had been placed there by a member of staff before leaving to collect his breakfast, which he proffered as evidence.

However, neither she nor her husband were having any of it, until, thankfully, the member of staff arrived with Sam's pot of tea and confirmed that he had indeed placed him at that table. However, this only served to make the woman even more hostile, initially refusing to move and then asking to speak to someone else to make a complaint, before her husband managed to be the voice of reason, telling her 'There are plenty of other tables,' and eventually convincing her to move. However she was clearly very angry at having being proved wrong and losing face and demonstrated this by issuing a stream of insults at Sam, who stayed very calm and simply replied by saying 'As my granny used to say, there's no point in being ignorant if you can't show it', which infuriated her even more, turning to her husband and asking, ' Are you going to let him speak to me like that?', which he did, shaking his head as he moved his irate spouse away.

Good start to the day, thought Sam. *It can only get better.*

Unfortunately, despite his optimism, his prediction proved to be just that, as on arriving back in the room and lying down on the bed to rest his head, he was startled by the hotel phone ringing loudly and persistently. He spontaneously lunged at it, nearly knocking it over in his clumsy, grasping attempt to secure it and managed to recover in time before it stopped ringing 'Hello' he said, still quite drowsy.

'Hello, Senor Meredith,' said the voice on the other end of the line.

'Inspector Delgado?' asked Sam, somewhat hesitantly and uncertain, due to still feeling tired, but it was indeed the Spanish official, who advised him that he and his colleague Inspector Herrera were in an office downstairs and that they; 'Would be grateful if you could join us.' Which Sam eventually did, after a shower *I've been here before*, he thought and accordingly decided that this time he would do things when he was good and ready and not in a state of panic or distress.

However, if truth be told, he had probably still not recovered from the shock and trauma of the previous day's events, and he was also feeling angry but wasn't quite sure why or who at.

On arriving at the room, Sam was welcomed and advised that he was not under caution and that he was being interviewed informally and asked if there was anything he required, to which he replied, in quite an annoyed and irritable tone and manner that he would like a pot of tea, which was duly provided. Sam drank his tea as the police interviewed him, questioning him about everything that had happened since his arrival in Tenerife; his involvement with Jill and Emily and the events and circumstances leading up to her dramatic death on the balcony, which Sam found very difficult and emotional. The police then informed him that the assassin had managed to evade being apprehended and they suspected that he had probably left the country using false documents. They had also found the rifle he had used to kill Emily, which had been abandoned at the scene, presumably having outlived its usefulness, if not its purpose. However, the sniper had clearly worn gloves as there were no prints on the rifle or anything else in the room that he had used as the vantage point for that very same purpose.

There were, however, traces of DNA found on a carelessly discarded cigar butt on the floor beside the rifle, which confirmed his identity, -information not released to the press or public, for political and security reasons, given his background and connections to the various factions involved from police to other perpetrators. The officials also informed him that after a forensic examination of the crime scene and discussion with Sam himself, the assessment being offered by the 'boffins' was that Emily's death was due to an unbelievable combination of circumstances, coincidence (again) and incredible synchronicity.

When Sam reacted to the pain in his mouth spontaneously, initially by jerking and then bending down to pick up what remained of his broken tooth, Emily had stood up at almost the same time to pour him a drink, resulting in the bullet that had been meant for him hitting her and ending her life in such twisted and shocking circumstances.

'This gunman is either one of the most incompetent or unluckiest assassins on the planet, fortunately for you Senor Meredith' said Inspector Delgado. 'But you Senor Meredith must be one of the luckiest or most charmed people alive', offered Inspector Herrera, and then smiling added, 'Somebody up there definitely likes you,' added Inspector Herrera.

But it didn't feel like that for Sam, 'You think so,really? So why don't I feel lucky?' he replied. It seems that every time I meet somebody I like, something terrible happens to them. It's like I'm being punished'.

'So, what have you done that you need to be punished for Senor Meredith,' asked Inspector Herrera, looking at Sam and holding his gaze. Sam didn't reply and avoided eye contact with both officers, hoping that he didn't look guilty.

'Being around you certainly seems to be a dangerous pastime Senor Meredith,' said Inspector Herrera. Sam didn't respond,

There's no point, he thought, *she's already made her mind up about me and she's just trying to get a reaction. Or maybe even a confession. Well, that's not going to happen.* And then he thought, *oh fuck it, I'm fed-up dancing around a flame* and decided to confront and challenge her the way that he had done with his twisted ex colleague. 'Look if there's something bothering you that you need to get off your chest now would be a good time to do it *Senora'* he said, deliberately not referring to her by her rank.'

'What do you mean,' Senor Meredith?'

'I mean that I am fed up with your insinuations and your snide comments, why don't you stop pissing about and just get to the point of whatever it is?'

'I don't know what you mean,' said the official,

'Really?' said Sam, 'Well in that case, Inspector Herrera, can we just give it a break with the uncalled for, sarcastic comments, unless you're prepared to put your conviction where your rather big mouth is?'

If looks could kill, the one he got from Inspector Herrerra was the equivalent of a dagger to the heart.

However, she said nothing, simply looking to her colleague for support, who managed a nervous smile, whilst attempting to diffuse the situation and to reason with Sam 'Look, I'm sure my colleague didn't mean anything Mr Meredith...'

The official was interrupted by a knock on the door, which was opened by the policeman standing next to it, allowing another man to enter. He was tall, dark, and slim, with an impressive suntan and he held himself with an air of confidence and authority. He also looked familiar to Sam, but initially he could not place him, but watched as he was greeted by both Inspector Delgado and Herrera.

At first, he thought that it was possibly the man he had seen smoking the cigar when he was out with Emily and then subsequently when watching football at Leonardo's. But as he watched him, he suddenly realised *exactly* who he was and involuntarily exclaimed, 'You're the person that I saw having coffee with Emily the day that she told me she was going shopping; the same day that I saw her talking to that little shit Akmal'. And then, unable to control himself and his emotions, he launched into a tirade. 'You were both involved in trying to kill me, weren't you?' That's why you were meeting in secret wasn't it?' She was supposed to set me up, but you killed her instead of me? That's what happened isn't it?' asked Sam, becoming more and more animated and almost hysterical, whilst moving towards him threateningly and asking, 'Who the fuck *are* you?'

'Sam this is Detective Inspector Holland from Scotland,' said Inspector Delgado, at the same time moving between them and attempting to calm Sam down.

I think that maybe you are still in shock Senor Meredith. 'Detective Inspector Holland is... was... a colleague of Senora Stafford,' said Inspector Herrera.

'Who?' asked Sam, of no one and looking even more confused.

'You knew her as Emily,' said Inspector Holland, holding his hand out towards Sam for him to shake and saying; 'Pleased to meet you Sam, I'm Max. And we weren't trying to kill you we were trying to protect you,' Sam however failed to offer his hand in return and Max, realising that he seemed totally disorientated, motioned for him to sit down, which he did.

'Would you like some water? Senor Meredith asked Inspector Herrera, to Sam's surprise and he nodded his assent, realising that his mouth was as dry as a brick. A bottle of water arrived and was passed by Inspector Herrera to Max, who opened it and handed it to Sam and then sat down opposite him, and waited until he had sated his thirst, before telling him, 'Emily is... sorry was... an undercover agent, like me Sam, who has... had... been shadowing you, along with myself, to keep you safe.

I had also been keeping an eye on you both, from a safe distance, as well as the person who had been hired to kill you, and me, as it happens.'

Sam, who looked as if he had suddenly woken up from a bad dream, looked at Max, askance and disbelieving, as the reality of the situation dawned on him, and said, 'So, what are you saying? That all that stuff she told me about her husband being married

252

to another woman was just nonsense? All lies? How could she do that? I believed all that shit, I felt sorry for her, I... Why would she...'

'It was a cover story Sam,' said Max, slightly surprised and not particularly welcoming or appreciating the extent of Sam's ire.

'Designed to get your sympathy and trust so that you become close and form a relationship quickly. Every undercover officer needs one that they must believe in if they are to convince anyone else. And she was particularly good at that part of the job, as you have obviously discovered. She thought that she had overdone it and had possibly pushed you away. Then she started to feel bad about deceiving you, which is not supposed to happen, but she really became very fond of you Sam, I mean she really liked you; she told me that she...

'Aye right, I'm sure, she did. I suppose that was just part of the plan as well, was it? All in a day's work for the lovely Emily, if that is even her real name.

As he said it, the expression on Max's face changed, and Sam realised that that was in fact the case 'You're fucking kidding me, right?' he said, looking at Max, who looked as if he was deliberating over whether to tell him more before eventually sighing resignedly and saying, 'Her real name is... sorry *was*... Lucy... Lucy Stafford, and she is... *was* a widow, he said cursing again under his breath.

He continued, 'Her husband died over twenty years ago. She never remarried and didn't have a family, instead throwing herself into her work before being recruited for undercover work which she did, very successfully, for over fifteen years. We worked together on quite a few occasions and became close friends – just friends and confidantes that's all,' said Max, seeing

253

the question in Sam's eyes and wanting to tell him, that he had loved her. But he didn't.

'She eventually retired about five years ago,' he continued. 'However, I needed a partner for this job, someone that I could trust and depend upon. Initially she wasn't interested, said that she was done with all the covert, undercover stuff and enjoyed being retired.'

'So why did she decide to do it. Did you threaten her, or do you have something over her?'

'What? no, no nothing like that,' said Max, aghast, his response making Sam clearly aware that he was angry at him for suggesting such a thing. However, he held himself in check and said, 'We were friends. I just asked for her help, as a friend and a valued agent, who is... *was*... reliable and very good at her job.'

'Oh, she certainly is,' said Sam, without bothering to correct the tense. 'She fooled me all right. I fell for the 'poor me,' stuff, hook, line and sinker, fucking idiot that I am.'

'Sam it was a job, just like yours,' said Inspector Holland.

'Aye right so it is, my arse. It's fuck all like my job, and a lot of other normal people's jobs too, apart from maybe eminent thespians, because that was an Oscar winning performance.'

'I mean that she was just doing her job Sam, and doing it bloody well too, hence your annoyance at being taken in by her professionalism,' said Max pointedly whilst at the same time knowing that Sam was right about their job not being remotely like ordinary peoples.'

'Is that what it was Max, eh, business as usual?' said Sam, using his first name for the first time, but not in a respectful way.

'Normally, yes it would've been, but she really liked you. She told me. That's why she couldn't sleep with you the first time, because…

'You know about that? she told you? asked Sam, surprised,

'Oh, for Christ's sake Sam, wake up, of course, she did, we're… fuck sorry… again… *were*… partners,' said Max, becoming increasingly annoyed with himself for his repeated use of the present tense and increasingly annoyed at Sam, for making him confront the unpleasant and uncomfortable truth of the situation. 'We must tell each other everything to do our job and to help each other stay… safe…' before realising what he had just said and becoming quite affected by it.

'Except that didn't quite work out that way, did it?' said Sam, and then seemed to grudgingly acknowledge Max's apparent emotional difficulty and eased off a little, before recalling his original statement and then asking, 'So why couldn't she have sex with me the first time? It was her who initiated it.'

'She felt bad about it happening in the context of an undercover investigation; like it was part of the 'job', because she liked you and she didn't want to have sex with you under those circumstances. She realised that it meant more to her than that and she was worried about how you would view her if… sorry… *when,* you found out the truth, as was her intention-ideally when it was all over and done with,' he said sheepishly and almost apologetically. 'So, she decided to use the cover story to get her out of the situation. Remember she had been inactive for some considerable period of time, so she was probably finding it difficult to adjust, to get back into the zone.

'Then, as she got to know more about you, she realised that she wanted to be intimate with you. And that's probably what got her killed.'

'What? What do you mean? Are you saying that it was my fault that she died? That I got her killed?'

'No, no, I'm not saying that at all Sam, and then, as if realising that he needed to say it out loud, replied, 'That's probably down to me, because if I hadn't used our friendship to get her to help me, she would be alive today. He then paused before adding, very emotionally.' 'Some friend I turned out to be, eh? She trusted me with hers. And now she's dead.'

'And it could've... should've been me that was killed,' said Sam, experiencing a mixture of anger and sadness.

'Well, yes, unfortunately you're probably right about that, but it's also the case that neither of you would have been at risk if she had told me that she was planning on meeting you as I would've had both your backs or I would've talked her out of it altogether, due to viewing it as unprofessional, which it was.'

And that is probably why she never told me, because she obviously wanted to keep it separate from the professional side of things. She obviously wanted to see you, probably to tell you everything, most likely because it was troubling her and causing her some level of emotional difficulty.

Sam's mind was racing all over the place but for some reason his gut reaction to the information he had just been given was to say;

'How do you know for sure that you could have prevented it'? What if he had managed to evade your surveillance and protection?'

'That was a chance we had to take,' countered Max.

'With *my* life, very brave of you both,' said Sam angrily.

'You had a much better chance of staying alive with us in your corner,' Max replied, attempting to reason with Sam.

'So why do I feel used?' asked Sam, still quite irate.'

'Sam, I'm going to tell you something and it's up to you whether you believe me or not, but it's true,' said Max, quite beseechingly. 'The only reason that she decided to help me was because as well as taking Lasenko out she was also helping to save two other people's lives; yours and mine. In fact, the main thing that appealed to her was stopping him from killing a totally unsuspecting and, as far as she was concerned, innocent person, in this case you, he said. 'That was her main motivation.'

But Sam still wasn't having it, 'That's bollocks, you set me up as bait so that you could keep track of Lasenko's whereabouts, and then take him out before he took you out, because you knew he had been hired to kill me. But it was your own skin that you were trying to save, not mine. You admitted that he had a contract on you too'.

'That's right he did, but I... we... we were also genuinely trying to protect you. Yes, we could just have used you to draw him out into the open until the opportunity arose to take him out, either before or after he had completed your contract. So, would you rather we had done that and just treated you as collateral damage?

'No, of course, not, that would mean that you would have been a... what is it? an accessory before the fact... like...

'Like Benidorm Sam is that what you mean? said Max,

'What?' said Sam, really taken aback initially, before recovering and then adding, 'No that isn't what I meant, and don't *you* fucking start with the insinuations now, if there's something you want to say to me just fucking say it... well is there ?' he added, not waiting for or receiving a response.

Max said nothing, whilst fixing Sam with a knowing look, before then continuing to explain, 'Sam, Lucy... Emily's job was to try and keep you as safe as possible, and to keep in touch with me because I had to keep a low profile as the assassin would have recognised me. She was also trying to keep you away from Jill'.

'Jill? Why? asked Sam, trying to look surprised but more or less convinced that his initial reservations were going to be vindicated. Max advised him that he knew that he had 'spent some time with her' with a wry smile. He then informed him that she had a long history of involvement in all kinds of crime, before providing Sam with some of the gory details of her lurid past. 'They also both have links to gangland contacts in Glasgow and the north of England, so we naturally suspected that she might have been involved in working with him and trying to set you up in some way. And we were right'.

Sam started to tell Max about the chambermaid, but he informed him that he already knew about it via Police intelligence, then adding that they believed Jill to be part of a contingency plan, following the chambermaid's failure to convince the police of his guilt.

'She is quite a girl; they both are to be honest; you did well to survive their attentions.' Sam responded with a very unconvincing smile, being all too conscious of his weakness and eventual compliance in succumbing to Jill's charms and seduction.

'But if she was supposed to carry out what the Chambermaid failed to then, why didn't she? he asked the undercover cop, who replied;

'We don't know that yet, but maybe something happened to change her mind or maybe she was given new orders because of what happened to the chambermaid; maybe it was considered to be too risky.

'We can't be sure until we interview her. And we might need you to stick around for a day or two more, depending on how things pan out,' said Inspector Holland, adding 'Don't worry, we'll take care of everything,' which brought back familiar and unsettling memories for Sam, which he tried to ignore, unsuccessfully. However, he managed to remain focused in the present, saying, 'And what about Emily... or I should say Lucy.'

'She's dead Sam,' said Max, and finding it hard to find any more words or in truth to speak, he placed his hand gently on Sam's shoulder in a sympathetic and supportive manner.

Sam neither acknowledged nor reacted to the gesture, instead simply saying; 'So what are you going to do about it?' in a very calm but forceful tone, which clearly expected a response. And it got one.

'I'm going to track her murderer down and kill him,' said Max, having recovered his composure, and then continuing, 'As I said before, I think he's probably not on the island any longer, as he'll have made his escape after what happened, because different people will be looking for him now, so he will want to lie low. But he won't give up, that's for sure, because he needs to try and save face and fix the mess he made. So, we need to find him and kill him before he kills you, me or anybody else'.

'I thought that you were supposed to arrest criminals and bring them to justice by prosecuting them via the Courts?' asked Sam.

'Too late for that,' said Max, pushing past him and leaving the room with a look of grim determination on his face.

Chapter 71

29 January 2018
Monday

It had been a long day and a lot had been said, which Sam needed time to consider and make sense of, so after taking his leave of the Scottish and Spanish officials, he headed back to his room to finish packing for his journey home the following day, which took him no time at all, with only the little, last minute things left to do, which he resolved to do later or in the morning. And so, finding himself with some time on his hands on what was a bright and warm evening, he made the decision to go for a walk along El Camison beach to clear his head which he found very relaxing and therapeutic, in that it helped to clear his head from the thoughts which had been troubling him. So, feeling more settled, he decided to keep walking, arriving at Las Americas beach and stopping for a beer at the same bar where he had met Emily, or Lucy, in what seemed like an age ago.

He shook his head disbelievingly as he reflected on how natural and spontaneous it had seemed at the time, when in fact, as he now knew, it had been all totally pre-meditated and contrived.

Also, if the policeman, Max, was to be believed, it was also all part of a clear and planned strategy designed to keep him safe from the killer, who had, allegedly and tragically taken Emily's life. Sam wanted to believe him, and he certainly had a persuasive and convincing argument however, he also thought that he had probably been in love with her, although he didn't seem to be keen to admit to it. Was it because of what had happened between him and Emily? he wondered, and then also whether that affected how the cop felt about him and if he should be concerned. After all, this guy had worked undercover as a hit man, and had openly expressed his intention to kill the man who had ended Emily's life, solely to take his revenge.

Sam headed back to his hotel to get changed and do his final packing and feeling confident that the hired assassin was no longer a threat, given Max's reassurance that he had probably left the country, he headed out to find somewhere for food. But first he needed to find Akmal, with the intention of getting more information from him about the recent developments, by whatever means necessary. He suddenly noticed that lights were starting to come on and realised that nighttime had arrived unannounced with singularly impressive stealth, in almost clandestine fashion, like a slow, creeping twilight wraith. Sam was interested to discover that Akmal, interestingly, was not at his usual post, with there being another man there in his place, also appearing to be of North African origin. However, he was also considerably larger and much fiercer looking than Akmal, and accordingly, Sam decided that he wouldn't run the risk of arousing his suspicion or ire by asking him questions about his absent colleague.

He also decided that there was nothing to be gained by making enquiries at Emily/Lucy's hotel, given recent events. And, it was also likely, he thought that the police would already have checked, not that they would have told him if they knew anything about his whereabouts, given that they were actively trying to discourage him from interfering any further in proceedings. So, after some very brief deliberation, he ended up having a drink at Harry's Bar before deciding that he would head across to the little Chinese behind the Safari Centre for food again and then watch Celtic's game against Hearts of Midlothian at Brahms and Liszt, one of the pubs nearby. And then, depending on the outcome of the match, he might just finish the night off with a few drinks in the Bull's Head. However, he resolved not to stay too late, as he had to be up early for his flight home the next day. As it turned out his team won 3-0, so he decided to do stick to his plan and accordingly headed off to listen to some live music.

The place wasn't that busy, and he was able to have his favourite seat at the bar whilst he was also delighted to find out that it was the band he liked best on stage. He ordered a beer, and settled in his seat, enjoying the band and the ambience in the room, which was gradually getting busier as the night unfolded thinking that things had picked up after such a difficult day. However, after his second beer, Sam's prostrate was playing up and he needed to go to the toilet, so he politely asked the barman if he could keep a watch on his seat and his beer, which he put a coaster over, as per usual, whatever that was supposed to achieve. Unfortunately, on returning, he found that there was someone sitting on his seat. And, unbelievably, on further inspection, it turned out to be the woman that he had had the run in with at breakfast in the hotel dining room at the hotel on the previous day. However, he remained calm and composed and approached her and her husband who was standing next to her and quietly said, 'Well, fancy meeting you again and I think you'll find that that is my seat again.'

Is this a particular hobby of yours, or is it just me that you've got it in for? She just looked at him astonished and said defiantly,

'I don't believe this, are you seriously claiming that this is your seat? I suppose it has your name on it as well, does it?' she said with a flourish and looking to her husband for support, who said nothing.

Sam just smiled and said, 'Sorry you're right, I apologise, what I should have said was 'I think you'll find that I was sitting there before I went to the toilet and pointing to the pint on the bar,' added 'and that is definitely *my* pint there with the coaster on it.'

And then, unfortunately for her, the barman then appeared and confirmed that Sam had indeed been sitting there before going to the toilet, that it was indeed his drink and that he had asked him to keep an eye on both his drink and the seat. The barman then turned to Sam and by way of explanation and apology said, 'I actually thought it was you she was with because you and her husband look quite alike.'

Sam hadn't really noticed it before, but now that it had been pointed out he supposed that they were similar in appearance and stature. His wife, however, was not in agreement responding angrily with, 'He looks nothing like my husband. And you can't keep seats, it's not allowed,' she repeated clearly unhappy and becoming even more annoyed.'

'I think that is up to pub to decide, don't you?' said Sam, much like the hotel did yesterday,' which only served to inflame her behaviour even more as she tried to slap him while her husband prevented her from doing so. 'I don't like violence of any kind,' said Sam, 'having been subject to it in the past, and I don't hit women, even one's that behaves as badly as you do. I prefer to take a new more radical approach. So, here's the deal for every time you slap me, I 'll slap him,' he said, pointing at her husband, and I can assure you I won't miss, and it'll hurt a

263

whole lot more. Which was pure bravado on his part.

'Are you going to let him speak to me, and you, like that?' she screamed at her husband, which Sam thought was in danger of becoming something of a catchphrase. Her husband however said nothing again. Accordingly, Sam assumed that he was probably used to her speaking to him like that – or worse. *The woman could start a war on her own,* thought Sam, and she was still going. Her husband then asked her to calm down which predictably, as before, just made her worse.

'Listen to your man he's giving you good advice,' said Sam, at which point the barman intervened and stopped her from trying to slap Sam again. She then turned on the barman claiming that Sam had been rude to her and accused her of 'stealing his seat'. 'I mean, who does he think he is? And he threatened my husband'.

'That would be after you tried to assault me,' said Sam, which really sent her into meltdown, resulting in her being told that if she didn't calm down, she would be asked to leave.

Unfortunately, this was a red rag to a bull, causing her to protest her innocence even more vehemently, screaming, 'It should be him that's asked to leave,' pointing at Sam and trying to hit him again. At which point her husband did intervene and got punched by her for his trouble, before the barman ushered both from the premises. She was still screaming as she was exiting -under extreme protest.

'Women, eh, they would get you shot,' said one of the other customers at the bar.

'Yeah, some of them would. But others would take a bullet for you,' said Sam as he headed out the bar, leaving the guy with a perplexed look on his face.

Chapter 72

Ivan Lasenko was born in Drogheda in Northern Ireland, to Lithuanian parents who had moved there from Liverpool, where they had settled on leaving their homeland some years previously. They had moved to Liverpool following them securing hotel work there, which they both had previous experience of in their native Lithuania. Some years later, with a son and a daughter, they made the decision to leave Drogheda along with their two children and head across the Irish Sea to Scotland, following them being successful in securing better-paid employment and conditions, as a joint management team running a hotel in Stranraer. They remained there for several more years before returning to Northern Ireland, again following them being offered more lucrative employment managing a bar/restaurant in Armagh. Tragically, they were both killed by a bomb planted in a nearby supermarket car park in 1989, whilst out shopping together.

Ivan, who had hoped to go to university to study medicine, suddenly abandoned his long-held ambitions in that sphere to apply to the police, citing his wish to give something back to the community which had embraced he and his family all those years ago. The well-mannered and seemingly determined young man impressed his interviewers and was successful in his application. However, had his interviewers probed him more intensely, they may well have taken the view that his motivation was of a much more personal and vindictive nature. Whatever his true reasons were at the time, he subsequently went on to serve as a regular policeman for over fifteen years, achieving the rank of Detective Sergeant, at which time he undertook the necessary training required to facilitate his entry into the shadowy and dangerous world of undercover work. As an undercover police officer, he infiltrated various organisations, including the Troops Out Movement (TOM), which campaigned for the British military to withdraw from Ireland.

During a two-year deployment, Lasenko rose rapidly to a senior position within the TOM before his position ended abruptly following his situation coming under scrutiny and being investigated by activists who suspected that he was an infiltrator. After a public enquiry, the police were criticised for infiltrating "an open, independent, democratic organisation engaged in lawful political activity" and highlighting accusations that undercover police officers had illegally infiltrated UK left wing groups for decades, and that they used these positions of trust to derail legitimate political groups. It was also revealed that the Metropolitan Police were employing people with criminal convictions, including assault, theft and drug possession.

Lasenko was also one of a significant number of undercover officers who had had sexual relationships with women without telling them their true identities, the inquiry commenting that 'The use of sex as a strategy is appalling, and the fact that it carried on throughout the decades is wrong on many levels.'

Lasenko then made the decision to leave the force after what he perceived as a lack of support from his superiors, who, he felt, had hung him out to dry by making him a scapegoat. Since that time, and following him going 'rogue', he has been implicated and/or associated with numerous contract assassinations throughout Britain and Western Europe, travelling freely under several different aliases. He has also evaded all attempts to track him down or arrest him, due mainly to a lack of evidence and the services of eminent criminal solicitors and barristers.

Lasenko's younger sister by only eighteen months, unlike him, was not academically inclined and had ended her education prematurely to the extreme disappointment of her parents, creating conflict and tension between them, which eventually culminated in her leaving the family home. Unfortunately, she then fell in with a bad crowd, becoming involved in petty offending before graduating into more serious criminal behaviour for which she later spent time in Mountjoy prison in Dublin.

Ivan visited his sister there; his previous contact with her having been at their parents' funeral, which she was given prison leave to attend.

Whilst he had hoped to reason with her regarding her behaviour, he found her to be totally unrepentant and determined to continue with her criminal lifestyle on her release, simply stating her determination, "Not to get caught next time". This statement was to prove both prophetic and definitive in terms of how her life would unfold in the future. And his.

Chapter 73

30 January 2018
Tuesday

Jill Gilchrist, when interviewed by Inspectors Delgado, Herrera, and Holland, confirmed all the information which had already been documented, as recorded by Sam's 'wire', whilst also elaborating further and providing extensive and valuable information, being of the view that that there was nothing to be gained by concealing anything anymore. She had also come clean about how she was supposed to seduce and then set Sam up to be accused of rape, whilst also acknowledging the subsequent change of approach following the arrest of the chambermaid and confirming the reasons why. She also claimed that she had been glad about that as she had become attracted to Sam and that it had affected her willingness to carry out the subsequent plan to set him up for the contract killer. However, she also conceded that she was too afraid not to comply for fear of the consequences from the people concerned, who had a well-earned reputation for being ruthless and unforgiving. And with whom she had significant history.

She talked constantly and animatedly without any need for prompting, bombarding them with information and explanations as to how she had originally become involved in a relationship with Lasenko when he was an undercover police officer, at the behest of gangland crime bosses, who were orchestrating a people and drug trafficking operation. She also alleged that after the debacle of the failed undercover operation, he had tracked her down and threatened to expose her involvement in illegal and corrupt practices to the authorities and to let it be known to certain gangland figures that she had been a police informer, which she hadn't, in order to ensure her compliance in subsequent seamy deals, deceptions, and contracts.

As she talked, pouring out endless details of her corrupt and criminal past, Max's thoughts drifted back hesitantly but inexorably to a particular memory, which initially he was having difficulty processing. However, the more he thought about it, the more it gradually came into focus and gained legitimacy, like a photograph being developed. 'It was you who he had the relationship with,' he said, almost disbelievingly.

'All those years ago, it was you,' he said again, looking into her eyes, as if trying to convince himself. And then he said it again 'You were the mysterious woman who sabotaged our undercover operation and then vanished without trace'. He said it almost as a question, looking for her to give it credence, which she subsequently did.

'Yes,' she said, smiling almost apologetically. 'But he made it his mission to find me, which he did surprisingly easily, given his connections, I guess. And he can also be very persuasive,' she said, but this time without any trace of a smile, just a look of sad resignation. I thought initially that he was going to kill me, but instead he just threatened me with exposure and worse, as I said. He said that I could be very useful to him, as he was planning to go into business for himself as a 'contractor', as he called it, as he was doing it anyway as an undercover, cop and it was much better paid. So, I was expected to do his bidding, whenever he needed someone to act as bait, or... whatever else it took' she said haltingly and surprisingly self-consciously. 'I didn't really have any choice…'

'But you didn't only work for him, did you?' asked Max. 'You did jobs for other people as well and this job was initially for someone else wasn't it?' 'What?' she asked, quite surprised and then eventually replying; Well… yes, on his recommendation apparently, and before he himself was asked to become involved, following the original plan not working out as planned. Look I'm not proud of myself, but okay, yes, I admit that I had earned a reputation for that kind of work over the years and when certain people come calling, it's hard to say no, particularly when they make a point of bringing up all your past indiscretions as a matter of course, just to let you know that they know and might just decide to do something about it one day. Or that they might just decide to pay you a visit one night when they decide that you're no longer of any use to them anymore. Or because you know too much'.

'You reap what you sow,' said Max, and then instantly regretted it, saying, 'I'm sorry Miss… I shouldn't have said that. I know what these people are capable of and that you wouldn't have had much choice. It's just that… the officer who was killed was my friend, and I'm still very angry. But I know that I shouldn't be taking it out on you, I know who's to blame. And I will make him pay for that.'

'I hope you do,' said Jill, adding, 'Let me know if I can help you with that'. Max looked at her with a curious expression on his face, seeming to be giving great thought to something, before standing up with great purpose and determination and then leaving the room.

He returned around 12/15 minutes later in a seemingly calmer

270

and more composed frame of mind. 'I have something for you,' he said to Jill, and sitting down at the table beside rather than opposite her.

'For me? What do you mean?' she said, confused and wondering what he meant, asking 'What? What do you have?'

'A proposition, Ms. Gilchrist. A proposition'.

Chapter 74

29 January 2018
Monday

'Why do you want to want to know if the club where I work has a fire escape?' Farouk asked his brother, who had picked him up from Glasgow airport, where he had called him from a public phone. As the car, which he had borrowed from a work colleague, made its way into the city centre in the early hours of the morning, Akmal outlined his plan. Farouk listened intently, initially with disbelief and then with growing interest and enthusiasm for the proposed strategy, which he thought was incredibly perilous and scary. And he couldn't wait to carry it out.

'I think we also need help from other people,' said Akmal.

'It won't be a problem, Bro,' said Farouk. 'He has made many enemies; people he has treated very badly and still he does. They will be happy to have a chance to take revenge against him. I will arrange this, leave it to me'.

***

The 'nightclub' where Farouk worked did indeed have a fire escape, which provided entry/ exit to and from floor above the actual lap dancing area, where the 'executive' or 'private' rooms were located.

Which is where you can, for a fee, spend 'private time' with the girls; normally just over an hour, unless you are 'connected' or a 'VIP', like Terry Lindsay, when you can spend as long as you like and do more or less what you want, no questions asked. Which he had been doing, sometimes three or four times a week, following the recent negotiation of the cessation of hostilities, even although the 'contract' on Akmal had not yet being completed, as agreed.

'He's just a sleazy old pervert' was the view from mostly everybody, and certainly most of the girls at the club. But contrary to popular belief, it wasn't about sex, it was about power, as he could get as much sex as he wanted from his own many and varied, corrupt 'business interests.' No, it was about control; it was about Terry Lindsay laying down a marker and letting it be known that he was still a player—a force to be reckoned with- even if there had been an amnesty agreed, for the time being at least.

And he treated the girls at the club like trash, often making perverted and extreme demands of them, whilst frequently using extreme force and being violent towards them, particularly if they didn't accede to his twisted demands. There was one girl that he had taken a shine to who, had so far resisted his extreme advances and attempts to humiliate and degrade her and unfortunately, had suffered the consequences.

However, he was clever and calculated enough to know not to bruise or damage her where it could be seen, unless she was naked, which then only served to cause her even more shame and humiliation.

Her name was Nalini, and she was from Mauritania, and she was also the girl that Farouk had become close to, whilst also managing to keep that fact under wraps, as he, like his brother,

273

had learned from experience. However, she had confided in Farouk, who, after speaking to his brother, had then contacted her and asked if she wanted to help him with a plan that he and his brother had come up with. Neither Nalini nor any of the other girls had ever made any complaints, as they knew that they wouldn't be taken seriously because of what they did for a living. But the main reason was because it was also well known that Terry Lindsay had well-established connections, and influence within the police. So, she and the many others were only too happy to seek justice via any other avenue which presented itself, particularly if it allowed them to exact their revenge on the disgusting lowlife, whatever that required and entailed. So, perhaps unsurprisingly, her response to Farouk's request was, 'When do we start?'

Chapter 75

30 January 2018
Tuesday

Terry Lindsay had contacted the nightclub to ask if Nalini was on 'duty' at the club, and on being advised accordingly, he indicated it was his intention to visit and that he expected to have her 'company'. Nalini, on being advised of this openly expressed her disgust and unhappiness to the other girls, even threatening to leave on the pretext of being ill, but ultimately agreeing that it was not advisable, given the circumstances. What she also did was to speak to Farouk, who was also on duty at the club, who then alerted his brother to the situation.

On arriving at the club, Terry Lindsay spent relatively little time indulging in small talk before asking for drinks to be brought to one of the rooms upstairs for himself and Nalini, who had joined him at the bar. She then advised him that she would head up to the room to prepare herself for him, which met with his approval.

However, prior to entering the room, she also opened the door leading to the fire escape, allowing Akmal to enter the premises unseen.

Whilst Nalini then went to the room to wait for Lindsay, Akmal was given access to another room where he changed clothes into the club 'uniform' and then remained there until Farouk arrived to give him the tray of drinks ordered by Lindsay.

When Lindsay entered the room, Nalini, who was still in the bathroom, shouted through to him to ask him to ask him to call the bar to ask if someone could bring her up a 'sanitary kit' from there, as there wasn't one in the bathroom. Whilst initially he was resistant, mumbling something about 'fucking stupid women and where are the fucking drinks we ordered?' under his breath, he reluctantly picked up the phone. At which point Nalini rang Akmal's mobile from hers, which buzzed quietly and was his queue to make his entrance, which he did, politely knocking first before announcing, 'Your drinks order sir'.

After making the call, Lindsay responded to Akmal, with 'About fucking time, what the fuck took you? Put it on the table and fuck off'. And then, looking at him and mistaking him for Farouk, which was what they had hoped and planned for, he said, 'Well look who it is, it's the whistle blower, or should that be,' Deep Throat' and I don't mean the film, you fucking moron. 'And talking about morons, how's your crazy brother by the way?' Which is when Nalini chose to emerge from the bathroom half naked, and saying, 'You won't believe it, but I found a pack in the bathroom, it was there all the time, sorry I'm an idiot,' she said smiling goofily.

'For fuck's sake, put some clothes on,' said Lindsay, gesturing towards Akmal, and walking towards her and pushing her back into the bathroom. 'And you fuck off,' he said over his shoulder to him.

At which point, he heard Akmal reply, 'No, you fuck of you pig. And I'm fine, and unlike your brother, I am still very much alive'.

'What the fuck did you...' was all Terry Lindsay managed to utter before he was smashed into oblivion by a blow to the head with a heavy cosh. Nalini just stood and stared at Terry

Lindsay's body lying on the floor, before kicking and then spitting on him.

'Help me carry him to the fire escape,' said Akmal, which she did, after they had checked that the coast was clear. Akmal then opened the door, dragged him outside and then spat on him too, before checking again that the street was clear and then kicking him off the fire escape. Akmal then descended the fire escape in more orthodox fashion and checked if he was still breathing, which he was. So, he covered his mouth with his hand until he wasn't any more saying, 'From one brother to another.' I hope you rot in hell you bastard', before checking once more that he was on his way there.

Chapter 76

Max had not initially been aware of Sam's alleged involvement in the brokering of the contract in Benidorm, although he was subsequently made party to that information and much more, which revealed and clarified the bigger picture, including the recently reported involvement of the Algerian "low life pimp" known as Akmal, if that was indeed his real name. Whatever it was, the authorities in Benidorm still wanted to question him regarding his knowledge of or whatever part he may have played in the situation. But that was their problem and no concern of his; he was more concerned with the here and now and the immediate threat to both himself and Sam. On being made aware of the contracts issued by Terry Lindsay on both him and Sam, Max also wasn't initially aware of Akmal's brother Farouk's link to the Glasgow underworld, however this information was acquired sometime later, via his contacts in the Glasgow criminal fraternity and another source within the police.

He *was* aware however that his colleagues in both the Vice and Serious Crimes Department had been trying to convict Terry Lindsay and some of his partners in crime for some time with no success, other than those convicted of arson several years earlier.

What Max wanted, more than anything, other than to take revenge and retribution against Lasenko for the murder of his beloved friend and colleague, was to obtain convictions against the bosses and ringleaders who were responsible for the illegal trafficking of people and drugs. And for them to get the lengthy prison sentences they deserved for ruining peoples' lives, either through the drugs that they peddled or by forcing them into a life of slavery and degradation. Lasenko was a different matter altogether however- as far as Max was concerned the only acceptable outcome of that matter was '*quid pro quo*'- a life for a life. But before he could take care of that piece of business, he needed to have another conversation with Sam Meredith.

Chapter 77

31 January 2018
Wednesday

Sam's flight home was due to leave at eleven twenty a.m., and he had set his alarm for seven thirty a.m., as he was being picked up at nine a.m. from outside his hotel. He had just showered and dressed when his doorbell rang, and on expecting it would be the maid, he searched for some Euros to give her as a tip. However, on answering it, he was met with Inspectors Delgado and Herrera offering to give him a lift to the airport. Just as a precaution, he didn't know whether to feel intimidated or reassured. He was also informed that there would be a police presence on the flight with both Inspectors wishing him a safe journey and advising him that someone would be in touch on his return home regarding his future security and wellbeing. Clearly, the view being taken was that he was still very much in danger of further attempts on his life. And now he also knew who from, and he wasn't referring to the assassin.

He was also conscious, however, that Max – sorry Inspector Holland (acknowledging that they weren't exactly best pals) – was nowhere to be seen. And then he thought, *why would he be? more than likely, he had more reasons than anyone to want to avoid me, he was probably glad to see the back of me'.*

However, at the same time, something told Sam that he had definitely not seen the last of his fellow countryman, and he didn't know how right he was, because after arriving downstairs and completing his check out Max Holland arrived beside him, lifted his case and told him that he would be accompanying him to the airport, as there were things he needed to tell him, and he did just that, as they made their way to the airport seated together in the back of the chauffeur-driven unmarked police vehicle, as Sam listened incredulously as the unbelievable details were disclosed to him.

On arriving at the airport, Sam saw, with some disbelief that the argumentative woman and her husband from the hotel and pub were also arriving at the terminal. 'God, no, please don't let them be on my flight,' said Sam out loud,' and definitely not in my seat'. On seeing Max's puzzled expression, Sam explained the reason for his reaction to him, at which Max smiled saying, 'That's the couple who were in your old room at the Med Palace, Sam. That's the man who was nearly killed and his wife who saved him,' said Max. 'They were also moved to the Mark Anthony after the incident as a gesture of apology and part compensation for the upset and trauma they suffered.'

Maybe there really is such a thing as coincidence, Sam thought to himself. Then he remembered a line from a novel which he had read some years before, *Coincidences are the scars of fate,* which he always thought sounded profound. The book in question was *The Shadow of the Wind* by the wonderful Spanish author, Carlos Ruiz Zafon, which was one of Kim's favourite novels.

However, if he was being honest, he didn't really understand it what it meant.

His attention was drawn back to the couple by hearing the woman shouting at and remonstrating loudly with her husband for whatever she considered that he had done to deserve it. As he watched, he recollected their eventful and dramatic time on the island and he heard himself spontaneously say out loud to no one in particular, 'No wonder she's so pissed off and bad tempered, and no wonder he puts up with her; she saved his bloody life. And thank God she didn't know who I was, or she would have done the assassin's job for him,' before involuntarily bursting out laughing, which caused Max to do the same.

'First time I've seen you laugh.' said Max, and hopefully not the last.'

'Hopefully, but I can't help thinking that's probably going to be more down to you than me,' said Sam, looking at him knowingly.

'I'll do my best Sam,' said Max, shaking his hand.

'I believe you will,' said Sam, saying his farewell, whilst also thanking him for the information and his honesty. However, despite the reassurances from Max and Tenerife's finest and his belief in their ability to offer him the necessary protection on the way home, he found himself casting nervous, furtive glances all around him, half expecting to see his would be executioner emerge from the throng of innocent holidaymakers − all of them oblivious to the potential threat to their blissful holiday experience − to finally fulfil his contract obligation.

Thankfully, however, there was no sign of such a dramatic scenario unfolding, at least to his uneducated eyes, and, he also hoped, to those of his more experienced and professional protector(s), whoever and wherever they were.

On boarding the plane and taking his seat, Sam was reassured to find that he was not seated beside the unfortunate couple from the hotel/pub and that he had the whole row to himself, in fact they were nowhere to be seen. Must be on another flight, he thought, most probably to Edinburgh—not that he had anything against the capital city or its inhabitants.

However, he found himself scanning the cabin and the passengers for anyone that looked like a policeman or an assassin, but abandoning it as pointless, particularly regarding the latter, realising that given his recent experience, they could very well be one and the same.

After he had put his case up in the overhead locker, he buckled up his seatbelt and tried to relax, opening his kindle, with the intention being to finally finish reading one of the books he had taken with him on holiday and hardly glanced at. However, he found that he was preoccupied with thoughts about the information given to him by Max Holland, particularly about Emily. The undercover cop had told him that he had known her for over ten years, when they had first worked on a job together, and then had done so many times after that, following her becoming more involved in undercover work on a regular basis. They had always got on well together from the very start, and he had supported her following her suffering tragedy in her personal life, when they had become even closer.

However, he claimed they had never been intimate or romantically involved with one another, which was true. He wasn't sure why, but it certainly wasn't because he hadn't found her attractive because he had and still did, but he had just never found the right time or opportunity. He had speculated further that it was possibly because he didn't want to ruin the positive working and personal working relationships that they had, or maybe it was because they respected each other too much; at least he hoped that she respected him as much as he did her. He advised Sam that he had trusted her more than anyone he had ever worked with in all his years working undercover, and she had trusted him equally, not judging him when he had had to agree to kill someone to protect his identity and that of others. He explained to Sam that he had been working on an undercover job for almost nine months, attempting to infiltrate a sex trafficking ring moving girls from Africa and Asia to various resorts in Spain, when he was given the job of carrying out a contract on someone in Benidorm.

He knew who the person was from his time working in Glasgow, and he also knew that he would be no great loss to the world, being involved in everything from drugs and prostitution to people and sex trafficking. However, he also knew that it did not justify killing him instead of bringing him to justice via the recognised processes of the Criminal Justice System. Unfortunately, he didn't have a choice - it was either him or Max- and he also knew that he was going to have to go ahead with it if he was to protect his and other agents' identities and all the work that had gone into the undercover operation over a long period of time.

So, he accepted the job – with the knowledge and blessings of his superiors – and whilst several convictions were subsequently obtained regarding the various criminal trafficking rings, they were again replaced by other equally as ruthless, morally corrupt criminals within a very short period.

When he had told his colleague about his dilemma and subsequent decision, she hadn't judged him and had been sympathetic to his plight, saying that she "understood that under the circumstances he had had no other choice," and that she would have done the same in his shoes. She had made him feel so much better about himself, and accordingly, he had never found her more attractive. And in that moment, he had wanted her like never before; and yet again, he had done nothing about it, and still, he had no regrets that they had not eventually become involved romantically or sexually, instead believing that it was simply not meant to be and being glad that they had remained very close friends.

However, he had informed Sam that he had never stopped loving her, and as they had remained in contact, he still got to see her regularly. Unfortunately, every time he saw her, his feelings just grew stronger, and he realised that he was eventually going to have to tell her how he felt.

Sam wasn't surprised to hear Max say that he loved her, as he had suspected as much. However, he *was* really taken aback to hear him – say that he had in fact decided that he was going to ask her to marry him – whatever the outcome – saying that he just needed to get it out of his system.

However, the real shocking revelation was that, as he listened to Max describing the events from their past something had gradually dawned on him, which Max sensed in his demeanour, and in response to this and Sam's eventual half whispered, half mumbled utterance of, 'Oh my god, it was you that …,

'Yes, Sam, interrupted Max, 'It was me who was paid to kill Rab Lindsay in Benidorm'.

Chapter 78

31 January 2018
Wednesday

Sam's flight passed without incident and arrived in Glasgow on time, with the landing being smooth and not remotely as jarring as the information provided by Max Holland, which had brought him right back down to earth with a bang, forcing him to confront the reality of his actions in Benidorm as never before. *It's not a coincidence,* he thought *it's Karma - and payback.* He had also suddenly felt exhausted by everything that had happened and had fallen asleep on a flight for the only the second time ever, waking up to hear the captain announcing that they were beginning their descent to Glasgow. It felt like he hadn't been on the plane for any time at all and that made him feel, probably quite forlornly, that maybe things were starting to look up for a change. It also, bizarrely, reminded him of the phrase; 'Timeless Flight' which was also the title of one of his favourite albums, by Steve Harley and Cockney Rebel.

Unfortunately, Sam also arrived home to deep snow and sub-zero temperatures, and, as if to add insult to injury, when he returned to his car, it was totally frozen, and he had a flat tyre. Whilst the key had successfully released the central locking, the doors wouldn't open because they were frozen, and he couldn't access the compressor in the boot to inflate the tyre. To make matters worse, he was wearing a cotton jacket that you could spit through. He decided that rather than just wait and freeze, he resorted to brute force and ignorance which as well as helping to make him forget about the cold, also yielded some success, as the driver's door eventually surrendered, probably more to his swearing than his physical exertions. *This shit never happens when the sun is shining*, thought Sam.

Earlier on the same day, Terry Lindsay's body was discovered by a postal worker in a back alley in Glasgow. The subsequently issued police report indicated that he appeared to have fallen from a fire escape outside a Lap Dancing Club.

***

Jill Gilchrist, after listening to Max's 'proposition', and giving it due consideration for a total of twenty seconds, then, quite unexpectedly, agreed to provide the authorities with all the information she knew about the various illegal operations and the people involved in running them. Even more unbelievably, she also agreed to become involved in a 'sting' to ensnare and prosecute the main gang bosses, and drug lords, and perpetrators in exchange for immunity, a new identity and protection under a Witness Protection Programme.

Informers and prosecution witnesses are frequently given new identities via the justice system, particularly in the event of them living in fear for their lives and the police believing that they or their families are in danger of violence from those whom they have informed or given evidence against. However, it is often not that simple or straightforward, as it is much more than just a new name, requiring provision of new medical records, national insurance number and bank accounts to minimise the likelihood discovering the person's identity either intentionally or by chance.

The person with a new identity will be given a past that is easy to memorise whilst anyone considered to be at serious risk and likely to be tracked down are often moved abroad, often as far as Australia and America. And that suited Jill just fine.

Chapter 79

February 1st, 2018
Thursday

Ivan Lasenko landed at Dublin Airport from Tenerife South on a false Spanish passport in the name of Ricardo Diaz. In order not to arouse undue suspicion, he stayed in Dublin for one more day before travelling to Larne in a black Ford Focus that he had hired at Dublin airport with a stolen credit card, before taking the ferry to Stranraer on other false documents in the name of Daniel o' Kane, under the pretext of being a football fan doing some sight-seeing prior to attending the Kilmarnock vs Celtic Scottish Premier League game on February 3 at Rugby Park, Kilmarnock. He then drove to Glasgow and checked into the Marriot Hotel in the city centre.

Over the next couple of days, Lasenko made several reconnaissance journeys to the leafy suburb where Sam Benedict lived in the outskirts of the city to familiarise himself with his intended victim's routine as much as possible. On one of those days, he also planted a gun, which it is believed he had collected from a contact in Stranraer, in the woods of a nearby park.

After Terry Lindsay's body was discovered and it being made public by the police, all staff at the club were instructed by the management to say that they hadn't seen anything and knew nothing about the situation (which many of them didn't) and told that anybody who said anything different would be instantly dismissed. There were only a couple of people, in addition to Farouk and Nalini that knew what had taken place, and they were saying nothing. The rest of the staff's true value was their genuine innocence and ignorance of the situation. However, in the event of it being discovered that Terry Lindsay had indeed visited the club, Farouk would be able to prove that he had been in the bar area all night, other than when he had taken the drinks to the room, after which Lindsay had made a call to the bar from there, proving that he was still hale and healthy at that point.

The explanation to be given for the phone call, which was not recorded, was that he had gone to the room to await the arrival of a girl, having told staff to 'surprise me'. However, when no one had arrived, because no one wanted to, he had become impatient and called down to ask why. Then, when Nalini had eventually gone to the room, he wasn't there, so everybody had just assumed that he had already left without anyone noticing. However, at that point, nobody had realised that he had left via the fire escape, so consequently they saw no reason to check it. There was also no evidence that he had had sex with anyone, forensic or otherwise, as he hadn't, and in fact the only evidence was exculpatory, thereby exonerating all the employees, within the club, at least. Also, Nalini had wiped down the en - suite bathroom in the room at the club, and then, when she had gone home, she had washed the clothes that she had worn and that had contacted Lindsay, albeit briefly. There were no surveillance cameras, legal or covert, anywhere inside or outside the premises, as far as they knew.

Akmal, meanwhile, had made his escape and was on his way to Glasgow airport to catch his flight to Gatwick, en-route to Houari Boumediene Airport in Algiers, on the same false passport that he had used to fly to Glasgow, which would take just over three hours. The main thing was that no one other than Farouk and Nalini knew about him ever being in Glasgow, apart from Terry Lindsay, and he wasn't saying anything.

The owners and management of the club were not sorry to see the back of Lindsay following his sudden and untimely death and, accordingly, there was no false outpouring of grief or fake sentiment expressed in that regard. There was, however, considerable concern that the situation could lead to a resurgence of the previous conflict and trigger a spate of retaliatory attacks, hence the reason for the continued denial, by the club's owners and management, that his death was in any way connected to the club. What they didn't know, however that there was no love lost for Lindsay within his own organisation, who had been plotting for a regime change for some considerable time and who saw this as a fortuitous opportunity to that very end.

They were also quite happy with the cessation of the hostilities between the opposing factions, viewing it as benefiting no one in the longer term. But that didn't mean that they were not prepared to use it to secure further concessions and advantages over their rivals in the weeks to come.

Chapter 80

2 February 2018
Friday

Sam had both awakened and risen early, having had a restless night, peppered with strange thoughts and dreams, but thankfully minus *the* nightmare. On looking out his kitchen window whilst eating his cereal and listening to his *Timeless Flight* album on his turntable, he observed and appreciated the familiar collection of assorted wildlife in the garden, a varied and colourful gathering of small birds fluttering in and around the very large tree, which also played host to cantankerous, feuding pigeons with attitude. And squirrels, one of which was albino and who were, as usual, helping themselves to the seed from the bird feeder. He had then heard and eventually seen one lone magpie, coincidentally, whilst a track called Black or White played in the background, as he awaited, with anticipation and hopeful expectation, the arrival of its mate, given the reputed implication of the sighting of a sole member of the species, in the event of you being of a superstitious nature, which, of course, he wasn't.

At least that was what he had told himself, trying to be rational and to dismiss it as the nonsense it was. At which point his phone pinged and on looking at the screen, he saw that he had received a text from Kim, his estranged wife, asking if they could meet for a coffee. They hadn't spoken since he had returned from his 'eventful' holiday in Tenerife, when she had called to ask if he had recovered from his experience and to get his version of the seriously dramatic events, which she hadn't been totally convinced about and which also appeared to cause her some consternation. Nevertheless, they had parted on good terms, wishing each other well and again promising to keep in touch, which they routinely never did.

Accordingly, her subsequent contact had given him pause for thought, and he didn't have a good feeling about it. Nevertheless, he had agreed to meet her at Metropolitan in the Merchant City for coffee, which turned into drinks at Blackfriars pub and then lunch at The City Merchant, which they decided to try on a whim, noticing that it wasn't busy and getting lucky.

Sam also couldn't help but notice a mean looking red Alfa Romeo, Guilietta, 1.6 TB Progression, parked nearby, and his photographic memory took him back to the first one he had ever seen, which was in a motoring magazine that he had read in his dentists waiting room, some thirty years previously, and from that moment he had wanted one, but sadly had never got round to it. And at fifty-three, he didn't think that he ever would, smiling ruefully at what Kim would say if he did;

'Having another middle-aged crisis are we'? As he looked at the car again, it also reminded him of a song from the same Steve Harley and Cockney Rebel album called; *Red Is A Mean, Mean Colour*, which contains the wonderful lyric;

Now here's a thing, a very silly thing
he says it's easy to make a million yeah,
here's a thing, a very silly thing
he says you steal from a broken Brazilian

Hardly what you would call sound career advice, mused Sam, but a wonderful album, nevertheless. As he admired the little Alfa, he thought that it probably belonged to the owner of one of the many bars or restaurants in the Merchant City.

After lovely food and some polite but slightly strained conversation, during which Kim told Sam that when she had read all about the events in Tenerife and his involvement in the situation, she felt like she had spent the day with him, whilst also expressing her concern for his ongoing welfare. However, he really didn't want to discuss the situation or even acknowledge the fact that he had his own concerns and not just for himself either.

Sam also wasn't sure whether her comment was a criticism or a compliment but felt that it was the opportune moment to change the subject and present her with the gift he had bought for her at Duty Free in Tenerife Airport, which was a bottle of Chanel perfume, saying 'It's just a wee thing'. However, she appeared to be both surprised and disconcerted by this, saying 'Sam I wish that you hadn't done this, there was no need'. Sam, whilst not expecting such a response nevertheless managed to respond calmly and managed a smile, saying; "Presents are made for the pleasure of the one who gives them, not for the pleasure of those who receive them'.

And then, seeing her confused look, asked her; 'Don't you remember who said that? On receiving no response, Sam said; 'Daniel's father in the Shadow of the Wind?' assuming that she would have recognised it. Unfortunately, this just made things worse, as she became really upset and burst into tears. 'What's wrong Kim, what did I say'? Sam asked, confused. However, she was too upset to answer him immediately and needed some time to compose herself, which she eventually did. Unfortunately, after gathering herself and her emotions she also managed to explain the reason for her response, which only served to confirm his previously held reservations and suspicions regarding the possible reasons for her contacting him. Kim, still clearly emotional, revealed the true purpose of her request to meet up; which was to tell him, face to face, rather than via a message or a phone call, that she wanted a divorce. Interestingly, however, she denied that it was because she had met someone else or that she was in a hurry to get married again. She just maintained that it felt like it was the right thing to do and the right time to do it. And, of course, he had no reason to disagree, so he wished her all the best for the future, saying; 'Be happy Kim'.

However, what he was thinking was; *Bloody magpie - I bet it was the bastard who steals the milk from my pint in the early hours -every bloody day.* He saw another one later in the day which had finally cleared up the question of whether you had to see two Magpie's together, rather than on separate occasions, for it to be a prediction of good luck- clearly it was the former. This also led him to wonder whether that meant he still had further bad news to look forward to.

He couldn't wait.

Chapter 81

2 February 2018
Friday

Following the police releasing the news of Terry Lindsay's body being found and it being identified as the brother of the 'businessman' who was killed in Benidorm the previous year, all the alleged connections and rumours surrounding Sam resurfaced, resulting in a flood of phone calls, emails and texts asking for his response to the discovery. They were all met with a polite, if firm, 'no comment', whilst pointing out that he had been in Spain when the murder was committed, according to the reported time of death. However, there were still a few persistent newshounds hanging around his home, so he just battened down the hatches, disconnected his landline and tried to weather the storm, which, thankfully, after a couple of days did settle down.

His employers had been in touch ahead of his return to work, and whilst also curious and maybe even hopeful of a 'scoop', they knew better than to cross the line and push him in that regard, being only too aware of his likely response to any attempted invasion of his privacy, having witnessed the distress and trauma he had experienced following the fall out of the saga in Benidorm.

They had been supportive of him then and would be again now and so when he insisted that had he had no knowledge of the situation or any association with the deceased, they respected his integrity and accordingly accepted his word in that regard, even if privately they found it hard to believe.

Sam had quite naturally assumed that the killing of Terry Lindsay was most likely related to the ongoing gangland feud. However, after further contemplation, another possible theory had slowly crept into his consciousness, including whether it was Max Holland's handiwork as part of his mission to clear up all the corruption and criminality in the world, or at least Glasgow?

Then he had begun to think about; *Who else would have a reason to want the gangster* dead? excluding himself obviously, which led to him to recall a conversation that he had had with Trish Roy in Benidorm, when he had asked her why she hadn't asked Akmal to kill Rab Lindsay. Her reply was that she 'didn't think that he was up to it'. However, the more he thought about it and the conversation he had had with the latter following the telephone call from his brother, the more his normally unerring gut instinct was telling him that maybe she had been a bit rash in her judgement. He had also been back to the car wash where Farouk worked, and he was nowhere to be seen.

As Akmal sat in the departure lounge of Gatwick airport, thinking over the events of the previous twenty-four hours, it seemed hard to believe what had happened, and what he had done, with everything having an almost surreal, dreamlike quality to it. But it had happened, he reminded himself; he had killed someone in cold blood; he was personally responsible for the murder of another human being.

In Benidorm and then Tenerife he had just been a gopher; a message boy, but this was different; this time he had planned and carried out a premeditated murder, something that he would never have believed that he was capable of. He knew that Farouk certainly wasn't capable of it and that's why he knew that he had to be the one to do it. It was self-preservation, he had reasoned; kill or be killed, acknowledging that the odds of him surviving otherwise weren't good. *And it might not be over, yet* he thought. But they would still need to find him, and he wasn't going to make it easy for them; he had disappeared before, and he could do it again. At least until the dust had settled, just like before.

And he wasn't alone; he had Farouk who it had been agreed, would not do anything hasty in terms of leaving the country immediately, believing that it would only draw unnecessary attention to him.

However, he hoped that he too would also soon be on his way home to join him.

Chapter 82

2 February 2018
Friday

With everything that had happened, Sam, who was due to return to work on Tuesday, 6 February had completely forgotten that he had agreed to look after his brother's dog, a German Shepherd called Dexter, for a few days whilst he and his family went on a long holiday weekend to St. Andrews, as the hotel they had chosen didn't allow dogs. They dropped the dog and all his accoutrements off on their way to the Kingdom of Fife, promising to call every day to check all was well with their precious pooch.

When Sam's work contacted him to ask how he was doing, he had indicated his wish to work from home for a few days to avoid having to go the workplace and encounter the more persistent journalists who were following him around, whilst, of course, failing to mention anything about the dog.

Thankfully, however, his request was sanctioned, and although there were still a few journalists hovering around outside his home, he dismissed them easily whilst the presence of such a large dog seemed to discourage their persistence even further, which Sam was extremely glad about, mainly because Dexter, being such a big dog needed to be walked. Also, his brother was as good as his word, calling the very next day as promised and to ask if all was well and to say they were having a great time - with no hint of drama or intrigue. *I really need to try that some time,* thought Sam. Dexter, who was an ex-police dog, had always enjoyed a run around nearby Queens Park, where he had taken him every day. And as the media interest had practically disappeared altogether, he decided that it was safe for him to venture out a bit further afield and that, for a change, he would take the car to Pollok Country Park, park it and take Dexter for a gentle stroll. He found himself involuntarily recalling that the last time he had visited the park was with Kim when they had gone to view the wonderful Burrell Collection.

Sam was able to let Dexter off the lead in Pollok Park, as there was less chance of him making a bid for freedom or disappearing into the woods and returning when he felt like it, usually covered in something dirty and smelly. However, his brother had been at pains to point out that he was getting on a bit now and wasn't quite as energetic as he had once been. *Tell me about it; I know how you feel pooch*, thought Sam.

Notwithstanding that however, when they arrived at the park, his canine companion bounded out of the car with energy and enthusiasm, which gave a lie to his advancing years and was clearly enjoying being there before settling into a much-reduced pace, which also suited Sam just fine.

The weather was quite dull and grey although it wasn't raining, and as he walked along the road through the park with Dexter, who he had put back on the lead because of the cars, the dog was stopping every few feet to sniff at or urinate on something.

Sam suddenly became aware of a noise and movement behind him and on turning round, he saw a black Ford Focus driving slowly behind him, so he moved to the right off the path and on to the grass. As he did so, the car moved forward and drew up alongside him, when he noticed the driver window being wound down. Thinking that the driver was probably looking for information or even directions, he moved towards the window to find that he was staring down the barrel of a gun with a silencer attached. As Sam saw the gun being raised and pointed directly at him, Dexter, who was an experienced guard dog trained to attack anyone pointing a weapon, began barking and lunged at the vehicle, pulling away from Sam and off the lead, causing the gunman to lean back and shoot from inside the car rather than pointing the gun out through the window, where Dexter could have grabbed it, and his arm. As a result, he missed his intended target, and the dog, thankfully, instead hitting a tree with both of his shots.

The shooter clearly wasn't going to get out of the car while the dog was there, as apart from being frightened of the beast, he also didn't want to draw any further attention to himself.

Surprisingly however, after an initial flurry of curiosity, all the people in the immediate vicinity had resumed their normal routine, totally oblivious to or realising the extent and serious nature of the dramatic events unfolding before their eyes. Sam, who was shaking, had grabbed the dog's lead back was struggling to pull Dexter away from the window of the vehicle out of concern for his welfare and out the way of another vehicle which was approaching from behind the Focus. As it drew up alongside the Focus, Sam saw the passenger side window slowly open revealing another similar handgun, also with a silencer attached, only this time it was pointed at the gunman in the other car. Seconds later, there was a flash and a quiet, muffled crack, followed by the driver of the Focus collapsing over the steering wheel covered in blood.

Meanwhile, the other car simply drove off into the distance, but not before Sam got a very clear sight of the driver and the passenger, with the latter looking directly at him. It was difficult to be certain, but he thought that he might have winked at him and smiled indeed, the only thing they didn't do was wave. Sam, who was still shaking like a leaf, trying to comprehend and process what had just happened, then realised that everybody else was still just getting on with their lives and daily routine as normal, still not having noticed the extreme and deadly scenario which had just been perpetrated in broad daylight within feet of them. Even Dexter had calmed down and had returned to his seemingly favourite pastime of finding something to urinate on, finally settling on a small tree stump. Accordingly, despite being traumatized, Sam decided that they should take their leave of proceedings and leave the glory of the grim discovery to some unwitting passerby. *Time for somebody else to get their name in the papers,* thought Sam. Dexter seemed to agree, happily following him to the car.

As Sam drove away and out of the park, he was sure that he heard a woman scream.

Chapter 83

03 February 2018
Saturday

Max Holland had driven to his secret bolt hole, a holiday home in Aberdour, Fife, which he had bought some years before and where he went to relax and escape from his 'everyday life', which of course, as determined by Sam, was significantly different from that of most other people.

As he sat looking out across the Firth of Forth on an unseasonably mild evening, with the sea sparkling and luminescent in the moonlight, giving it an almost alien, other worldly appearance, he reflected upon his decision to tell Sam Holland about his involvement with the contract on Rab Lindsay in Benidorm. He had had a clear reason for telling him; he had thought that because they had shared feelings of affection and grief for the same person that Sam might feel able to share or confide in him about his own alleged part in the same crime, perhaps as a cathartic, conscience-cleansing exercise.

But then he realised that it was more than that; he had found himself, for some reason, wanting to… no, needing to make Sam understand how he had become involved and why he felt the way he did about Lucy/Emily, who had made him feel valued as a human being. They had both experienced grief in their lives Lucy's husband, who was also a policeman, had been killed after responding to a burglary, only a year and a half after they had married. Max had subsequently shared his own childhood trauma with her, and they almost immediately developed a bond and friendship in both their work and personal lives, which had stood the test of time. And now she was gone.

And he had no one that he could trust or turn to for anywhere near the same kind of support or understanding. Maybe that's why he had told Sam because he needed to know what his response was; basically, he needed his validation. He wasn't normally given to worrying about what other people thought of him, but for some reason the whole situation had left him questioning his worth as a person, which had never, ever happened before.

He wondered if it was because of the guilt he felt about Lucy's death and perhaps he hoped that getting it out and sharing it with someone would have some kind of therapeutic effect and benefit. He wasn't sure whether that it had or not, but what he was sure about was that killing Ivan Lasenko definitely had and he wasn't sure how that made him feel about himself. Unfortunately, whilst it had also brought him some form of closure, it had also led him to question what he had done with his life; undercover work was something that he felt as if he had been doing forever and which had become second nature to him and which he believed that he had done for all the best reasons.

Except that now he wasn't sure that he could carry on doing it anymore. Unfortunately, it wasn't easy to simply walk away because you didn't just leave such a profession, particularly while there were still contracts on your head. *And let's face it*, he thought ruefully, the odds against him surviving weren't great. In fact, he mused *Compared to him the Christians were even money.*

Meanwhile, Sam had not responded to his openness in kind, as he had hoped, and was continuing to play things very close to his chest, giving nothing away. Fortunately, there was still another possible avenue to be explored in that regard.

Chapter 84

03 February 2018
Saturday

Sam Meredith watched as the world moved around him, a study of perpetual motion which begged the eternal question of 'Where the hell was everybody going?' However, he observed that whilst normally everyone seemed to be in such a desperate, hectic rush, particularly at this time of day, he thought that today the world seemed quite calm, with there being an almost silvery stillness about it. And then the heavens opened, and the rain fell like it had been programmed—heavy, constant and seemingly unrelenting. It was almost like a perfect demonstration of what real rain should be like. And it showed no sign of stopping anytime soon. Thankfully, he had brought a large golf umbrella—not that he played; he had tried it a couple of times but decided it wasn't for him, as he wasn't able to cope with the constant frustration and disappointment. Whilst other golfers were looking for their lost balls in the rough, Sam was looking for his club, following him launching it into the air in a fit of rage and frustration.

After the discovery of the "assassination" of Ivan Lasenko in Pollock Park, the media were in a frenzy, frantically looking for any connection between the two deaths, occurring as they had within such a small space time of each other and fabricating what they didn't know, claiming that the death was drug related and referring to it as the 'Narcs in the park' murder. *Anything for a headline,* thought Sam.

Subsequent Closed-Circuit Television (CCTV) footage from the two days before the attempted assassination of Sam revealed that the gunman had spent several hours disguised as a Local Authority Council refuse worker, picking up litter to observe Sam and his movements. Separate surveillance tapes also showed Ivan Lasenko, dressed in black and lying in wait outside the house hours before the attack. Police speculated that the presence of reporters in the vicinity had dissuaded him from attempting any attack on Sam at his home.

However, the tapes were destroyed and never released to the media as it was not felt to be in the public interest; nothing to do with the gunman being an ex-undercover policeman who had just been terminated by an ex-colleague and serving undercover policeman of course. Sam had also decided that he wasn't going to mention to his brother how close he had come to getting both himself and his beloved dog killed, and thankfully Dexter could keep a secret too.

Sam had often thought about getting a dog of his own but didn't like the idea of leaving it at home on its own, having read somewhere that dogs suffer from separation anxiety, which made him feel bad.

If only dogs could get jobs as well, he had thought, and then immediately realised that, of course, they did; Police dogs, like Dexter, guide dogs, sheepdogs, sleigh, dogs and even dogs selling insurance for God's sake. Loads of opportunities, he thought; no reason at all for them to be lying at home like draft excluders doing nothing.

And then, getting carried away on a flight of fancy, he began wondering if the dogs with jobs looked down on the ones that were idle and routinely gave them a hard time whenever they met them something along the lines of, 'Away and work, you lazy, good for nothing growler. *Maybe that's where the phrase, "dog's abuse" came from*, he mused, suddenly laughing at his own witticism and being surprised by the sound, realising that it was the second time he had laughed in as many weeks. Things are looking up, he thought.

Chapter 85

10 February 2018
Saturday

In contrast to the media, the police, for obvious reasons, were playing down any possible link with the two deaths whilst also insisting that they had no interest in contacting or interviewing Sam Meredith, which also helped diminish the press's interest in him. Social media, on the other hand, was a riot, with all sorts of unsubstantiated theories and allegations being slung around with impunity and absolutely no consideration or thought given to the consequences. *There really needs to be some regulation introduced sooner rather than later,* thought Sam. Also, despite their claims, the police were very much interested in interviewing Sam and had, in fact, contacted him, as he had been advised they would by both Spanish officials before he left Tenerife. But they hadn't told him who it would be contacting him. Consequently, when he found out the identity of his sole visitor, his reaction was one of both pleasure and intrigue, in equal measure, particularly as they were working solo.

Sam took the train from the South Side to Glasgow Central and after a short walk arrived, far too early at Viva, the Italian restaurant in Bothwell Street, in Glasgow City Centre where they had arranged to meet. So, rather than wait outside on what was a quite a cold and 'drizzly' day, he thought; *I have time for a pint* and headed to Viva Brazil on the next corner, where he ordered a pint of Brahma, which he proceeded to drink half of in a matter of seconds. At which point he realised that he was feeling quite anxious about their meeting and took a deep breath and tried to calm himself.

He made the drink last until roughly ten minutes before they were due to meet and headed out into what was now quite steady rain, taking shelter in the doorway of the restaurant, rather than go inside and risk the embarrassment and indignity of his 'date' not turning up. *It's not a date you moron it's an official interview*, he told himself

Thankfully, however, that scenario did not materialise, and she arrived within minutes, greeting him with a smile and asking, 'What you doing standing in the pissing rain? Shall we go in?' closing and then shaking her umbrella as she led the way.

'After you,' said Sam, smiling sardonically, gesturing accordingly and standing aside to let her pass and catching a whiff of her fragrance as she did so. She smelled fantastic.

Sam liked Indian food and two of his favourite restaurants, Indian or otherwise, were the Dahkin in Blackfriars Street and the Madha in Albion Street, both in the Merchant City area of Glasgow, both of which he had originally suggested when she had contacted him, advising that they needed to meet up to talk and suggesting that they do it over lunch.

He had also asked her if she knew anywhere, they could get a decent Welsh Rarebit, but she hadn't answered, seemingly ignoring him and not taking the question seriously, before recommending their current destination.

Sam, who also liked Italian food, was happy to both meet and eat there, particularly as she had offered to pick up the tab. He had never previously eaten there but had heard good reports from various friends and family and had intended to visit but had just never had a date when it was convenient. He had also never been to the Spiritualist, the pub that she had also recommended they visit after their meal for cocktails.

She was dressed very simply, but the transformation from the person that he remembered from Benidorm only a few months before could not have been more pronounced. She looked so different much more glamorous and feminine. As she removed her winter coat and handed it to the waiter, it revealed a stylish black knee-length dress which complimented her slender but shapely figure. She wore elegant black shoes with a small heel, which made her nearly as tall as Sam and she looked as if she was wearing sheer black stockings rather than tights. *But maybe that's just wishful thinking on my part,* thought Sam.

She also wore very little jewellery, other than a watch on one wrist, a bracelet on the other and a very fine and delicate gold chain and cross around her neck. And he thought that whatever she had done with her make-up and her lovely dark brown hair, which looked very lustrous, tumbling on to her shoulders, the effect was quite stunning.

She looked sensational, but for some reason he stopped himself from telling her so perhaps because he still wasn't sure what the deal was. And he was also wondering whether she just scrubbed up well or had she made a special effort for him?

After they were seated, the waiter arrived with menus, and they ordered a bottle of red wine, which Sam let his companion pick, and they also ordered some water for the table.

'Well, well, long time no see Inspector Powrie,' said Sam, just to lighten the mood and the tension that he was experiencing, settling into his seat and accepting a menu, which the waitress had just handed him. 'The 26 of November 2017, in Benidorm, to be exact Mr Meredith, and can we please dispense with the formalities, it's Vanessa today,' she said smiling and opening her menu.

'Fine with me, and that being the case, you can call me Sam,' and pausing before adding 'today', and wondering where this was going, at which point Vanessa announced that she was going to the ladies' room to powder her nose and brush up on her Italian vocabulary. This drew a puzzled look from Sam and a smile and an amused look from the detective as she rose from the table.

The waiter, who had arrived at the table with the water and the wine as she headed to the restroom, had obviously overheard her comment and explained to Sam with a grin that 'Learn how to speak Italian.' Linguaphone-style recordings were played constantly in both the men and women's washroom for people's education or amusement whilst they performed their ablutions.

He then proceeded to take an age to open the wine with one of those small corkscrews that looked like a utility knife, which Sam could never use without injuring himself. The waiter, who looked about seventeen, whilst struggling with the wine, admitted to Sam during subsequent, idle small talk that he didn't speak a word of Italian and was in fact Irish.

When the very apologetic but pleasant and charming young Celt eventually managed to open the bottle of wine, he poured a small drop into Sam's glass, looking at him to taste and indicate his appreciation, however Sam just told him to pour the rest, which elicited a gentle smile from Vanessa as she returned to her seat at the table.

After the waiter had gone Sam lifted his glass towards Vanessa and said 'Cheers', which she reciprocated, clinking her glass gently against his, looking at him and saying 'So... I see you've been busy since we last met, running up even more of a body count, your fecundity is impressive. I would have thought that after you're experience in Benidorm you would've been keen to pursue a much quieter existence.'

'And you would have been correct,' said Sam, 'but for some reason, that just seems to be something that eludes me, despite my best efforts. But you will already know that, as I'm sure your colleague, Inspector Max Holland, the passenger in your lovely red Alfa Romeo, Guilietta,1.6 TB Progression- very discreet and inconspicuous by the way would testify to, when he's not assassinating people that is. And, as you will also know, the body count is down to him and his ex 'colleague', who, as we both know, was the unfortunate and most recent beneficiary of his expertise and skill- with a little help from his friend. Am I to assume that he now has a new partner?'

'What? No, no... said Vanessa, hastily and earnestly. I was merely there for practical help... and insurance purposes, given the circumstances and complex political nature of the transaction' she said, before adding, 'and ten out of ten for observation about the Alfa, my only real indulgence, I didn't know you were into sports cars.'

'I'm not, I'm into detail, description and effect,' that's my job... and... self-preservation... which I thought was your job.'

'Well, you are on a roll today, Sam,' said Vanessa and then adding, But I think that we did our bit in that respect at Pollok Park.'

'On the contrary,' said Sam. 'I think a German Shepherd named Dexter saved my life whilst you, and your friend were taking care of some personal 'insurance' business' and mocking her by making a quotation sign with his fingers, before adding, 'But he was definitely in the self-preservation business, in order to extend his own very precarious existence.' 'I take it, he took care of Terry Lindsay too?' said Sam.

'Actually, no he never, believe it or not,' said Vanessa. 'And we're not sure who did either. But we will find out eventually,' she said calmly. As she spoke Sam was again reflecting on his own thoughts as to who else might be responsible but had no intention of sharing it with her at this time.

'Are you ready to order now?' asked a waitress who had replaced the waiter, having suddenly materialised at the table with considerable stealth and no little poise.

She also had a quite lovely smile, as far as Sam was concerned whilst his appreciation had not gone unnoticed by his lunch guest. As neither of them had even looked at the menu due to being too involved in their verbal jousting, they both did so very quickly and placed their respective orders with the waitress.

After she had gone Vanessa looked at Sam and said, 'She's very pretty, isn't she?' looking at Sam enquiringly.

'Who?' asked Sam, trying to look innocent and failing miserably.

'What do you mean who?' she laughed, before continuing with 'the waitress that you couldn't take your eyes off, of course, that's who,' before suddenly asking, 'when was the last time you were intimate?'

'Pardon me?' said Sam, really taken aback.

'It's not a complicated question,' said the Inspector.

'Do you mean sexually intimate? asked Sam, because he wasn't sure what else to say.

'As opposed to what,' laughed Vanessa.

'I mean to what extent?

'I suppose that's what I'm asking *you,*' she replied.

'Why are you asking?' Sam countered.

'I'm just curious,' said Vanessa, and trying to take the

conversation in a more light-hearted direction, said jokingly, 'I thought that you were looking at that waitress with a very hungry look in your eye.'

'Only for food Inspector,' said Sam, lying, and deliberately not using her first name. Then, with perfect timing their order arrived, which both looked and smelled lovely and which they then proceeded to devour in relative silence, apart from agreeing that it was delicious.

It was Vanessa who both finished eating and spoke first,
'The good news is that there haven't been any more arson attacks or any kind of violent repercussions in response to the death of Terry Lindsay- so far-and long may it continue.'

'Absolutely,' he replied, looking pensive, before saying; 'And what about the likely response to the death of Ivan Lasenko?'

'Well, without wanting to give you false hope or optimism, there's reason to believe that there may not be any appetite for vengeance or to pursue Terry Lindsay's personal vendettas within the existing regime, and it may well work to your advantage,' said Vanessa.

'Also, they'll all be too busy jostling for position and power, which could get quite messy - and trying to find out where he has stashed his money- knowing him he probably keeps it under his mattress,' she laughed sneeringly.

'And his conscience in his pocket,' replied Sam.

'Sorry?' said Vanessa, looking puzzled.

'Nothing, just a lyric from a song,' said Sam, still singing the corresponding Steve Harley song inside his head and thinking that at this rate he would soon have gone through the whole album.

'Oh, right,' said Vanessa, not at all interested. 'Well, anyway, so far so good in regard to that situation and hopefully no news is good news, but we will be keeping our eyes and ears open, so watch this space.'

'I intend to, with great interest. Does that mean we will be seeing more of one another?'

'Well, we will still be observing you; from a distance- for the time being,' Vanessa said, with a wry smile, whilst asking for the bill.

'I think I prefer this more close - up personal observation.'

'Are you propositioning me Mr. Meredith?'

'Sorry... Sam,' she corrected, smiling.

'Would you mind?' asked Sam.

'Would you care?' replied Vanessa.

'Would I care about what?'

'If I minded?'

'Of course, I'm only interested in people who are interested. And you seem to be interested.'

'In you?' asked Vanessa,

'In my sex life,' said Sam.

'Touche,' she replied, before taking ownership of the bill from the waitress and confirming that both their meals had been delicious, in response to her asking, 'How was your meal?'

'As you said, I'm on a roll. Are we still going for cocktails?'

'There's something I need to ask you first,' said Vanessa, looking suddenly serious, whilst handing payment and a tip to the waitress, who had again appeared at the table with the stealth of a panther.

'Is this you finally cutting to the chase?' asked Sam.

'I suppose so, if you want to put it like that,' said Vanessa, adding, 'did you have anything to do with Rab Lindsay's death in Benidorm last…

'No,' said Sam, before she had finished the question.

'That's it, that's all you have to say?'

'Yes.'

'Just, no?'

'As opposed to what?' Yes?'

'No as opposed to an explanation why it wasn't you.'

'Because it was Trish Roy, as you know.'

'Do I?'

'Yes, otherwise you would have charged me by now. But you can't do that on your own, so if you had been intending to, you wouldn't have come alone.'

'We haven't charged you because we have no evidence, that's not the same thing.'

'You don't have any evidence because there isn't any. That's the only thing.'

'We don't have any evidence that you killed him, but that isn't the only thing.'

'What else is there?'

'Conspiring, incitement, facilitating…'

'And do you have any evidence of any of *them*?' She just drew him a look which said. *You know I don't.* 'Maybe if we could speak to your friend Akmal, or even his brother Farouk, if that is their real names.'

'Why, what do they know?' said Sam, trying to look both ignorant and innocent but probably not quite managing either, before adding, 'and he's not my friend.'

'Apparently, it was them who blabbed about what happened in Benidorm,' she advised, 'but then you have probably already worked that out for yourself,' looking at him for validation but instead getting a question.

'How do *you* know that?' asked Sam.

'Let's just say we have eyes and ears everywhere,' she replied, smiling before continuing, 'however, unfortunately we can't speak to them because they have both vanished. I don't suppose you know where they are? I only ask because you and your friend Akmal seem to have a knack of finding each other.'

'Pure coincidence,' said Sam, his own belief in that particular concept having changed significantly over recent weeks.

'And I have no idea where either of them is,' said Sam. The last I heard 'our' friend, Akmal, was heading back to Algeria.'

'Mmmmm... you might be right,' said Vanessa, looking pensive. 'I don't suppose you know if he or his brother used any other names or aliases?'

'No, I only ever knew them by those names,' said Sam, shrugging his shoulders whilst holding Vanessa's gaze, as she stared at him. Vanessa broke the silence with an impatient puff of her cheeks, saying; 'According to them you arranged the 'hit' on Rab Lindsay with Akmal, using Trish Roy's money.

'And you believe that?'

'Terry Lindsay did. That's why he put a contract out on you. But then you already know that as well, don't you? Sam again ignored the question, instead replying, 'Maybe he was just looking for somebody else to blame. In addition to your new partner in crime that is,' said Sam, and this time it was Sam who was staring at her.

'Ah, yes, that. I don't know why he told you that. Well actually I do but he probably shouldn't have.' Sam just gave her a knowing look, before adding, 'But he did, whatever his reasons were. But don't worry, your... sorry, his... secret is safe with me,' said Sam, and then, making firm eye contact with her again, he thought that he saw something; maybe a reaction to what he said but he wasn't quite sure why.

'Why do I get the feeling that there's something you're not telling me?' he asked, but as she didn't respond or acknowledge his question, he continued, 'and why isn't he here with you? And why *did* you arrange to meet me on your own?'

'I was interested'

'In what?'

'In what you had to say, why did you agree to meet me?'

'I was interested.'

'In what?'

'In you,' said Sam, looking into her eyes again.

'Was?' she asked, again holding his gaze.

'Could still be, given some encouragement,' said Sam.

'Am not sure that would be wise,' said Vanessa, moving her chair back from the table.

'So, are we all done then?' said Sam.

'Unless you have anything else for me,' she asked, rising from the table and asking the waitress for her coat, which was on a peg next to the bar.

'As a matter of fact, I do,' said Sam, lifting her coat off the peg before the waitress could, whilst giving her a friendly, if mischievous smile.

'What?' Vanessa asked, looking surprised.

'A proposition,' said Sam, holding out and helping her on with her coat, whilst at the same time gently pulling her towards him and kissing her softly on the mouth, which she responded to by reciprocating accordingly, if briefly.

As they left the restaurant Sam stopped, turned, looked at her and said, 'Thursday, 25 January 2018.'

'What?' said Vanessa, looking confused.

'Thursday 25 January 2018. It was the last time I had sex,' said Sam.

And then, realising who it was that Sam had been intimate with on that date, Vanessa said, 'I'm sorry Sam, I didn't mean to be insensitive, I was just…'

'It's okay, it's not a problem, Inspector… Sorry Vanessa,' said Sam, stroking her cheek and then kissing her again, which this time she responded to more definitively and lastingly.

They didn't bother with the cocktails.

Chapter 86

Detective Inspector Vanessa Powrie had wanted to believe Sam Meredith when he said that he hadn't been involved in the killing of Rab Lindsay in Benidorm. So, when he said that he hadn't, she chose to do exactly that, possibly against her better judgment and despite the now mounting allegations to the contrary. However, she had also reasoned that they had been made by people who, it could be argued, had their own agenda and reasons to be vindictive, whilst also reminding herself that there was still no evidence against him. She also acknowledged that she had found herself very attracted to him from the start and believed, rightly or wrongly, that it was mutual because of the way they had interacted in Benidorm. Accordingly, when he had confirmed it in Viva, she was so relieved and happy that she hadn't been unable to resist his advances.

And if she was being totally honest with herself, she hadn't tried that hard. She just hoped that she didn't live to regret it. However, she also wasn't against using whatever attraction and affection they had for one another, to her advantage.

She and Max had met with their superiors, and it was agreed that it made sense for her to try and get him to discuss or at least acknowledge what part, if any, that he played in Rab Lindsay's death, the thinking being that he was more likely to do so if it was just the two of them. Max had previously had similar thoughts and hopes that Sam might have opened up during their meeting on the way to the airport when he had revealed his own involvement, but that had not been the case, with Sam remaining tight-lipped. And, accordingly, for that, and other reasons, he had made the decision not to be totally honest and transparent with Sam about the situation in Benidorm.

Equally, Vanessa, despite her decision to share physical intimacy with Sam, had also chosen not to disclose certain crucial information that had serious implications for everyone involved in the dramatic events in Benidorm, Tenerife and now even Glasgow.

It'll keep for now, she told herself, but she still had a job to do, and it definitely wasn't case closed. Not by a long chalk. Also, she still had to find somewhere that made a decent Welsh Rarebit.

Epilogue

Jill Gilchrist subsequently provided the authorities with vital information about how drugs were imported from Spain into Scotland hidden inside machinery, whilst also supplying them with valuable details about sex trafficking routes and locations. Police subsequently went on to seize cocaine, cannabis resin and herbal cannabis with a value of upwards of £2m, leading to several convictions being secured. The drugs were hidden and then transported in lorry trailers run by a variety of individuals and companies. This often involved contacting transport firms using an alias and a fake company name.

Three Algerian nationals were arrested when officers raided their flat in Bathgate, West Lothian, discovering approximately £50,000 in cash and five kilos of cocaine, hidden behind the toilet panel in the bathroom, which when cut, would carry an estimated street value of £53,000.000. The police also found firearms and ammunition hidden under the floorboards in a cellar of the ground floor flat. The men were sentenced to five and a half years for possession with intent to supply Class A drugs and received a further sentence of thirteen years for drugs and firearms offences.

Jill Gilchrist was subsequently, as promised, given a new identity under the Witness Protection Programme. Unfortunately, her identity was revealed by a corrupt police officer to one of the associates of Terry Lindsay, who had been one of the people allegedly involved and charged with, but not convicted, in the earlier drug and people trafficking case. She was found dead some weeks later in a beach house in Florida, having been strangled with a garrotte.

END